BETWEEN A WOK
AND A HARD PLACE

Also by Tamar Myers
in Large Print:

Gruel and Unusual Punishment
The Hand that Rocks the Ladle
Eat, Drink, and Be Wary
The Crepes of Wrath

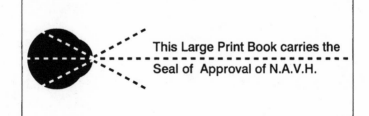

BETWEEN A WOK AND A HARD PLACE

A PENNSYLVANIA DUTCH MYSTERY WITH RECIPES

TAMAR MYERS

Thorndike Press • Waterville, Maine

3 1923 00417614 1

Copyright © Tamar Myers, 1998

This is a work of fiction. Names, characters, places, and incidents either are the product of the author's imagination or are used fictitiously, and any resemblance to actual persons, living or dead, business establishments, events, or locales is entirely coincidental.

Published in 2002 by arrangement with NAL Signet, a member of Penguin Putnam, Inc.

Thorndike Press Large Print Mystery Series.

The tree indicium is a trademark of Thorndike Press.

The text of this Large Print edition is unabridged.
Other aspects of the book may vary from the original edition.

Set in 16 pt. Plantin by Al Chase.

Printed in the United States on permanent paper.

Library of Congress Cataloging-in-Publication Data
Myers, Tamar.
    Between a wok and a hard place : a Pennsylvania Dutch mystery with recipes / Tamar Myers.
        p. cm.
    ISBN 0-7862-4640-5 (lg. print : hc : alk. paper)
    1. Yoder, Magdalena (Fictitious character) — Fiction.
    2. Women detectives — Pennsylvania — Fiction.
    3. Pennsylvania Dutch Country (Pa.) — Fiction.
    4. Hotelkeepers — Fiction.   5. Pennsylvania — Fiction.
    6. Mennonites — Fiction.   7. Cookery — Pennsylvania.
    8. Large type books.   I. Title.
    PS3563.Y475 B47 2002
    813'.54—dc21   2002027180

ACKNOWLEDGMENTS

I would like to acknowledge all the members of the Wednesday Workshop, as well as Mignon Ballard, Gwen Hunter, Misty Massey, James Werrell, David Lyon, and the staff at York County Public Library. I am particularly indebted to the real live Pooky Bear, who is nothing like the one in this book.

CHAPTER ONE

I was a virgin until I married at age forty-six. Use it, or lose it, my sister Susannah always said. Maybe she was right.

Of course this is none of your business. I am a God-fearing woman and I certainly do not intend to discuss my sex life with you. It is imperative, however, that you understand I was still in a state of shock when the events I am about to relate happened. After all, I had been married only a month, and what Mama had only hinted at paled in comparison with the real thing. I was born and raised on a farm and had seen animals — cows and horses — but never a naked man. How was I to know they looked like that? Thanksgiving is forever ruined for me. I can't even look at a turkey neck now without feeling embarrassed.

So, perhaps you can understand why I was distracted enough not to notice the young woman lying in the intersection of North Main and Elm streets until I was almost upon her. I swerved sharply, and it was the curb I hit, not her. I'm almost positive. And surely she was already dead by then, because she was lying flat on her back with her arms folded across her chest, a white cotton handkerchief spread across her face.

Even Melvin Stoltzfus, our chief of police, seemed to believe me, and that's saying a lot. Rumor has it that Melvin was kicked in the head by a bull he was trying to milk. Of course he was just a teenager then, but the adult Melvin is not a whole lot brighter. Scarcely over a month ago he tried out a new chain saw — intended for me as a wedding present — and met with an unfortunate accident. Melvin was surprised when the limb he was sitting on not only parted from the tree, but took him with it.

"Tell me the story again, Yoder," he said, limping around the body to view if from another angle. "What were you doing driving through Hernia at four o'clock in the morning?"

I sighed patiently. "My name is Magdalena Miller, now. Mrs. Aaron Miller. You were at the wedding — actually you weren't. Come to think about it, Aaron and I never did get our present!"

"Yoder!"

"Oh, all right. It's like I just said. Aaron had a ten-thirty flight to catch out of Pittsburgh last night. I took him to the airport in my new car, but as you well know, Melvin, it's at least two hours from Pittsburgh to Hernia, and along about midnight I got sleepy and pulled over into a rest area to grab a few winks. But I must have been really tired because —"

Melvin had the audacity to tap on his cast with his cane. "The highlights, Yoder. I want only the highlights."

If humoring him meant I could at least go to bed, so be it. "Well, I was driving through town, minding my own business, and suddenly there she was. But I did *not* run over her."

"Mmm. Have you ever seen her before?"

I looked at the body again. The victim had been a beautiful Asian woman, probably in her midtwenties. Her thick, black hair was cut short, but it suited her. Her complexion was flawless, but in the early-morning light, at least, it had a bluish cast. She was dressed on the shabby side; jeans, a Coca-Cola T-shirt with a few brown stains sprinkled across the front. She was wearing no socks, and her brown loafers were scuffed gray along the toes. The only distinguishing mark that I could see was a small blue rose tattooed on the inside of her left wrist.

"I've never seen her," I said.

"You sure?"

"Positive," I said, my patience wearing thin.

Hernia, Pennsylvania, (population 1,532) has a remarkably homogeneous population of Swiss and German ancestry. The majority of us are Amish and Mennonite, although we do have a Methodist, and even a Presbyterian church. Our only minorities are the members of the First and Only True Church of the One and Only Living God of the Tabernacle of Supreme Holiness and Healing and Keeper of the Consecrated Righteousness of the Eternal Flame of Jehovah congregation out by the turnpike. None of them are Asian-Americans.

"Then she's from out of town," Melvin said.

"Brilliant deduction," I muttered.

"What was that?"

"Nothing." I feigned a warm smile.

"What was that grimace for, Yoder? You didn't tell me you were hurt in the accident. How bad is it?"

"Don't get your hopes up, Melvin. I'm not hurt, and I *wasn't* in an accident. Can I go now?"

"Well — uh — I — uh —"

A stammering Melvin is a dangerous Melvin. If I'd been any brighter than him, I would have made a dash for it. The Maryland state line is less than fifty miles away.

"Spit it out, dear," I said kindly.

"Yoder — you — uh — well, have a good head on your shoulders. And folks around here seem to like you. Some even respect you. In fact, I —"

"Thank you, Melvin, but you're too late. Aaron and I are still happily married."

It *was* true, I'm sure. Besides, even if it weren't and Aaron and I went our separate ways, I would never marry again. First of all, it would be a sin, and second, I would never want to see another naked man. A body can only take so much shock. Perhaps that's why the good Lord instituted marriage as a lifelong commitment.

Melvin probably glared at me. It is hard to tell these things because Melvin has enormous green eyes that operate independently of each other. He also has an unusually skinny neck, a long torso, and knobby joints. I am not the only one in Hernia who thinks he resembles a very large praying mantis. But at least he's a male praying mantis, so I wasn't in danger of being eaten.

"I wasn't proposing to you, Yoder. I was about to ask you a favor."

"*Moi?*" Coming from Melvin, that was a greater shock than a marriage proposal.

His left eye swiveled to fix on my forehead. "You're making this hard for me, Yoder."

"Okay, okay. Ask me your favor so I can go home."

"I want you to be my assistant."

I jiggled my ears with my pinkies. Surely I had not heard right. Melvin is my nemesis, a fact which I have made very clear to him over the years.

"Melvin, dear, you already have an assistant. Zelda Root. Besides, I have a full-time job. I own and operate the PennDutch Inn, remember?"

"It would only be temporary, Magdalena. Just for this case. Just until this cast comes off."

I don't think Melvin has called me by my first name since we were kids. The man was obviously desperate.

"And Zelda?"

"Zelda does a great job on the small stuff, so don't get me wrong. Last week she tracked down Rita Stutzman's missing scarecrow. It turns out a raccoon had hauled it off into the woods because Rita had used a real cob of corn for the nose." He lowered his voice to a whisper. "But Zelda is not so hot on the big, important cases."

It's a good thing I was wearing bloomers under my pantyhose. An admission like that

14

was guaranteed to knock my socks off, as Susannah so quaintly puts it. Not only are Melvin and Zelda engaged to be married, they exhibit a fierce sort of loyalty not often seen outside of the animal kingdom.

"I'm flattered that you asked, Melvin, but I have no police training. Not that I'm incapable of passing the course, mind you — what color would my uniform be? Navy? Frankly, I look much better in royal blue. Baby blue is all right, too."

His right eye focused on my chin. "There wouldn't be a uniform, Magdalena. Not unless you made it yourself. This would all be unofficial."

"And my salary?"

The truth is, I didn't need any. At the risk of sounding immodest, I seem to have a flair for business. After my parents died — a tragic death, squished between a milk tanker and a semitrailer loaded with state-of-the-art running shoes — I turned the family farm into a highly profitable bed and breakfast. Thanks to a couple of good reviews and my inflated prices, the Penn-Dutch Inn has become *the* destination for the rich and famous who yearn for solitude. In fact, I now have a two-year waiting list.

A lot of my guests are in show biz, although I prefer not to deal with the Holly-

15

wood crowd. But as long as they possess healthy bank accounts, I feel it is wrong to discriminate. Indeed, the reverse is true. It is my Christian duty to administer to their spiritual needs. We are to be a light unto the world, and believe you me, there are a lot of dark places in the minds of some of those folks who hail from the "Hills."

Of course, a number of my guests have nothing whatsoever to do with Celluloid City. Some are attorneys, some politicians, some both. Their minds could use a little light, too, and believe it or not, a number of them have mended their ways after spending a week at the Inn. After spending only three days with me, one infamous divorce lawyer not only gave up a million-dollar practice, but became a missionary to a remote region of Zaire.

And then there are the plain old business types. They may be less flashy than the aforementioned folks, but — and I say this in all modesty — they admire my business acumen. Some very important tycoons come just to study at my feet. Take that little Texan with the big ears, for instance, who thinks I'd make a good Vice President.

Few of the above are anywhere near as wealthy as the televangelists, however. Mama would turn over in her grave if she knew I was charging men of the cloth for the privilege of sleeping in her bed. But she'd be spinning like a gyroscope if she knew just how tightfisted some of those guys — and gals — are. And no matter what they say, religious tracts and complimentary testaments do not count as tips!

"There'd be no salary, Magdalena."

"Well, in that case . . ." I shook my head.

"You'd get to carry a beeper."

"Whatever for?"

"To let you know that I have something important to tell you. Then you come or call in as soon as you can."

"Ah, I see. I get to come running like a dog that has been whistled for. I think not, Melvin."

"Please."

It was the first time I'd heard the word "please" make it past his lips, and it was a surreal experience. I wouldn't have been any more surprised if the street lamp near me had spoken.

"What did you say?"

"Don't make me beg, Magdalena," he pled. "What say I call you as soon as I get the coroner's preliminary report?"

"Melvin, I —"

"Have it your way, Yoder. I'll call in a special investigator. It'll cost the taxpayers something, of course. Chances are he'll be English — an outsider. He won't know our ways."

I sighed deeply. He had me between a rock and hard place. Aaron *was* out of town, and even though the Inn was full, my cook, Freni, was more than competent. Helping Melvin with a case might actually be fun. On the other hand, it was sure to be aggravating. Although possibly not quite as aggravating as higher taxes and a meddlesome outsider.

"All right," I said, and then immediately regretted it.

CHAPTER TWO

"Ach du leiber!" Freni shrieked. "You did what?"

Seventy-five-year-old Freni Hostetler is Amish. Her pacifist traditions originated in Switzerland four hundred years ago. She lives a life of simplicity and modesty, not much different from that of her forebears who settled Pennsylvania in 1738. Her home is without electricity, and she and her husband drive a black, horse-drawn buggy instead of a car. Freni wears ankle-length dresses, has never cut her hair, and is never without a white prayer cap to cover those silver tresses.

I am a pacifist as well, but being a Mennonite, I have a bit more latitude. The Inn has electricity, and I drive a car. My dresses can be any length, as long as they remain below the knee. Some members of my denomination have even taken up wearing slacks, but if I ever did that, Mama would spin so fast she'd raise the earth's temperature by five degrees and melt the polar ice caps. My light brown hair brushes my shoulders, and I never wear a hat unless my head gets cold.

Freni and I spring from the same stock,

however. Unlike some Mennonites, my people are of Amish descent. In fact, Freni and I are related through both of my parents. Freni is also related to her husband Mose, who is related to me, and I am related to my husband, Aaron, who is related to both Freni and Mose. The four of us in turn, are related to 80 percent of the Amish families in America.

Although this may sound confusing, it has its advantages. I am, in fact, my own cousin. I can be alone and still be at a family reunion. Throw in a sandwich and it becomes a family picnic. And who needs baby pictures when I can simply gaze upon all the towheaded youngsters in the community? I'm not claiming that these children are interchangeable, but Rebecca Neubrander, who came home from church with the wrong toddler, didn't notice the difference until two years later. By then it was too late to do anything about it, and little Samson had her name changed to Sarah.

My point is that not only do Freni and I have fewer genes than a one-legged man, we are genetically challenged. Being a pacifist does not come easy to either of us. Sometimes it is a struggle to be the cheerful, even-tempered woman I present to the world. Freni, I know, feels the same. In fact, she had only recently confided to me that she was making a special effort to curb her tongue. Apparently her daughter-in-law, Barbara, had complained to the church elders that Freni's tongue was sharper than a two-edged sword. Freni was doing her level best to rectify the situation, but it was a monumental task.

"Calm down, Freni," I said to my cook and kinswoman, "it's only temporary. Poor Melvin can barely hobble around with that cast. Have you seen it?"

"*Ach!*" Freni exclaimed, and then her jaw clamped tighter than a pit bull on a mailman's leg.

"So, how are the guests doing?" I asked pleasantly.

Freni was rolling out dough for fresh yeast cinnamon rolls on the heavy plank table in the middle of the kitchen. Dough, rolling pin, and table were all getting a vigorous workout while she pondered her answer.

"You told me I wouldn't have to cook for children," she said, without moving her lips.

She had me there. I did have an "adults only" policy. The brochure I sent the Dixons had stated that quite clearly. But what was I to do when they showed up for their scheduled week with three children in tow?

"But these children have famous parents," I said.

The rolling pin came down with a thud that shook the rafters. "I never heard of them."

"Angus Dixon is a Pulitzer prize–winning photographer," I explained patiently, "and his wife Dorothy is a very popular children's book author."

She stopped pounding and began slathering butter on the dough. "Bible stories?"

"*Minerva the Mermaid* books," I said reluctantly. "I hear they're best-sellers."

Freni stared at me. "There is no such thing as a mermaid, Magdalena. What kind of a parent would put such crazy ideas into a child's head?"

"Actually, she seems to be a very good parent. But then, what do I know?" I added quickly.

Freni took a handful of cinnamon and sprinkled it liberally across the dough. "The children are hard enough to cook for, Magdalena, but that movie star! He wanted to know if the vegetables we serve are organic." She tossed a handful of sugar after the cinnamon. "Are they?" she asked hesitantly.

My heart went out to the woman. To her,

food is food. I had only recently convinced her that cheese was not a fruit. We had yet to tackle organic gardening.

"Yes, our vegetables are organic." It was the truth. We grow our own vegetables, and I much prefer to use the free fertilizer our two milk cows provide than to pay good bucks to get similar results out of a bag.

"So now I'll tell the movie star." Freni actually smiled, and began rolling the dough into a long, thick coil. It reminded me of something and I glanced away in shame.

"Terry Slock is not a movie star, dear. Susannah says he's a former child actor from that popular TV show, *Mama Wore Pearls*. After that he made one or two guest appearances on a soap opera. *The Young and the Spiteful*, I think it was. He played a vampire. Anyway, Susannah says he hasn't been on TV for years."

My sister Susannah knows these things because, unlike Freni or I, she watches television. It will undoubtedly shock you to learn that my sister is not a Mennonite. Her apple not only fell far from the tree, it rolled into another orchard altogether. Susannah is a Presbyterian — and a lapsed Presbyterian at that!

I fully expected Freni to go ballistic upon hearing that Terry Slock had played the role of a vampire; Amish theology and vampires don't mix. I glanced back at the table just long enough to see that Freni was calmly slicing the offensive coil.

"Well, at least the movie star is a nice man," she said. "That's more than I can say about the doctor."

"Oh?" I said, leading her tongue into temptation.

She grabbed a wad of butter and rubbed it vigorously along the insides of several baking pans. For a brief moment self-discipline and self-expression battled it out. In the end, experience won.

"He is not a friendly man, Magdalena. Yesterday I asked him a simple question about my bunions, and he told me to make an appointment with a podiatrist. When I told him we didn't have one in Hernia, he said I should see my *primary care physician.* He didn't even offer to look at my feet."

"Your feet are beneath him, dear. Wilmar Brack is a world-famous osteopath."

"Famous shamus," Freni mumbled as she plopped the rolls into the pans. "I saw that back brace he invented, and I wouldn't put that on a plow mule."

"It won him a Nobel prize," I said.

"And made him millions," Freni said, and gave me an accusing look.

"Man does not live by bread alone. Or even cinnamon rolls."

Freni limped over to the oven, a pan of rolls in each hand. "As far as I'm concerned, you have only one good English in this batch."

I knew exactly what and who she meant, and she wasn't referring to the rolls. To the Amish *all* outsiders are English. Without a doubt the good one in this case was Ms. Shirley Pearson, a high-level executive of Silver Spoon Foods. I'm sure you've heard of them — they make that new breakfast cereal Chocolate Troglodytes, of which Susannah is so fond. At any rate, I am all for women in high places, and if the truth be known, I jockeyed my applicant's list around and bumped her ahead of a few very wealthy, but less wholesome folks.

"Ms. Pearson is very pleasant," I agreed.

"She dresses sensibly."

"Maybe too sensibly."

The oven door slammed. "*Ach,* what is that supposed to mean?"

"She dresses plain," I said.

I didn't mean that as a slight, merely a statement of fact. Ms. Pearson with her midcalf skirts, and her elbow-length sleeves, could have traded dresses with the "plain" women of a number of Pennsylvania Dutch

25

sects. Her shoes were boxy brown oxfords, the kind Susannah referred to as clodhoppers. And it wasn't only her clothes that set her apart from past and present female guests. Ms. Pearson was totally devoid of ornamentation, be it cosmetics or jewelry. She wore her dark blond hair in braids piled at the back of her head and held in place with bobby pins. It was not the look I expected to see from an important executive.

"Yah, plain is good," Freni said stubbornly.

"Freni, the woman is —"

I was interrupted by a high-pitched wail that could only mean one thing. My sister was home. I whirled.

Susannah swirled in. I mean that literally. My sister wears neither slacks nor dresses, but outfits consisting of yards and yards of flowing fabric. Just one of her getups could clothe an entire, small, third world country. And so as to not speak critically of my sister twice, I will tell you here that she owns a very small and nasty dog, Shnookums, which she carries around in her purse and, upon occasion, in her bra.

"You're home!" Freni and I chorused. Susannah had only recently been hired by a paint company in Bedford, Pennsylvania, to name their color chips.

26

"I was fired!" Susannah wailed, and flung herself into my arms.

There followed a pitiful yelp, which led me to conclude that the despicable Shnookums was spending the day aloft.

I steered the poor girl over to the nearest chair. "Tell me what happened."

"I told you, Mags. I was fired. I worked there for only a month, and then they fired me."

"Why?" Susannah, much to everyone's surprise, had loved the job and thrown herself into it.

"Oh, they did some stupid survey and it said that sales were down on account of my color names."

I patted her comfortingly. There was not much I could say. I had tried to warn her that Mucus Mellow was never going to replace Buttercup, and as for Gonad Green — I shuddered at the thought.

"*Ach*, there'll be other jobs," Freni said. She peered into the oven, willing the rolls to rise further and turn a light golden brown.

Susannah sat slumped in her chair, like a pile of unfolded laundry. "What jobs?" she asked weakly.

"You could help out here."

It was a radical thought. Before our parents died a dozen years ago they wisely left the farm under my control. Even at age twenty-four my sister could outlaze the most shiftless of teenagers — not that all teenagers are shiftless, mind you, but you know what I mean. Susannah could sleep for thirty-six hours and not have to use the bathroom. When she was awake, her spine was incapable of supporting her in an upright position.

I am ashamed to admit that my sister did not outgrow this adolescent characteristic, until the paint chip job came along. That first day, when she got up with the chickens, Freni and I both went into shock. Even Freni's husband Mose, who is never shaken, examined Susannah's pupils with a flashlight to see if she was sleepwalking.

"Yah, I could use some help," Freni said. "What with your sister taking off to play policeman."

Susannah sat up. "What?"

I filled her in. It was already clear I had made a colossal mistake. Two, in fact.

"How much will you pay me to help out?" Susannah asked.

The nerve of that girl. She gets a hefty allowance, plus room, board, and the occasional use of my car just because we share more genes than two pairs of identical twins.

"I'll double your allowance," I said generously, "but you have to earn it."

"I'm thirty-six years old, Mags, and I still get an *allowance!* I want a salary."

"Then call it a salary, dear. Already you get enough money to support two Democrats or one Republican."

The oven door slammed, although nothing had been taken out. "Why Magdalena Portulacca Yoder Miller! I slave over a hot stove for you day and night, and do I get my salary doubled?"

"Freni, please! I pay you plenty."

Freni yanked the oven mitt off her right hand and wagged a finger at me. "I want my *allowance* doubled, too. On principle."

That would make Freni the highest-paid professional cook in Bedford County, but since I could afford it, and she was both family and a friend, why not?

"Okay. But you have to stop serving headcheese to the English just to see their reactions."

Freni nodded. Among her kind, that was as binding as a vow.

"No fair," Susannah wailed. "I'm your sister, so I should get mine tripled then."

I sighed wearily. I was breaking. I would have admitted to being Anonymous if anyone had asked.

"Fine. Just get to work."

"Magdalena?" Freni was staring at me through flour-dusted glasses.

"Freni, you'll still be making more than Susannah. She really was getting only an allowance. I mean —"

The oven door slammed and a pan of half-baked rolls came crashing down on the heavy plank table. "I quit!"

CHAPTER THREE

I woke up from my mid-morning nap with a splitting headache. The phone was ringing.

"What?" I may have snapped.

"Mags?"

It was Aaron. My husband. My Pooky Bear.

"So how is Minnesota?" I asked, after we had exchanged a few intimate words which I will *not* share with you.

"Cold. I wish I was back home."

"Aaron, it's August, so it couldn't be that cold. And if it is, why don't you come back home?"

There was a long pause which, had it been pregnant, would have doubled the world's population. "So, you've started nagging again, have you?"

"I'm not nagging, dear. It's just that I don't understand why you had to go there in the first place."

"I told you, Magdalena, I had some loose ends to tie up."

"What kind of loose ends?"

Those were wasted words. Aaron's lips were sealed tighter on the subject than a clam at low tide. All I knew was that Aaron had once spent several years in Minnesota, between the Vietnam War and his repatriation in Hernia as the Prodigal Son.

Aaron was born and raised a Mennonite, and as a member of an officially recognized pacifist group, could have done alternative service to the military. Instead, my Pooky Bear had actually volunteered, thereby breaking his pop's heart. I didn't even know he still had Minnesota on the mind, until just three nights ago when the phone rang. Aaron took that call, so I had no idea who it was, or why. Had I been strong enough to use a crowbar on my hubby's mouth, I might have given that a try. The silence was deafening.

"Well, if you keep that up, I'm not going to be able to get a word in edgewise," I said. I said it *playfully*. I was trying to lighten the mood a little.

"I should have expected something like this," he had the nerve to say. "Pops warned me."

"Pops?"

That did it. The old coot he calls Pops was living under my roof, and sponging off my generosity. I had given Aaron Sr. a place to stay even before I married his son because I felt sorry for him — and because I loved Aaron. But it was mismanagement, pure and simple, that cost Aaron Sr. his farm. It wasn't like he fell on hard times through no fault of his own. Yet here he was, accusing me of —

"Just what did your father say?" I demanded.

I could hear my Pooky Bear gulp. "That just sort of slipped out, Magdalena. I mean, Pops was only looking out for my welfare."

"Well, Pops is going to be looking out for his own welfare, if he doesn't watch his tongue," I said, not watching mine.

There was another silence during which the population of the world tripled.

"Magdalena?" he said at last.

My pregnant pause wouldn't have populated Rhode Island.

"Yes?"

"I don't want us to fight anymore. This isn't how I imagined it."

"Me either."

"I'll be back soon, Magdalena, I promise. And I'm bringing back a surprise."

Well, that was more like it! "All wrapped up with pretty bows?"

Aaron laughed. His laughter had the ability to make me think impure thoughts. But then again, now that I was married, they weren't impure after all, were they?

I laughed, too.

It was a good thing my mood had improved when I answered a persistent knocking at my door an hour later. It was none other than Pops. The old coot himself.

"Yes?" I asked calmly.

Aaron Sr. was once a handsome man like his son. Now that the black hair has turned white, and the broad shoulders are slightly stooped, he is only a little less handsome. The widows at Beechy Grove Mennonite Church agree with me, and have made him their summer project. The fact that he is poorer than a church mouse's debtor hasn't dawned on them. Or perhaps it has, and they think the old geezer will outlive me, and somehow inherit my estate. Fat chance.

"I need to talk to you, Magdalena." My Aaron's eyes were blue as well, only brighter.

"I'll say." I ushered him into my room and offered him the only chair. I sat on the edge of my bed. The door was wide open, in case you're wondering.

"Now, what's this I hear about you warning Aaron not to marry me?"

He looked genuinely surprised. Startled even.

"Well, never mind that. What did *you* want to talk about?"

"Do you believe in flying saucers, Magdalena?"

"You're serious?"

"Yah. Do you?"

What a question. We Mennonites tend to believe that while God created a vast and wondrous universe, he created only one *world*, if you know what I mean. On the other hand, so many of my guests have reported close encounters of their own, that I have decided to reserve the right to be skeptical. Believe me, this is stretching the envelope for someone of my background.

"I don't believe they exist," I said honestly. "But I'm not sure they don't. Is that answer good enough for you?"

"Yah, that's a good answer. I would have said the same thing yesterday."

"And today?" I asked. It is possible there was a trace of impatience in my voice.

He smoothed an imaginary wrinkle in his gray polyester pants. "Last night — early this morning, really, I saw a flying saucer."

I stared at him. As much as I hate to admit it, there was a difference hearing those words come from my father-in-law's lips, and, let's say, a Harvard-educated man who makes over a million dollars a year. Or even a high school–educated movie star who makes ten million dollars a year.

"Pops —"

"Oh, I know, Magdalena, now you're going to think I'm crazy, on top of being meddlesome, but I saw what I saw."

"Little green men with big bald heads?"

"I didn't see the occupants. I only saw the saucer."

I decided to humor him. After all, he was my Pooky Bear's father. Besides, if I was eighty-one and the Easter bunny came to visit, I would want someone to listen to me.

"Do tell," I said politely.

"Well, I only saw it for a few seconds. It landed in my pasture across the road."

Poor man. That cow pasture wasn't even his, but belonged to a corporation called The Beef Trust, composed of Pops and his sisters. The farm, under Pops's care, had lost money over the years. When the farm sold, most of the money would go to repay debts. Pops's undoubtedly small share wouldn't even see him inside the front door of Hernia's Home for the Mennonite Aged, much less keep him there the rest of his unnaturally long life.

Enter a developer who showed a keen interest in Pops's property. Unfortunately the man was threatening to build Hernia's first *real* shopping center smack dab in the middle of it. I say threatening, because several Amish families had banded together and were preparing to make Pops an offer he couldn't refuse. The odds were though that the Amish offer would fall far below that of the developer and would not be accepted. Of course that would be a shame — although it would be nice to have a Wal-Mart and a Payless within walking distance. One must consider progress, after all.

Or would it be so nice? What would the rich and famous prefer to view as they rocked on my front porch; a giant parking lot, or a green pasture dotted with grazing cows? It didn't take a genius to figure that one out. No doubt even Melvin Stoltzfus would come up with the right answer if given three tries. Although Aaron Jr. might not be happy with my decision, I was going to figure out some way to get the Amish families to raise a donation large enough to impress the developer.

"Magdalena? Did you hear what I said?"

I smiled. "Of course, dear. You saw a flying saucer land across the road. How nice for you."

Aaron Sr. muttered something that sounded vaguely insulting and left the room.

★ ★ ★

I had two missions now, one foisted on me by Melvin, the other placed on my shoulders like a mantle — well, it *was* sort of a revelation. At any rate, I certainly didn't have time to shmooze with Wilmar Brack, the back specialist. He had no business lurking in the hallway just outside my room.

Allow me to describe the PennDutch briefly to you. At one time it was a large, two-story farmhouse built by my great-great-grandfather, Jacob "The Strong" Yoder. At that time it had four bedrooms to house himself, his wife (my great-great-grandmother, of course!) and their sixteen children.

It had undergone extensive remodeling since then. Guests are required to enter through the front door the first time, and when they do they find themselves in a vestibule that contains a counter topped with a cash register and a rack of colorful and informative brochures describing area attractions.

A door on the right opens into a large sitting room, complete with a stone fireplace. This is the least changed room in the place. Great-great Granny Yoder used to cook stews in a large cast-iron kettle suspended from the hearth. Legend has it she hid the baby under the pot when they were attacked by Delaware Indians. The pot, now spilling over with a plethora of petunias, graces the front porch of the Inn.

Adjacent to the sitting room is the recreation room, the newest addition to the Inn. While I would prefer that my guests amuse themselves with Scrabble and quilting, they have a preference for treadmills and television. But it is my establishment after all, and the waiting list is long. The treadmill they got, the television they did not. Call me old-fashioned, but the road to hell is paved with remote controls.

To the left of the foyer is the dining room, with its massive table, around which my guests are expected to take their meals *together*. Behind the dining room is the kitchen which, for as long as I can remember, has been Freni's domain. Even when Mama was alive, Freni cooked for us. Back then it was her job to feed the farmhands.

Directly in back of the vestibule is the only downstairs bedroom — until recently *mine*. Of course now I share it with Aaron. If the truth be told — and this must never get back to Aaron — I was actually looking forward to having it back all to myself for a few days. I hadn't realized just how luxurious, and perhaps decadent, it is to be able to sprawl completely across a bed and not brush up against anyone. I believe firmly in a biblical hell, and the best metaphor I can come up with for it is a shared bathroom. Mine should be the only hair to clog the shower drain.

Upstairs are all the guest rooms, along with Susannah's room, and the suite I had built for Pops. Before you criticize me soundly for having stashed an octogenarian upstairs, at least allow me to state that we now have an elevator connecting the two floors. The impossibly steep staircase of yesteryear is still there, however, because it adds a certain quaintness.

Outside, in back of the Inn, where the old six-seater outhouse (the largest in the county) used to be, there now stands a white, wooden gazebo. To the left of that there is the chicken coop, then the barn, and then acres of cornfields backed by acres of woods.

My point is that there is plenty of space for my guests, and there was absolutely no reason on earth for Dr. Brack to be lurking outside my private door. When I opened it, I nearly jumped out of my skin.

"Ha, I must have scared you," he said.

"Can I help you?" I snapped.

Even under the best of circumstances, Dr. Wilmar Brack gave me the willies. Primarily it was because his age was indeterminate, probably due to extensive plastic surgery (believe you me, the frailer sex is not above going under the knife these days!). Judging by the amount of glint left in his eyes, however, I presumed that he was possibly in his fifties. He had thick gray hair that grew everywhere it was supposed to except for the crown of his head, which was capped by a perfectly round, shiny circle, looking for all the world like the photos of alien landing pads in the British papers. Three long hairs had been trained across the pate from right to left, and then lacquered into place.

At any rate, Dr. Brack didn't even have the decency to appear taken aback. "You promised to let me bend your ear for five minutes."

"My ears are already folded, stapled, and stamped. Besides, I'm really very busy."

"Two minutes of your time, then."

I let out a sigh that was heard as far away as Oregon, and led him to the sitting room. I gestured to the most uncomfortable hardback chair in my collection.

"Bend away."

Dr. Wilmar Brack lit up like a two candle jack-o'-lantern-lantern. "You know who I am, of course."

"You won the Nobel prize. You've told me that five times."

He squirmed. The chair was as hard as I had hoped.

"I said I was *nominated* for the Nobel prize. I didn't actually win. Still, it's quite an honor, don't you think? After all, the Nobel prize is worth far more than some damned Pulitzer."

I winced at his language. One more time, and I'd have to chide him.

"I'm sure it is. Who nominated you?"

He squirmed again. "The nominations are confidential, but I can tell you, it was one of the most thrilling moments of my life. Almost as thrilling as that time in Africa when I assisted Dr. Schweitzer in surgery. He was my mentor, of course, although some say that Al should have shared the prize with me that year."

"You don't say."

Even if Dr. Brack shared Cher's plastic surgeon, it was doubtful he was more than sixty. Since Dr. Schweitzer won the Nobel prize in 1952, that would have made Dr. Brack fourteen at the time.

"But enough about me," he said with a cap-revealing smile, "I want to talk about you."

"Me?"

"You have the worst posture I have ever seen in an adult woman not afflicted with scoliosis."

It was a good thing the windows all had screens, or I might have caught a mouthful of flies.

"You were aware of that, weren't you?" he asked, just as casually as could be.

I found my jaw muscles. "Well, I never! That was the rudest thing anyone has ever said to me."

"Oh, but I meant it in the nicest way. With your back and my brace, we could make millions."

I stood up, as straight as a flagpole. "I don't think so."

"But I found a factory in Honduras that will make the brace for pennies per piece."

I walked away.

"You'd make the perfect poster girl," he called after me. "We could show a before shot without the brace . . ."

43

CHAPTER FOUR

I was not in a good mood when I answered the phone. "PennDutch Inn!"

"Magdalena, this is Melvin —"

"My nemesis?"

"You pantsed me in seventh grade. You started it."

It was true. I had tugged on Melvin's overalls, but only because they were unsnapped. He was asking for it. Had Melvin been the decent guy he claims to be, he would have done me a favor and not worn underwear that day, in which case, I would still be a single woman.

"What is it, dear?" I asked patiently. "Is your cast itching you again."

With uncharacteristic maturity, he ignored my jibe. "The preliminary coroner's report is in. Of course it's a little complicated — the language and all — and I wouldn't expect you to understand everything —"

"Read it to me, Melvin."

It wasn't complicated at all. Anyone with as much English as a New York cab driver could understand the report. It was distressing, however. The body, as yet un-

44

identified, showed a bruise that corresponded to a horse's hoofprint, and another linear bruise an inch and a quarter wide. The latter was possibly two bruises, one superimposed and slightly overlapping the other.

"Sounds like our mystery lady was run over by an Amish buggy," I said midway through the report.

Melvin snickered. "The first rule in police work is not to jump to conclusions, Magdalena. There are other possibilities."

"It wasn't Santa and his reindeer," I snapped.

"There was *one* linear bruise, Magdalena, not two. Hernia area buggies have two sets of wheels."

"Yes, but the wheels are at least four feet apart. Clearly, the buggy ran over her with just one set of wheels."

"Will you let me finish, Yoder? There is a lot more."

I let him finish. There was indeed a lot more. Before being run over by the buggy, our mystery woman had been strangled.

"By what?" I asked.

"It doesn't say. This is just a preliminary report, remember?"

"Well, I can tell you right now, it may have been an Amish buggy that ran over

45

her, but it wasn't an Amish person who strangled her."

The static I heard next was Melvin bristling, I'm sure. "What makes you an expert so suddenly?"

It was time to backpedal a little. As much as I disliked dealing with Melvin, helping him with the case would be preferable to having my ear bent by Wilmar "Bragging" Brack.

"Of course I know nothing about police work, dear, but I do know something about the Amish. It just doesn't fit."

"Yeah? Well, there have been documented cases of Amish committing homicides, you know."

"Yes, but aren't most, if not all, of those victims Amish as well?"

Melvin has the world's only telephonic sneer. "There is always a first time for everything."

"Melvin, dear, do you want my help, or not?"

The silence that followed was long enough to ripen a melon. A more pious person would have knitted during the dead time. "Idle hands are the Devil's playground," Mama always said. Just what she meant by that, I wasn't sure. But given how far off she was in her veiled allusions to my

46

wedding night, I don't ever want to know. From now on I would have my knitting bag handy whenever I called Melvin.

"Of course," he said at last. "But keep them close to the chest, Magdalena."

"I beg your pardon!"

"Your cards. The few facts we do know. When you talk to the Amish give away as little information as possible. Make them give *you* the information. That's how you trap them."

I tried to visualize Melvin the monstrous mantis preying on a swarm of black buggies. The buggies kept getting away.

"Whatever you say, dear," I said sweetly.

It was indeed fortunate that I had been conscripted to help poor Melvin on the case, since Melvin was not privy to the Amish grapevine. That's putting it mildly. The man has, through every fault of his own, managed to put the entire vineyard out of his grasp.

Although the Amish strive to love their neighbors — even the English — and are famous for turning the other cheek, they are only human. And alas, Melvin has, over the years, taxed their patience beyond human endurance.

The Amish would never tell you this, so it is up to me, I suppose. The first day on the job Melvin started writing warning tickets to those Amish whose vehicles had emission problems. In other words, the horses left deposits ("road apples" we used to call them as kids) on the streets of Hernia. Melvin wanted the horses to wear giant diapers when they were in town. The Amish obediently complied with this demand and swaddled their horses' hinies with squares of black cloth. But this was not enough for Melvin, who insisted that the diapers had to be fluorescent orange. Melvin claimed this was necessary in order for him to tell at a glance which horses were clad, and which weren't.

But fluorescent orange was far too worldly for the Amish, and the day after this ridiculous dictum the diapers disappeared altogether. Melvin then began writing tickets — thirty-seven in all — and the Amish meekly paid them. It wasn't until a visiting Amish bishop — who owned a prolific horse — was ticketed three times in one day, that the Amish put their collective feet down. If their horses weren't welcome au natural, then neither were they. Since the few businesses in Hernia depend heavily on Amish patronage, *and* contribute substantially to Melvin's salary, reason won out.

Of course the Amish forgave Melvin, but

they didn't forget. I have heard Amish children refer to Melvin as *mischt kaupf* — which even a polite person would be forced to translate as "manure head." Since the Amish rarely make disparaging remarks, there can be no doubt about his lack of popularity. So you see, Melvin needed me.

I ignored several of Melvin's suggestions and decided to begin my investigation by interviewing Annie Kauffman. Annie is a short, but ample, woman, about my age, with a beak that would put a hawk to shame. She is an excellent cook with a reputation for the best shoo-fly pie in Bedford County. She also has an exceptionally sharp tongue for someone of her religious persuasion.

Normally — being the shy and retiring sort that I am — I tend to give folks like her wide berth. But, Annie, I have observed, receives even more than she gives, and as a consequence is privy to more information than a plethora of peeping priests. Not a thing goes on in Hernia that Annie doesn't know about, and of course she has an opinion on everything. It was time to pay her a visit.

I drove out to Annie's place in my brandnew fire-engine red BMW318I. Actually, it was a wedding present Aaron and I gave ourselves, but if the truth be told, I paid for it. And, while I'm being so frank, the car was Aaron's idea, not mine.

My Pooky Bear had originally promised me a honeymoon trip to Japan, a country that has always fascinated me, but the day after our wedding he inexplicably changed his mind and suggested that we buy the BMW instead. His timing was impeccable. I was still in such a state of shock that I signed on the dotted line in a virtual trance.

Believe me, I never would have picked red on my own. No doubt Mama is still turning over in her grave over that decision. Sinfully Red, Susannah calls this shade, and she ought to know. At any rate, I'm the first practicing Mennonite in Bedford County to own a red BMW and you can see the tongues wag when I drive through Hernia.

Between you and me, I sort of enjoy the attention. Of course I know that this is a form of pride, and therefore a sin, and I truly am sorry about that. But since Aaron insisted that I sell my gray 1978 Chevy sedan, I have no choice but to drive the new car. I'm sure that God makes allowances for circumstances such as mine, although I suppose I could just solve the problem by becoming a worldly Presbyterian. But five hundred years of religious history is a lot to give up, so until the Good Lord smites my engine, I'm going to consider this new car one of my life's many blessings.

At any rate, I found Annie Kauffman squatting on her haunches in back of her farmhouse, plucking chickens. She was observed by a flock of free-ranging chickens, none of which seemed particularly upset by the murder of their companions, and two small children, one of whom was presumably the last of Annie's brood of eight. Annie stood up when she saw me, wiping her hands on her apron.

"If it isn't Magdalena Yoder."

"Miller," I said. "I got married last month."

"Yah, that's right. I heard. You finally found yourself a man."

"Aaron was worth waiting for, I assure you."

"Let's hope you didn't wait too long. Even for a young woman it wouldn't be easy having children with hips like yours."

"What's wrong with my hips?"

"*Ach,* you're nothing but skin and bone, Magdalena. And all of it up and down. Even Jonas, our scarecrow, has better birthing hips than you."

The children twittered.

I glared at the barefoot urchins. One had the decency to hide behind Annie's skirts, but the other insolently stared back.

"Who says I even want children?"

"That's in the Bible, Magdalena. Be fruitful and multiply, it says."

The staring child was now sticking her horrid little tongue out at me.

"Perhaps some of us are meant to be fruitful without multiplying," I said.

"Why, Magdalena, your mother would turn over in her grave if she heard you say something sacrilegious like that."

"You leave Mama out of this. You barely even knew her!"

The beak recoiled, temporarily rebuffed at my passionate outcry.

"You may be prolific," I added, "but your children are rude. Especially this one."

"*Ach*, that's little Mary, my neighbor's child. She's English, but she likes to dress our way. She comes over almost every day to play with my little Lizzie."

A missile came hurling at me from behind Annie's skirt. I yelped and clutched my knee.

"*Ach*, you were always a strange one, Magdalena. So English in your ways."

"Me?" I shrieked. "Your precious little Lizzie just threw a stone at me."

Annie stared at me in horror. Despite her razor tongue, she was a pacifist through and through. Yet, with one fling of her arm, little Lizzie had overcome five hundred years of breeding and gone where no Amish had dared go before.

"*Ach*, Magdalena! I'm so sorry! Lizzie —"

The little girl scampered off, Mary at her heels.

"Lizzie! Mary!" Annie was clucking like a hen whose chicks refused to obey.

"I'll be all right." I limped over to the Kauffmans' unpainted porch and sat down.

Annie seemed to stare at me, but I could see that her mind was racing. How could she possibly undo the unspeakable? She started toward me, froze, and then a second later spun around and swooped up the half-plucked chicken.

"A wedding present," she panted, as she thrust the fowl at me.

I blushed. Chickens, turkeys, it was only a matter of size. And this one, as chickens go, was unusually well-endowed.

"Thanks, but I didn't come here soliciting gifts. I just wanted to ask you a few questions."

She literally jabbed me with the dead bird. "Take it. It's rude to refuse a gift, and my range-fed chickens are said to be the best in the county."

I took the chicken reluctantly, holding it

by one scaly orange leg. Annie had just committed the cardinal Amish sin of pride, and I am ashamed to admit that it pleased me.

"Thank you."

"Now, what is it you wanted to ask?" she asked, and sat down next to me.

I had rehearsed my first question all the way from home. "I — uh — well — uh . . ."

"Out with it, Magdalena. I haven't got all day. Eli will be in from the field soon, and expecting lunch on the table."

"Well, this might take some time. Perhaps I could talk to you while you work."

She shrugged. "If you insist."

"What are you making for lunch?" I asked pleasantly.

Her long plaintive sigh was worthy of a teenager in top form. "Well, we were going to eat the chicken you're holding."

It was my turn to thrust the chicken. "Here. I want something else for my wedding present. Something wrapped."

She took it without protest and immediately resumed plucking. Feathers flew everywhere.

While she worked I explained that there had been a "disturbance" in town the night before involving an Amish buggy. Did she know of any situations — emergencies, possibly — that might have required an Amish person to drive through town in the middle of the night? I purposely did not tell her that a young Asian woman had been killed. Play it close to the chest, Melvin had advised, and with a figure like mine that meant smack against the sternum.

Annie shook her head vigorously. "First you become an innkeeper, Magdalena. What are you now, a policeman?"

I spit out a mouthful of feathers. "In a manner of speaking," I said too proudly for my own good.

"Who ever heard of a woman policeman," Annie sniffed. "It's not in the Bible."

"I'm not a policeman, dear. I'm a policewoman. Well, actually I'm not even that — I'm just helping out."

"Who?"

"Our local chief of police."

"*Ach,* a friend of Melvin Stoltzfus," she said, shaking her head.

I smiled brightly. "I seem to recall that Melvin's mother and your father were first cousins."

Her feathered hands flew to her face. "*Ach,* how you talk! They were *second* cousins."

"Blood is blood," I said.

"I see that marriage has not tamed your tongue a bit."

"Nor has it yours, dear. Please, we were getting along so nicely. I simply want to know who drove through Hernia in the middle of the night."

She looked down at the chicken, pretending to search diligently for pin feathers she may have missed. "Why do you want to know? Was there a disturbance?"

"You might say so," I said just as cagily.

"Are you sure it was Amish?"

"Just as sure as you are, dear."

She glanced up at me, and then away. "I keep my eyes open, Magdalena, but I don't see everything."

"Perhaps not, but how's your hearing?"

Annie mumbled something about the English and their nosiness. I prudently let that one slip on by.

I stretched out my injured leg. It no longer hurt, but I grimaced anyway. Please don't get me wrong. I am dead set against lying, which is a sin. Feigning an injured leg, however, is not the same as lying. Birds feign injured wings all the time, and animals, as any God-fearing person knows, are incapable of sin.

My little exhibition was wasted on Annie, who was staring off into the distance. If she was looking for the urchins, she was wasting her time. I could hear them giggling just around the corner of the house.

I was forced to groan loudly to get Annie's attention.

She whirled. "What's the matter?"

I grimaced again. "This thing's killing me. You wouldn't happen to have a pair of crutches, would you? It's a long way back to my car."

Okay, so it was fighting dirty. But Annie was a harder nut to crack than I had anticipated. Maybe if she thought her monstrous Lizzie had done me serious harm she might soften.

Annie blanched. "Yah, we have a pair in the barn. Homemade crutches. Eli broke his ankle this spring when he was plowing. Are you hurt that bad?"

I had hoped for guilt, not a solution. "Well — maybe if I just sit here a while longer the pain will go away. What are you serving with the chicken?"

Annie declined to give me the menu, and scurried off to get the crutches. As soon as she was out of earshot the giggles got louder.

"I don't think it is very funny," I said loudly. "I could have gotten hurt by that stone."

Before the words were out of my mouth a second stone came flying at me from around the corner of the house. Had I not been just skin and bones, I'm sure it would have hit me.

"Des macht mich bees," I said in Pennsylvania Dutch. That makes me mad.

The giggles gave way to guffaws.

They may have been just kids, but that hiked my hackles. I wouldn't have dreamed of throwing a stone at a grown-up when I was that age. If Annie wasn't going to teach them good manners, I would. I hopped agilely off the porch just as Annie emerged from the barn.

"Why, Magdalena Yoder! You aren't really hurt, are you?"

Sometimes I'm actually grateful my sister Susannah parted from our pacifist ways and became a Presbyterian. Had she not, I never would have learned such useful slogans as "offense is the best defense."

"Why, Annie Kauffman," I shouted, my hands on my hips. "You should be ashamed. Your little Lizzie just stoned me again."

Her face reddened and she dropped the crutches. *"Ach!"*

"And you talk about *me* being English," I said. "Just wait until I tell the ladies in my Mennonite Women's Sewing Circle about this!"

"*Ach,* it's little Mary's fault."

"Blaming a child are we, dear?"

"Yah, but —"

"Perhaps we could come to an agreement, Annie."

Dark eyes flashed warily on either side of the beak. "What kind of agreement?"

"Tell me what you suspect happened in town last night, and my lips are sealed. As far as I'm concerned your little Lizzie is the patron saint of pacifism."

Despite her predatory features, Annie sang like a canary. It was not a pretty song, and it was one I had heard many times before.

Amish society, as strict and disciplined as it is, allows its teenagers tremendous freedom. The intent is to let them get rebellion out of their systems before they are baptized into the faith as adults. It is not uncommon for Amish teens to own cars, smoke cigarettes, and even drink during this period of flirtation with the world. Once they are baptized, however, they must toe the line, or face excommunication and shunning. Still, over eighty percent of Amish youth choose to be baptized and submit to *Ordnung,* the ordinance by which the community lives.

As a Mennonite teenager I envied the

Amish kids. They ran around in "crowds," racing their buggies up and down Hertzler Lane where we lived. They even held hoedowns — something Mama viewed as a date with the Devil. At least I didn't have to make an all-or-nothing choice when I was baptized; I have always straddled the fence between tradition and the world. But frankly, just between you and me, fence-straddling can be uncomfortable, and sometimes I even envy Susannah, who fell off the fence and into the arms of the first Presbyterian to ask her out.

"Don't you have a son who is about that age?" I asked gently.

She stared at me.

"Samuel, isn't it?"

How was I to know she would burst into tears? Crying is simply not something I think about a lot. In fact, I'm sure I haven't indulged myself since Mama and Papa's tragic accident. Annie, on the other hand, shed tears like a petunia in an onion patch.

This may surprise you, but I have never been the nurturing type. "There, there," I said, and patted her on the back.

"Oh, Magdalena," she wailed, and threw herself into my arms.

CHAPTER FIVE

ANNIE KAUFFMAN'S DUTCH COUNTRY CHICKEN AND CABBAGE

INGREDIENTS

1 pound chicken, boneless leg or breast, or mixture

2 1/2 teaspoons paprika

1 tablespoon olive oil

1 small head cabbage, cored and finely sliced

Pinch of salt and a turn of freshly ground black pepper

1/4 cup fresh lemon juice

1 medium onion, peeled and finely sliced

1 red apple, washed well, cored, and thinly sliced

1 teaspoon toasted caraway seeds

1 cup plain yogurt (optional)

DIRECTIONS

Remove all skin and visible fat from chicken. Cut into bite-size pieces and dust with the paprika. Heat a large frying pan, add oil, and swirl to cover surface. Add chicken and quickly sauté to sear surfaces for about 1 minute; add cabbage, mix with chicken over high heat for about 30 seconds.

Lower heat, add seasoning and lemon juice. Place onion and apple slices on top and cover tightly. Simmer mixture for 15 minutes and then sprinkle with caraway seeds and lightly mix. Replace lid and cook 10–15 minutes or until vegetables are tender. Add a little hot water as necessary.

Serve with or without plain rice or pasta. Drizzle top with a little plain yogurt (optional), which may be offered in a separate serving bowl.

Serves 4.

CHAPTER SIX

I hugged Annie and got the front of my dress wet, but I did not get the confession I wanted. According to her, "little" Samuel spent the night safely tucked in his trundle bed. She was crying, she would have me believe, because she was a sensitive soul and could empathize with the mother of the real hooligan.

Of course I believed her. I believed Mama when she told me that babies were found under cabbages. But I was only twenty then and afraid to ask questions. Fortunately I had grown up a lot in the intervening years.

"You have more empathy than a nursery full of squalling babies," I said kindly.

She dabbed at her eyes with her apron. "You're trying to trick me into something, aren't you?"

"Absolutely not, dear. Well, even if I was, it would be for a good cause. Some mother out there is really going to have a broken heart when her son gets hauled off to the hoosegow."

Annie stared at me with bleary eyes. There is nothing more unattractive than a woman with red eyes — well, perhaps there is, but that's not my point.

"What does hoosegow mean?"

"Jail. Prison."

"They could do that? Put an Amish boy in prison just for having a good time?"

"I'd hardly call a hit-and-run accident a good time. I'd call it a crime."

"An accident? Is that what you said?"

"Yes. But I'm not free to give you any details." Not that she needed any, I'm sure.

The bleary eyes blinked several times. "What would happen to such a boy if he confessed to his crime?"

"Well, I'm not sure, except that the punishment is undoubtedly lighter in cases where the criminals turn themselves in."

"Criminals." She said the word slowly, letting its three syllables become acquainted with her tongue.

"I'm sure you know as well that hiding a known fugitive is a crime in itself. Heavens, the Hernia hoosegow could be filled to overflowing before this case is through."

"*Ach,* but I . . ." He voice faced away, and the tears welled up again.

"You what?"

She shook her head vigorously. "Nothing."

"If you know something, you should tell

64

me now. I came here to help, Annie."

"Enos Mast."

"Who?"

"Isaac Mast's son."

That's all she would say. Further prompting caused her to snatch the chickens — one still half-plucked — and head for the house.

"What about lunch?" I called after her. "I'm available."

The screen door slammed behind her.

Not only was it lunchtime, but I was missing a cook. My guests pay big bucks, and expect high returns. Fortunately, it is atmosphere they expect, not service. Until Freni saw the error of her ways and came crawling to me on her knees, I would have to implement an emergency measure. It was time to resurrect ALPO.

I smiled benevolently at the group assembled around Great-granny Yoder's solid oak table. Thank the Good Lord the urchins had settled for peanut butter and jelly sandwiches and were already outside screaming and hollering loud enough to wake the dead in China. And since I was in a grateful mood I gave thanks for the fact that Susannah cleaned exactly one room before falling fast asleep on a pile of dirty laundry.

"It means Amish Lifestyle Plan Option," I said, ignoring the hungry looks on my guests' faces. "It's the quickest way there is to get to know the Amish."

"I still don't get it." Wilmar Brack was a pain in the back.

"Oh, I do, and I think it's marvelous." Shirley Pearson, who was used to speaking at board meetings, stood up. "You see, Mrs. Miller has generously offered to let us experience the authentic Amish lifestyle. We get to cook our own meals, clean our own rooms, and do our own laundry, and it will cost us only fifty dollars more a day."

"Cool. I can dig it." Terry Slock, former child star, seemed genuinely pleased.

It never failed to surprise how much abuse people will put up with if they can view it as a cultural experience. Well, most folks.

Wilmar Brack stood up as well. "I think it's the dumbest thing I ever heard."

Shirley bestowed an icy smile on Dr. Brack. "I still have the floor, I believe."

"Floor shmore. This isn't some damn boardroom."

"There'll be no swearing in my establishment," I said sternly.

Dr. Brack backed down.

Dorothy Dixon raised her arm, as if she

were a schoolgirl. "Will we get a chance to meet the *Aye*mish? Besides, Mrs. *Hoax*stetler, the cook, I mean. You see, I've been thinking that the *Aye*mish would make a wonderful setting for a series of children's mysteries. What do you think of *Hattie Hoaxstetler and the Hernia Hex* as my first title? Hattie would be *Aye*mish, of course."

The woman was creative, I'd give her that. I have always been a voracious reader, and as long as I can remember, authors have been my heroes. That was true right up until the day I met my first live author, a bizarre, paranoid woman who traveled with a contingent of six bodyguards and a pet cheetah. Since then I have come to understand that authors are just folks like the rest of us, with the same quirks and foibles, although in some cases the foibles are more pronounced. Okay, let's face it, most writers I know are more neurotic than a kitten raised by pit bulls, but I try not to judge.

In all honesty, Dorothy was far more normal than most writers I'd had as guests at the PennDutch. She was an attractive woman in her mid-thirties who didn't appear to be any stranger than yours truly. I could say something equally complimentary about her husband, Angus Dixon. If they hadn't shown up with their urchins in tow, I might well have liked them.

I tried to smile pleasantly. "That's *Ah*mish, dear. And yes, perhaps something could be arranged. Perhaps a visit to Annie Kauffman's farm." That would serve her right for not inviting me to lunch.

"Wonderful!" Shirley exclaimed.

"Will there be photo opportunities?" Angus asked. He seemed rather shy for a Pulitzer prize-winning photographer.

"I'm sure." It isn't a lie if you don't go into specifics.

"Costumes!" Terry Slock sat up, suddenly excited. "Man, that could be real cool. We could all wear Amish costumes to help us get in the mood."

"For what?" Maybe Susannah is right when she says I never have a clue.

Terry gave me a sympathetic look. "It's like method acting."

Shirley graced him with an executive smile. "Wonderful. Where could we buy some of those charming outfits, Mrs. Miller?"

"The Amish around here make their own clothes," I said. "Although you can find the fabrics they like at Miller's Feed Store."

She looked expectantly at me.

"It's a very distant relation. You won't get a discount."

Shirley nodded. "Anyone here know how to sew?"

It was time to put a stop to the nonsense. "They'll think you're mocking them, if you copy their dress. Like I said, the best way to learn about them is to live like them. Right here. The ALPO plan."

Dorothy had her hand up again. "That's redundant," she said politely when called on. "Calling it the ALPO *plan*. But, what I want to know is, can we still visit that farm?"

I smiled away my irritation. "Of course, dear. And you," I said to her husband, "could photograph the week's activities."

"That could be a photo essay," Angus said pensively. "*Life* magazine might go for it."

"Count me out," Dr. Brack bellowed. "I'm not washing dishes and cleaning rooms on my vacation, just to get my picture in some damn magazine."

He stomped out of the dining room just as Freni stomped in. The two nearly stomped into each other. If I was a betting woman, which of course I am not, I would lay odds on Freni, and not just because her center of gravity is lower.

"Magdalena Portulacca Yoder Miller. I want to see you. Alone!"

I excused myself from the group and obediently followed Freni back into the kitchen. It would not do to have my guests see two pacifists lock horns. The lucrative ALPO plan would fizzle then for sure.

"Freni, what are you doing back?" I whispered, hoping that she would take the hint.

"*Me?*" she practically shouted. "What are all those people doing in there? I haven't called them to lunch yet."

"Freni, dear, you don't even work here anymore. Remember?"

"*Ach,* throw me out just because I'm old. Well, I may be eighty years old, Magdalena, but I'm not useless."

"Stop padding your age, Freni. It's not going to get you my sympathy. Besides, you *quit.* I did not throw you out."

"Magdalena, please, we shouldn't argue about the meaning of words. Life is too short, and you and I are close blood relatives. Not just distant cousins, like some."

"Ah, I think I see. It's your daughter-in-law, Barbara, isn't it? The two of you not getting along again? Freni, you really should consider getting some professional counseling. It isn't easy having one's in-laws living in — believe me, I know — but you're going to have to accept the woman. She's been married to your son John for twenty years."

She stared at me through two little round

lenses supported by plain wire frames. "You may be hard to work for, Magdalena, but you're going to need my help with this bunch. So, as a favor to your mama — may she rest in peace — I *un*quit."

It was time to stand my ground, or forever give way to the Amish wolverine. "You can't decide that on your own. This is my kitchen, and we can get along perfectly well without you."

Freni sucked in her breath sharply. "Ach! So that's it. You're trying to sell the English ALPO, aren't you?"

"Maybe, maybe not."

"Magdalena, you should be ashamed of yourself for taking money from them like that."

"I tithe," I said stubbornly. "And anyway, they can afford it. Whatever they spend here means less money for sex, drugs, and alcohol somewhere else."

Freni nodded slowly. Although neither of us had much firsthand experience with the evils of the world, we knew they cost money.

"How much is ALPO costing this time?"

"Fifty extra a day."

"How about a modified ALPO? Tell them that they still get to clean their own rooms, but I'll not only cook for them, I'm willing to teach them how to bake pies from scratch for an extra twenty-five."

"It's a deal," I said, and then realized too late that the Amish wolverine had just weaseled her way back into my kitchen.

Everyone was pleased with the modified ALPO except for Dr. Brack.

"I'm still not interested in your damn plan," he snarled. "And who the hell wants to make pies on their vacation?"

"Watch your language, buster," I snapped. To her credit, Mama always said I thought fast where money was involved. "But that's a real shame, because for that extra twenty-five dollars a day I was going to let you shovel out the barn."

"Who do you think you're kidding?"

I feigned confusion, something I am skilled at. "What I mean is, you could shovel it wearing one of your famous braces. You would wear it without your shirt, of course. When that picture gets published — well, you know what they say about a picture being worth a thousand words."

Dr. Brack chewed on that for about ten seconds. His mama had raised no dummy, either.

"Shirtless, eh? And there would be pictures of me in my brace plastered across the pages of a national magazine?"

"That's the point."

"Hmm. This guy Dixon really any good?"

"He wasn't just nominated for his prize, dear. He won."

Although Dr. Brack glared at me, I could tell he was hooked. "Okay, but you have to wear a brace, too."

"I beg your pardon!" I had never gone shirtless in my life, and I wasn't about to make a debut as a topless tootsie for a quack with a back fetish.

He smiled, and for the first time I noticed that he had three gold crowns. Until then, I didn't even know he had teeth.

"I don't mean you need to go shirtless, as well. I just want you to try wearing one. You'll love it, you'll see. By the end of the week you'll swear by them. Who knows," he shrugged dramatically, "you might even allow me to stock some literature about my invention in the information rack in the front office."

I shrugged, albeit less dramatically. "Who knows."

But I knew. I might consent to wear one of his braces, if it meant his participation in ALPO, not to mention shut him up, but I was never going to mix his sorry little pamphlets in with those of area attractions. Melissa Frances, curator of the Pennsylvania Living Museum of Newts and Salamanders

73

would never forgive me if she found out. Neither would Horace Schnicklegruber, organizer of the Bedford County World's Smallest Pumpkin Festival.

Susannah, much to my surprise, took the termination of her new job in stride. Actually, she took it lying down, on the job. I mean that literally. She was still sacked out atop a pile of dirty shirts when I found her. I'm sure no one else even noticed her, thanks to the fifteen feet of flowing fabric she was wearing that day. They just happened to match some of my sheets.

My sister yawned. "Easy come, easy go," she said. "But fired from two jobs in the same day, that has to be some kind of a record."

I patted her shoulder. "You weren't fired, dear. I just don't need you to strip beds and wash sheets."

She yawned again. "I wasn't going to wash the sheets. I was just going to switch them around. You know, take the blues from that room, and put them on the bed in there, and takes those pink ones and put them where the blue ones were. It's energy efficient, don't you think?"

I complimented her on her ingenuity. "Perhaps some of the guests might prefer clean linens," I said gently. "You could show them how to use the washing machine."

"Okay."

I couldn't believe my ears, and decided to test them. "I know they could use a few tips on vacuuming and dusting. Why don't you demonstrate for them?"

"Sure, whatever."

Something was seriously wrong with my dear sister. Lethargy I could expect, but never cooperation. Where was the true Susannah, the slovenly, slatternly slut I loved so much?

I threw myself down on the pile of soiled linens and clasped her to my meager bosom. "What's wrong?" I wailed.

She didn't even have the will to struggle from my embrace. "Nothing."

"Before, in the kitchen with Freni, you had more gumption," I said.

"That was then, this is now."

I clasped her tighter. Suddenly it dawned on me that the little rat dog she carries in her bra had yet to yelp. In fact, I hadn't heard as much as a snarl.

I released Susannah. "Where's Shnookums?"

She barely shrugged. "Don't know."

"*What?*" Since getting that minuscule mutt six years ago, my sister has never let

75

him out of her sight. She even showers with him, stashing him under a glass cake server to keep him dry. One of the worst days of my life was when she took such a long shower that poor Shnookums ran out of air. Because Susannah was so hysterical, it fell on me to give the carnivorous cur mutt mouth-to-mouth resuscitation.

"He's around here someplace," she mumbled. Her eyes closed and she began to snore softly.

I shook her. "Susannah!"

There was no response.

Of course I was scared. Susannah is, by her own admission, a party animal. I'm not saying the Presbyterians are to blame, but the one she married did like a beer or two on the weekends, and I'm sure it was him who first introduced her to sin in a bottle. Yet despite her life of devil-may-care debauchery, my baby sister was not into illegal substances. Or was she?

There have been many times I wanted to slap Susannah's face, but this time, when I finally had a legitimate reason, I had to force myself to do it.

"What?" she moaned.

"Susannah! Are you on something? If you are, don't be afraid to tell me. I won't be mad, I promise."

No response. I'd give it one more try, and then call 911.

"Susannah! What are you on?"

"A pile of dirty sheets."

"That does it! I'm calling for help."

One eye opened halfway. "Don't be silly, Mags. I'm not *on* anything. I'm just depressed. Now, go away."

Believe it or not, I could relate to that. In school I was always good in English, and for as long as I could remember, fostered a secret desire to be a writer. In high school I won an award for making the highest overall grade in my creative writing class. I even got a short story, "Good Girl," published in *Ladies' Home Journal*. So, when I got that scholarship to Northwestern, why did my parents insist that I attend Bedford Community College instead?

At any rate, my freshman year of college I was so depressed I felt like I was walking around under water. I had the weight of the universe on my shoulders, including all the solar systems yet to be discovered. I didn't want to be an English teacher at Hernia High! That was their vision for me; it had nothing to do with my goals, my plans for living happily ever after.

I don't recall what lifted me out of that deep funk — it certainly was no one thing.

Time was perhaps the chief factor, and just maybe the fact that Harvey Plank, with the curly blond hair, was my lab partner for Biology 101. Harvey and I didn't actually ever date, but he made me laugh, and sometimes I would catch him looking at me, and not through the microscope.

"Get up, Susannah," I said in a firm voice. "We need to find you a man."

I couldn't believe I had said that, and neither could 153 Amish Mennonite forebears, Mama among them, who simultaneously turned over in their graves. Although there was nothing in the paper about it the next day, I know for a fact that the Hernia area experienced a small earthquake. Even Freni said the glasses in the kitchen rattled.

Susannah, however, went back to sleep.

CHAPTER SEVEN

Isaac Mast was a harder nut to crack than Annie Kauffman. I found him in the barn shoeing a horse. The man had a reputation for being the best at this task in the county, which was no surprise. When I was a little girl, Papa would take our mare Sadie (my family had both a horse and a car in those days) to Isaac's papa, Enos, to be shoed. Isaac grew up watching his papa at work, and playing with the children of his father's customers.

I was always afraid the nails Enos pounded into Sadie's feet would hurt her. Each time we went, Papa had to explain again that a horse's hoof is like a very thick toenail, and has no nerve endings. Like a toenail, a hoof is always growing, and Mr. Mast would file and shape the hoof before fitting a shoe to it.

Somewhere around the fourth grade I stopped being concerned about Sadie and started noticing Isaac. The boy went to a private Amish school, but I could tell he was about my age. He had the blondest hair, eyebrows, and lashes I'd ever seen. His blue eyes were so pale I could see the faint tracery of pink veins webbing across his corneas. We had a boy at my school with his coloring whom we called Whitey.

Isaac and I got along just fine. After the shoeings, while our fathers, who were some sort of distant cousins, chatted, Isaac and I would play. He was the oldest of five siblings, and most of our play consisted of chasing his siblings away so we could play in peace. Once Isaac and I found a nest of mewling kittens stashed in a niche between some hay bales in the loft of his barn. When the kittens were old enough, I got to choose one and take it home with me. I named it Isaac. But he was *never*, as Susannah claimed later, my boyfriend.

"Pretty day," I said, as I entered the barn.

Isaac glanced up from his work. "Magdalena."

"You have a minute?"

"*Nei*," he said. "Jacob Stucky will be returning soon for his horse."

"This will only take a minute. And we can talk while you work."

"Talk."

"Well, you see — okay, Isaac, I'm not going to beat around the bush. A couple of Amish boys may have gotten into trouble last night in Hernia."

"Yah? What does this have to do with me?"

80

"Was your Enos out last night?" I wanted to add the words "and acting like a teenage hooligan," but of course I am much too polite.

"My Enos did not go to town last night."

"Are you sure?"

"Yah. There was a volleyball game over at the Troyer place. Enos and his brother went to that."

"Yes, but I mean *late* last night. This morning, really. Would you ask him if he did?"

Isaac regarded me with eyes that had faded to the color of water. Perhaps they saw me seeing through him.

"Enos is a good boy, Magdalena. He has his fun, but he is not wild like some."

"You mean the Kauffman boy?"

"*Ach*, Magdalena, I will not mention names."

"Suit yourself. But Enos could be in trouble."

He put the horse's foot down, and patted her affectionately on the rump. The mare snorted her appreciation.

"What kind of trouble?"

Before I could answer, my pager went off. I am ashamed to say that my bladder almost did, too. The horse, however, had less control than I.

"Ach!" Isaac deftly dodged the deluge. "What was that?"

"It's my beeper. It's an electronic gizmo, one of the new English inventions to make life miserable."

A good Amish man, Isaac was not about to join me in a little English-bashing. I, who have one size ten foot firmly planted in the world, while the other is still stuck in tradition, would do well to follow his example.

"Were mailboxes hit again?" Isaac asked.

"It's much more serious than that. There was an accident; a woman is dead."

I wouldn't have thought it was possible for Isaac to get any paler, but he did. Dressed in white, against a background of snow, he would have faded away altogether.

"What kind of accident?"

"A buggy accident. Someone hit the woman and drove off."

"An English woman?"

"In a manner of speaking. So, what do you know about this?"

"Enos has said nothing about this." He turned his back and picked up another hoof.

"Of course Enos would say nothing," I snapped. "It's just like the army and gays."

That had Isaac's attention. He put the

hoof down, and the horse snorted again. She wanted the manicure done as soon as possible.

"You do not make sense, Magdalena. Are you saying Enos is —" He could not bring himself to say the word "gay."

"I'm not talking about his sexuality, Isaac. I'm talking about the 'don't ask, don't tell' policy you have. If I had a teenage son, I'd want to know what he was up to."

"It is easier not to know, Magdalena."

"Except for now. There is a dead woman, Isaac, and Enos may have been involved."

"*Ach!* Enos would never kill a woman."

"I believe that. But I need to talk to him about last night."

"Why you, Magdalena? Are you a policeman now?"

"No, but I'm helping Melvin Stoltzfus investigate the incident. You heard about Melvin's accident, didn't you?"

"Yah." Isaac's mouth twitched, and I knew he was trying to repress a grin.

"May I speak with Enos?"

He froze.

"Or would you prefer that Melvin talked to him?"

Isaac blinked. There still wasn't a trace of color in his lashes.

"Enos is visiting his cousins."

"Where?"

"Ohio."

I sat down on a wooden stool intended for Isaac. From that perspective a horse looked preposterous, all bulging belly suspended above narrow ankles. It was a wonder they could even walk, much less gallop at speeds exceeding twenty-five miles per hour.

"We were friends once," I said. "I didn't think you'd ever lie to me."

"*Ach,* Magdalena! I am the boy's father. I cannot say any more."

Maybe if I gave a little, so would he. Melvin would blow a gasket if he found out I wasn't playing my cards close to my chest. Well, it was a risk I would have to take. And anyway, as long as he had that cast on his leg, I could outrun him.

"This woman was run over by a buggy, Isaac. But she was already dead when that happened. We just want to question the driver of the buggy for clues. Maybe he saw something that will help with our investigation."

"My Enos is a good boy," he said doggedly.

I had to admire his loyalty. Papa would have been like that. Mama might have been a different story. When she smelled the cigarette smoke Harriet Schlabach blew on my new sweater one day after school, Mama thought the world was coming to an end. I barely escaped being branded the Whore of Babylon and cast out into the Wilderness of Sin. Because of something I didn't even do, I had to memorize thirty-six Bible verses, all of them having to do with smoke, none of them to do with cigarettes.

While I may share several bloodlines with Melvin, the obvious does finally manage to percolate through my callused cranium. This was one nut I wasn't going to crack. As much as I might want it, Isaac Mast was not about to throw himself, sobbing, into my arms.

"Well, it looks like justice may not prevail after all," I said bitterly.

"The way of the Lord is not just," he said, quoting from the Book of Ezekiel.

Had I known my Bible better at the time, I would have realized he was quoting the verse out of context. I turned to march from the barn indignantly (an action I've perfected over the years) when my glance fell upon a buggy wheel with a bent rim.

"What is that?" I asked, pointing to my discovery.

"*Ach*, just a wheel," Isaac said.

It would behoove men of that complexion

to turn away when they lie. Caught in his second lie, Isaac's face turned the color of Freni's pickled beets. Remembering the boy Isaac, my playmate from the hayloft, I almost felt sorry for him.

"You know where to find me," I said. "And now I have a scripture verse for you. 'The truth will set you free.'"

I made a detour past the scene of the crime on my way to the police station. Melvin was sitting behind his desk, facing the door. His eyes were open, but he was so still he may have been asleep. If he had been waiting patiently immobile for his next victim to enter the tiny office, he was out of luck. I wasn't in the mood to be pounced on.

"Yoder! It's about time. I beeped you twenty minutes ago."

I yawned. "It takes fifteen minutes to get from Isaac Mast's barn to here. Plus which, I had business to attend to."

Melvin's left eye fixed on my bosom. Since I am not blessed in that department — "carpenter's dream" they called me in high school — I chose to interpret Melvin's action as unintentional. Alas, most of what he does is.

"What kind of business?"

"None of your business," I said calmly. I was not about to discuss my necessary visit to the Masts' outhouse. The Masts, incidentally, should be thoroughly ashamed of the facility. It is only a two-seater, and in such bad repair, I risked life and limb just to make myself beeper-proof. And it wasn't even clean. There was simply no excuse for that.

It is gone now, burned to the ground by a crazed Presbyterian minister's wife, but we Yoders used to have the finest outhouse in the county. Ours was a six-seater, built by Great-grandpa Yoder for his sixteen kids. Its heaviest usage was before my time, but nonetheless, in my day that place sparkled. Folks used to come from as far away as Lancaster to admire it. "You are what you eat," the saying goes. We Yoders chose to take that saying one step further.

It was a fluke that both of Melvin's eyes met mine. "Damn you, Yoder —"

"That does it, Melvin. I refuse to stand here and listen to your profanity. Does your mother know you talk like this? Because if she doesn't, I'd be happy to clue her in."

It was a safe bet (not that I bet, mind you) that Melvin's mother did not know her son had a sewer mouth. Elvina Stoltzfus was a good Christian woman, a pillar of Beechy

Grove Mennonite Church. Zelda Root may be the heavenly body around which Melvin's heart orbits, but his mother exerts a stronger gravitational pull. If that were not the case, Melvin and Zelda would be married, and Zelda would be *the* Mrs. Stoltzfus who trims Melvin's toenails on a monthly basis.

Melvin's mandibles masticated madly, but in the end he minded his manners.

"Did you learn anything from Isaac Mast?"

"He definitely knows something, but of course his lips are sealed. My guess, though, is that his son Enos was driving the buggy. It may be coincidental, but there was a wheel with a bent rim in his barn."

"You talk to anyone else?"

I told him about my visit to Annie Kauffman.

"I never did trust that woman," he said. "In high school she let me copy from her chemistry exam, but she purposefully wrote down the wrong answers!"

"That was a different Annie Kauffman, dear. This Annie Kauffman is Amish, remember? She's never been to high school."

There are, in fact, eight Annie Kauffmans that I knew of in Bedford and neighboring Somerset counties. There are probably a good deal more, since the name Kauffman is more common in that area than Smith.

"All the same," Melvin muttered, "a Kauffman is a Kauffman."

I wisely refrained from pointing out that if you prick a Stoltzfus, a Kauffman is sure to bleed.

"What about you?" I asked. "You were going to interview the people on North Main and Elm streets. Did you?"

"Of course I did, Yoder. I'm a professional."

"And?"

He treated me to a monocular glare. "No one heard or saw a thing. The world has already gone to hell in a handbasket, if you ask me. No one wants to get involved anymore. Everyone claimed to be sleeping."

"It was the middle of the night, Melvin. They probably were sleeping."

Unless they were Aaron. Mama hadn't warned me that even God-fearing men were capable of experiencing certain urges at inappropriate times. After forty-six years of having a bed to myself, I found it unsettling to turn over and not only come face to face with a wide-eyed Pooky Bear, but to discover Pooky Bear Jr. standing at attention.

"It could be part of an Amish plot," Melvin said.

"*What?*"

"I saw it on TV. Only then it was the Mafia —"

"Bye, Melvin," I said, and headed for the door.

"Wait, Yoder! I didn't tell you yet why I paged you."

"Speak. And it better be good."

"It seems that our victim was Japanese."

"Or Chinese. Or Korean. Maybe even Thai or Vietnamese. Melvin, you can't just look at someone and tell."

That was especially true of Melvin, whose only encounter with anyone of Asian descent was at the Dairy Wok in Bedford. Three years ago when the Dairy Bar Softserve went under, the Kim sisters bought it and briefly made it a go. The industrious sisters, well into their sixties, began serving a Chinese menu along with the ice cream. Although the Kim sisters were Korean, they were a quick study and their version of Chinese food was surprisingly well received. Gradually they began to introduce Korean items to the menu, and the small restaurant continued to thrive. The Kim sisters were so encouraged by their success, they sold the business, moved to Harrisburg, and opened Seoul Food. Unfortunately, I heard that it failed almost immediately.

Poor Mr. Yamaguchi, who bought the Dairy Wok from the Kim sisters, wasn't even that lucky. Perhaps if he had followed the sisters' example and started out with a more familiar Chinese menu, things might have been different. Or perhaps he should have dropped the dairy items when he added the Japanese delicacies. It was definitely a mistake to combine them. Serving sushi shakes the first day he was open was not a clever move. Ditto for eel-sicles.

Melvin smiled smugly. "The woman was Japanese."

"And you're a praying mantis, dear," I couldn't help but say.

"Sticks and stones may break my bones, Magdalena, but they won't change a word on this fax I got from Harrisburg. It says that while they haven't found a match for our victim's prints, a Japanese tourist, last seen in Erie, has gone missing. Her name is Yoshi Kobayashi and she's twenty-three years old."

I willed my chin back into its proper position. "Let me see that."

It was all there in black and white.

"Well?"

Triumphal smirks do not become most folks, but this one actually improved Melvin's visage, and I told him so. I said it kindly, as a sort of penance for having maligned him with the mantis moniker a few minutes earlier.

"Is that all you've got to say?" he asked.

I was stumped. Okay, I had jumped to an erroneous conclusion, but I hadn't hurt his feelings. Trust me on that one. The man has no feelings. To concede that he does would be to assume culpability for years of well-deserved observations.

"What else should I say?" I asked crossly.

Melvin sighed deeply. Somehow he managed to squeeze a tear from each of his giant orbs.

"You have a sharp tongue, Magdalena, you know that?"

"*Me?* Look who's calling the kettle black."

"You should try walking a mile in my shoes, Magdalena. See how you feel then."

"I'd have blisters, of course, since your feet are far smaller than mine. I'd probably have athlete's feet as well."

"You see what I mean?"

"And you don't think you ever hurt my feelings?" I asked.

His eyes converged on my forehead. "Maybe you're right. We're a real pair, aren't we, Magdalena? Have you ever imagined what it would be like if the two of us had ended up together?"

"How do you mean?"

"You know, married."

"In your dreams, buster."

I slammed the door as hard as I could, and I'm sure I would have succeeded in breaking the glass if my foot hadn't been in the way.

CHAPTER EIGHT

Parking is at a premium at the intersection of North Main and Elm, so I limped the two blocks over to the scene of the crime. The First Mennonite Church, the First Baptist Church, and the First Presbyterian Church claim three of the four corners. Yoder's Corner Market occupies the fourth. Even on a slow day this busy intersection, which is the hub of Hernia, sees at least twenty cars an hour, and a handful of buggies. Even tourists from New York City have told me they are bewildered by all the traffic.

Because there are no residences on the corners, it hadn't surprised me to hear that Melvin had failed to uncover any eyewitnesses. The nearest domicile is the Presbyterian parsonage on Elm Street, but Reverend Sims has taken to shutting out the world ever since his wife Martha burned down my six-seater outhouse — with me in it!

I was after something specific, and I found it almost immediately. In the grassy median in front of the First Mennonite Church, only a yard or so from the intersection, I found a rut that could well have been made by a buggy wheel. The grass was thick, so it was not a well-defined rut, but I have an eagle eye for such things, thanks to Susannah. Occasionally I let her borrow my car, and despite my anti-smoking rule, she does so nonetheless. I have learned that accusations based on odor alone carry no weight in her rolling eyes. Consequently I have become skilled at detecting microscopic pieces of ash that would make a Mars-studying scientist proud.

Not only did I find the rut, but a scratch on the curb edge nearest the intersection, and then later where the wheel veered back into the street, a whole series of scrapes and scratches. They were faint, all of them, but the latter continued on down the block to the corner of Main and Poplar, where they faded into the dings and nicks of one of the worst maintained roads in the state of Pennsylvania.

Buggy wheels have a metal rim with a wooden outer surface. It didn't take a genius to figure out what had happened. Young Enos Mast (with a Kauffman boy as a companion) had been racing his buggy down Main Street in the wee hours of the morning. Suddenly he saw a body (or perhaps it was the horse that saw it first) and swerved, but not quite in time. One side of the wheels rolled over the body, up on the curb, over a brief stretch of median, and back in the street. It was on making contact with the curb that that wheel bent. The scratches and scrapes that blended into Poplar Street were the result of an asymmetrical wheel being forced along at high speed.

I was so satisfied with my conclusion that I didn't notice I had company until one of them spoke.

"This town has truly awesome vibes."

I had a few vibes of my own, and after crawling back into my skin turned my tongue on Terry Slock. "Don't ever sneak up on me, dear."

He grinned, a boyish forty. "Man, I don't blame you for spacing out. This place is really something."

"Fabulous!" Shirley Pearson was positively beaming. I might have looked that joyful on my wedding day if someone hadn't left the cake out in the rain.

The Dixons were there as well. Only Dr. Brack was missing.

"What is this, a group tour?" I didn't see a guide, but it wouldn't have surprised me if Freni or Susannah had popped out from behind a poplar tree.

"It's an exceptionally clear day," Angus

said. "The light was perfect for photography. They volunteered to come along."

"We couldn't just sit around and wait for you," Dorothy said accusingly. "I, for one, needed to gather material for my first Hattie Hoaxstetler book."

I glanced around. Some of the two-story Victorian houses had gingerbread porches, and here and there I could see a planter of past-prime petunias. Other than that, there was nothing I could see to inspire pen or camera lens. Hernia is a nice place to live, but you wouldn't want to visit there.

But since all four of them had stars in their eyes, there was no sense in disillusioning them. "Gather away," I said pleasantly.

Shirley Pearson cleared her throat as if to address a board meeting. "Perhaps you would like to fill us in on some local history and color."

"Yes!" the other three chorused.

I sighed. My dogs — especially that one I slammed in Melvin's door — were barking. All I wanted to do was to get back to the PennDutch Inn, and take a long relaxing bath before supper.

"I'd be happy to list you on the acknowledgment page of my book," Dorothy coaxed.

"All right. Hernia was founded in 1762 by my great-great-great-great-great-great grandfathers Christian Yoder and Joseph Hochstetler. Of course their wives helped with the founding."

"Of course," Terry said, his eyes shining. He reached out slowly and reverently touched my right arm with his fingertips. I casually shrugged it off. I may be piling up the years, but I am not a historical relic.

"Right there" — I pointed to a gray shingle house, an anomaly among the Victorian clapboards — "is where Christian built his log cabin, and down there" — I pointed to the First Mennonite Church — "is where Joseph built his."

It wasn't strictly true, but close enough for the good Lord not to mind. We were standing in the general area of the first cabins, which had long since disappeared, and it is the spirit, not the letter of the law, that counts, isn't it?

A station wagon packed with kids drove by and everyone craned their necks to get a look at the occupants, who as it turned out, weren't even Mennonites.

"Baptists," I said.

Next came a van. The driver was the only occupant.

"Presbyterian."

98

There was another load of Baptists, a load of Methodists, and three Presbyterian vehicles before a Mennonite motored by. It was Edwina Stucky in her brand new Lincoln Town Car.

"Mennonite."

"Are you *sure?*" Shirley sounded like she'd been handed a bad stock report. "She was wearing a halter top."

"Edwina Stucky is the organist at the First Mennonite Church. Of course she's General Conference Mennonite, which means she's pretty liberal. I belong to the Beechy Grove Mennonites."

"Mennnnnn-onite," Terry hummed. "Ahmmmmmish. They sound like mantras. You Mennonites are pacifists, aren't you?"

"Yes." I flushed. If Jimmy Carter was guilty of committing adultery in his heart, then I was guilty of biting, kicking, maiming — possibly even murder. "Pacifism is one of our basic tenets."

"And Amish are pacifists, too, right?"

I thought of Freni, whose heart's desire for the past twenty years has been to wring the neck of her daughter-in-law Barbara. But, of course, Freni never acts on that impulse, and deep within her ample bosom there beats a heart of gold — well, at least cast iron.

"Amish are definitely pacifists."

"So Amish and Mennonites are very much like Buddhists, right?"

"Excuse me?"

"Trust me. I spent six weeks in Thailand, and the similarities are striking."

"Well, uh — are you a Buddhist, Mr. Slock?"

It was time to lay our religious cards on the table, just to know what we were dealing with. Every now and then, I find myself engaged in a religious discussion with one or more of my guests. Just last week there was a couple who insisted that the Amish were a sect of Hassidim who shaved their mustaches. After arguing senselessly for half an hour, it was revealed that the female half of the couple was a Reform rabbi.

"Oh, no, I'm not a Buddhist," Terry exclaimed quickly. "I've left that scene behind. I'm into OUT now."

"You mean you're gay and proud?" Angus asked.

"I've always hated riddles," I wailed.

"OUT," Terry said, and spelled it for us. "The Oneness of Universal Thought."

I had no trouble dishing up a blank look.

"You know, my oneness and your oneness join together to form the thought patterns of the universe. Likewise, my me-ness

100

and your you-ness combine and become the our-ness of mankind. In other words, I am you, and you are me, and we are both that starling up there on the telephone line. Deep, isn't it?"

"And getting deeper," Dorothy said, and wandered back down the street toward its junction with Main.

"Do people ever convert?" Shirley asked.

"All the time. Believe me, it's the fastest-growing religion in Hollywood."

I nodded. I'd met a fair number of that crowd, so I could believe that.

Shirley gasped. "Oh my, I didn't mean your OUT thing. I was referring to Amish and Mennonites. What do they think of outsiders?"

As I opened my mouth to tell her, an Amish buggy turned the corner at Main and headed in our direction.

"Please, out of the way!" Shy Angus was waving his arms at us, shooing us like Mama used to chase cows from the cornfield.

"Well, I never!" I huffed, but obligingly stepped aside so he could get a clear shot with his camera at the approaching vehicle.

"Perfect!" Angus gushed.

"Splendid!" Shirley hissed.

"Ahmm," Terry moaned, his eyes closed in religious ecstasy.

"Follow that buggy!" I shouted.

It was Enos Mast behind the reins.

My guests had parked even further away than I, and by the time I limped back to my car and located my keys in the quicksand of my purse, the buggy was a part of history. Hot, tired, and desperately wanting that bath, I pointed my horseless carriage in the direction of home.

The PennDutch is only five miles from the center of town, but there are times when it feels a world away. I can't adequately describe what a relief it was to get away from the hubbub of Hernia. The Victorian houses became ranch houses and ranch houses farmhouses, and finally there was the PennDutch with its two giant maples on either side of the driveway. I couldn't imagine how Susannah had once forsaken the tranquillity of our birthplace for the bright lights of hectic Hernia.

I was seconds away from pulling into my peaceful driveway with a song of thanksgiving on my lips, when I heard the siren. I pulled in anyway and stopped. A moment later Zelda was rapping at my window.

Taking a cue from one of Susannah's many stories, I rolled the window down slowly and smiled. I did not, however, bat my eyelashes or purse my lips like a howling monkey.

"Good afternoon, Officer."

"Clocked you going thirty-five in a twenty-five-mile per hour speed zone," Zelda said, and whipped out a pad.

That did it. That hiked my hackles for sure. Not only do I believe that speeding is wrong, I believe it is a sin. The good Lord made it clear that we are to obey the laws of man as long as they do not interfere with his divine law, and nowhere does the Bible require us to speed. Okay, so it does say to "make haste" a couple of times, but I assure you those references have nothing to do with speed limits.

Because I believe this strongly, I refuse to drive a mile over the speed limit, even when there are trucks barreling down on top of me. Aaron thinks this is foolish and has warned me that I could get killed. So be it. I will not stoop to break the law just because someone else does.

My point is, I was so mad at Zelda for her false accusation that I rolled up my window. She rapped again, this time using the notepad to cushion her knuckles.

"Roll that down, Magdalena."

"I wasn't speeding!"

"Okay, you weren't. That was just an excuse. But I need to talk to you."

I rolled it down an inch. "Make it snappy, Zelda."

"Magdalena, I need your help."

The window came down. I may not be much of a fashion statement (Susannah claims I will never be until I stop wearing opaque hose), but even I could benefit someone like Zelda. Since she's almost always in uniform, her problem isn't a matter of dress, so much as it is grooming and hygiene. Zelda cuts her short dark hair herself with a pinking shears and then plasters it against her head with an inch of grease. She has tweezed away her natural eyebrows and replaced them with penciled arches. If she used a gold pencil instead of brown, she would be an advertisement for hamburgers. Now, it is no shame to be born with lips no fuller than a chicken's, but Zelda uses a fuchsia liner to extend her hen's mouth from just above her chin to the base of her nose. When she talks only part of her "mouth" moves, so who is she trying to kid?

"Scrub it all off and start again," I said gently. "Work with what the Good Lord gave you. If you grew your hair long you could wear it in a nice attractive bun. And let those eyebrows grow, they were meant to keep bugs out of our eyes. Unfortunately there's not much you can do about those lips, dear —"

"Magdalena! I'm talking about Melvin."

I sighed. A few makeover tips were not going to be enough for him.

"I'm afraid he's a lost cause," I said gently.

She nodded. "That's what I think. I thought he loved me as much as I love him, but I was wrong. It's not me he loves at all, but Susannah."

"*What?*"

She raked her fingers through the jelled do, and they emerged glistening. "Oh, yeah. He admitted it last night. He's been in love with her ever since high school. The day they started going together last year was the happiest day of his life. Then when they broke up, it nearly killed him."

"You don't say." I was grateful to be sitting in an old car that didn't have bucket seats. If I fainted and fell sideways I wouldn't hit a console.

"He asked me out on the rewind."

"You mean 'rebound,' dear."

"No, rewind. I went over to his house one day after work to help him with his VCR. It wouldn't rewind. I fixed it for him, and while it was rewinding he asked me out.

That was the happiest day of my life."

"How romantic." I noticed that her large, hazel eyes were brimming with tears. "I'm so sorry for you, dear. Is there anything I can do to help?"

She nodded vigorously. "Yeah. Get my studmuffins what he wants."

"I beg your pardon?"

"Get him your sister. Reunite him with Susannah."

I tried to faint — sideways, of course — but had forgotten to unbuckle my shoulder harness. A bruised bosom was all I had to show for my efforts.

"Well? Will you help me?" she wailed piteously.

It was worse than having to chose between fried liver and boiled turnips. Despite what I may say about her, I love my sister deeply, and her welfare is always on my mind. But how could I possibly choose between allowing my dear, sweet sister to wallow in the depths of despair and sending her into the arms of a maniacal mantis? Mama, how could you do this to me? And you too, Papa! You had no business dying before your jobs were finished. A tanker full of milk and a truck full of shoes is a flimsy excuse if you ask me.

"Magdalena!"

Zelda's tear-stained face was now just inches from mine. She may not have bought them at the golden arches, but she had definitely eaten onion rings for lunch.

"Okay, I'll do my best," I said.

Deep within my bruised bosom I knew I had made the right decision. Perhaps not for me, but for my baby sister.

CHAPTER NINE

I heard the faint moans and rhythmic thuds while I was still on the back porch. When I opened the back door I had my second chance to faint, but with nothing to break my fall, I just stood there and stared.

Freni Hostetler was sitting in a ladder-back chair, which in itself is not unusual, given her age, but she was taped to it. With duct tape. Yards and yards of it had been wrapped around her ample frame. Fortunately her face had not been covered, except for a small strip across her mouth. She looked like a gray cocoon topped with a Hostetler head.

Mercifully, after a few seconds my brain switched me over to auto-pilot.

"Dial 911," I said calmly. "Walk over to the phone and dial 911."

I didn't. And not just because Hernia doesn't have 911. I mean, I could have called Melvin, who would have sent Zelda zinging right back. But it was the tape over Freni's mouth that diverted me. Once when I was sleeping Susannah had taped my mouth closed — just as a joke, mind you, because I was snoring — and it was the most uncomfortable sensation I ever experienced, my wedding night excluded.

Driven by empathy, not caution, I ripped that tape off my cousin's mouth.

"Ach du heimer!" Freni shrieked, and with good reason. I had quite forgotten that she had a mustache any fifteen-year-old boy would be proud to call his own.

"Sorry, dear. Can you breathe?"

"Of course I can! I'm talking, aren't I? Unwrap me this second, Magdalena. When I get my hands on them, they'll wish they'd never seen this old Amish woman."

"Who is *they*, Freni?" I was unwrapping as fast as I could, but duct tape is hard to part from cotton clothing. "Robbers? Where is Susannah?" My heart was pounding and my fingers were shaking, which didn't make the unwrapping any easier.

"How should I know where Susannah is?" Freni barked. "Maybe they have her wrapped up, too."

"Oh, my baby sister," I wailed. Then a horrible, but quite possible situation occurred to me. "They didn't — uh — well — are you all right?"

"Gut Himmel! Of course I'm not all right! I'm seventy-eight years old, for crying out loud. Just wait until you get to be my age,

Magdalena, then you'll see."

"You're not seventy-eight, for pete's sake, you're only seventy-four. I wanted to know if you were *raped*." I whispered the word.

"*Ach du leiber!* They're only children, Magdalena."

"The robbers were children?"

Freni shook her head in despair. She was unbound, but still at the end of her tether. "*Snitzkaupf,*" she said, rapping her head with her knuckles.

"So I have a head full of dried apple slices," I said humbly. "Please explain."

Through a mixture of Dutch and English I learned that the villains were the three Dixon children. Apparently they had come into the kitchen looking for sweets, and Freni, who is usually such an obliging person, had refused their request because she didn't have their parents' explicit permission. Shortly after that Freni had sat down — just for a minute, mind you — and the next thing she knew they were wrapping her up like a mummy.

"And they took the whole cookie jar," she wailed.

I comforted Freni as best I could, promising to find the missing cookie jar, pay for her damaged clothing, and read the Dixons the riot act. I would not, however, promise to summarily show the Dixons the door. There are at least two sides to everything, after all. Now I'm not saying Freni deserved the treatment she got, I am merely stating a fact. Freni Elizabeth Hostetler is capable of generating strong, and sometimes un-Christian emotions in people who rub her the wrong way. Of course she has no idea this is a two-way street. Frankly, I wouldn't have been surprised had she told me her own daughter-in-law, Barbara, had done the dirty deed.

"Either they go, or I go," Freni shouted at my retreating back.

Until she paid me what the Dixons did, it wasn't even a choice.

I found Susannah still in the hallway, still sleeping on top of the dirty bedding. I shook her gently, but she didn't stir. I shook her as if I were the paint mixer at Home Depot.

She opened one sleep-swollen eye. "Go away."

"Not until you hear what I've got to say."

"Don't waste your breath, Mags. I know I'm a slothful, slovenly slut. You've already said so a million times." The eye closed.

Of course I was taken aback, possibly even ashamed of myself. I had thought those things about my sister, certainly, but I don't think I ever said them. In my defense I told her that.

"Of course you did," she said, both eyes closed. "Maybe not with your words, Mags, but you know what they say about actions."

That hurt me to the core of my already bruised bosom. "What kind of actions?" I wailed.

"You don't trust me, for one thing. Last summer when I asked to borrow your car, you told me I couldn't."

"It was still in the body shop, Susannah! You backed it into a telephone pole, remember?"

"Well, that wasn't my fault, Magdalena. Jimmy's foot accidentally hit the gear shift, and he would have stopped it, except that his zipper got caught on my belt."

I may as well be arguing with Freni. If I was going to save her, it would have to be at the expense of being right.

"You're right, and I'm sorry. I'd like to make it up to you now."

One eye opened. "You'll let me drive your new BMW?"

"When pigs fly, dear," I said gently.

"Then my life is over."

I prayed that it wasn't. "I've come to give you my blessing, Susannah."

"Your what?"

"My blessing. I've come to tell you that from now on you can do whatever you want with your life, make any horrible mistakes that you want, and I won't interfere."

"Yeah, right."

"No, I mean it. If I didn't, would I be telling you that Melvin and Zelda have broken up?" Well, it was close to the truth. At any moment Zelda would break Melvin's heart.

The other eye opened and she lifted her head weakly. "No way," she said, yet there was hope in her voice.

"Way, dear," I said mimicking her speech. "They are splitsville. Not only that, but a little birdie told me that Melvin is carrying a torch for you."

"That's silly. This isn't even an Olympic year." Her eyes closed and her head drooped. Had she been a plant I would have rushed off to find some water.

"He's still in love with you, Susannah. It's you he wants, not Zelda."

My sister popped up like a jack-in-the-box. "Melvin? Me?"

I know, it is a sacrilegious thought, but it occurred to me that the Good Lord might have told Lazarus there was a woman waiting for him. Someone other than his sisters, I mean.

"Take it easy, dear," I said. "You might want to attend to some essentials before you charge off to collect your knight in shining armor."

"Like what?"

I wrinkled my nose. "You've been sleeping on a pile of laundry, for one thing. And" — I looked around — "where's Shnookums?"

"Shnookums! My baby!" Susannah wailed. "Oh, Mags, I'll die if something's happened to him."

"Don't worry, I'll help you find him."

I couldn't believe those words had come from my mouth. That cowardly cur had been the bane of my existence ever since Susannah first brought him home in her purse. This just shows you how strong a force love can be. If that pitiful pooch made my sister happy, then I would forever hold my peace. About the dog, I mean. After all, Susannah is the most important person in the world to me, with the possible exception of my Pooky Bear. Okay, so maybe my Pooky Bear would win out if I was given one of those drowning scenarios in which I could save only one person. *Maybe.* But while I gave my solemn promise to cleave unto my Pooky Bear until death do us part, theoretically at least, Aaron and I could go

114

our separate ways. Susannah and I, however, would remain sisters forever.

Having said that, I did my sisterly duty and virtually tore up the Inn looking for two pounds of mouth and one pound of sphincter muscle. The cows were coming home, and so were the guests when I finally located that mangy mongrel. I found him just in time, too.

"Have you seen a little dog anywhere?" I asked one of Dixon urchins, who was sitting on the back porch steps, her head in her hands. A half-dressed doll lay at her feet.

The girl's name was Caitlin, mispronounced to rhyme with Kate Lynn. I guessed her to be about four, certainly no more than six.

"No *gou*," she said.

I froze my frown. It wasn't her fault if her parents allowed her to speak baby talk. Mama goochy-gooed Susannah until she was a teenager. Not that Mama neglected her parental duties, mind you. Susannah went happily off to high school committed to drinking eight glasses of wa-wa a day.

"He's a very tiny dog," I said patiently.

"No *gou*. Just *lao shuu*."

"Can the baby talk," I said sweetly, "and speak to me in English."

"I seen a rat," she said, and giggled.

115

"Not here you didn't, toots." I wondered if she was too young to sue for libel.

"Yessum, I did so. His name is Mickey. I dressed him up in my dolly's favorite dress, and we was playing tea party, only Bradley come along and took him away."

My heart began to pound. More than one guest has mistaken that snarling snippet for a rat.

"Was he black? Was he ugly? Did he growl and bite?"

She nodded solemnly. "He was my bestest friend in the whole world."

"Where's Bradley?" I shouted.

Her face clouded over, and her chin began to quiver. Since my shouts have been known to make grown men bawl like babies, it was time to back off a little. I squatted on my haunches so that we were eye-level.

"Where did your brother take the rat, sweetie?"

She shrugged. "Him and Marissa is going to give him a ride."

I breathed a prayer of thanksgiving that Susannah was still searching inside. "What kind of ride, sweetie?"

"A popochute."

"Say that again, sweetie. I didn't quite catch it."

"A popochute."

"What on earth is that?"

She scrunched her little face into a look of total disdain. "Don't you know nothing, lady?"

I glared at her. "A lot more than you, toots. If you ever want to see Mickey again —"

"There!"

I looked in the direction her stubby finger indicated. At first all I could see was the barn. Then just below the hayloft window, a full thirty feet from the ground, I saw a white speck.

"Popochute," the tyke said.

I gasped. Then, much to my credit, I sprang into action. At the risk of sounding vain, Carl Lewis has nothing over me. I covered the ground from the house to the barn in five seconds flat. By my reckoning I had the sixty-second mile down pat. Even then, I got there just in time to catch the little parachute before it crashed heavily into the earth.

The Dixon kids might have been bright, but they were not versed in the laws of aerodynamics. A single man's handkerchief is not going to offer enough air resistance to give a three-pound pooch a safe ride to the ground from the upper story of a barn. It was a close call.

Poor, pitiful Shnookums. My heart, which was pounding like a drum along the Mohawk, almost went out to the beast. He looked almost cute, clad as he was in a lacy pink doll dress, with matching bonnet

At least the Dixon urchins had been thoughtful enough to supply a green plastic strawberry basket for the pooch to sit in. It wasn't like they tied the strings directly to his ears and tail like I might have done. Back when I was a child, I mean.

"Is Susannah's widdle Shnookums Pookums okay?" I cooed.

Shnookums snarled and snapped at my shnoz, thereby ending any chance we had of bonding. I almost handed him back to the terrible two.

"Give me back that rat!" Bradley demanded.

"Yeah, give it back you big, ugly witch!" Marissa pointed to her nose and rolled her eyeballs back until only the whites showed.

The terrible two had inadvertently saved the cur's ungrateful carcass. Nobody speaks that way to me and gets away with it. I know, I am supposed to turn the other cheek, to be long-suffering, meek, and a host of other virtues. I try to behave like that, I really do, but I seem to have a threshold that is lower than that of my coreligionists. Perhaps, as a visiting psychiatrist once told me, I am the victim of my parents' upbringing. Dr. Alice Well should know, since she is the author of the best-selling book *Everything I Didn't Need to Know, I Learned From My Mother*.

But I digress. "Go straight to your rooms," I ordered. "March! And not one word of back talk, or you won't get any supper. As it is, there's no dessert for either of you. Now get!"

Simply said, they got.

"Brava!"

I whirled.

Dr. Brack was standing there, his hands arrogantly on his hips, an amused smile tugging at his mouth.

As I caught my breath, I prayed for deliverance from Mama's upbringing. Dr. Brack is a paying customer, after all. And his only crimes were lurking about and trying to peddle that preposterous posture contraption.

"Guess I scared you, didn't I?" He chuckled.

The patience I had prayed for was slow in coming. "Scare me again and you won't get your dessert, either."

"Hmm. What's for dessert?"

"Upside-down caramel apple pie."

"In that case I'll be more careful to announce my presence. I've always had a sweet tooth."

"Supper's at six o'clock sharp. That's half an hour from now. Even if the others — say, why aren't you in town with the others?"

"I'm not a tourist," he said, suddenly indignant. "I didn't come here to gawk, I came to relax."

I glanced over at my newly paved parking lot. It is a recent addition, and cost a pretty penny, but it has cut down substantially on complaints from customers about their cars being dinged by gravel. At any rate, Dr. Brack's Pontiac with the personalized plate bearing his name was now parked there in all its gleaming splendor, whereas it had not been there upon my return from town.

"Well, in that case you may want to try out one of those rockers on the front porch. They are very comfortable, and you can see the pond across the road from the porch. I paid good money for those rocking chairs, but I might as well have poured it down the drain."

Frankly, it irked me that this was the squirmiest bunch of guests I could remember. *Schusslich*, Freni called them. Not one of them could stay still long enough for a fly to land.

Dr. Brack shrugged, proving my point. "We each relax in our own way, don't we? I, for one, prefer a nice drive through the country over rocking. How do you relax, Mrs. Miller?"

I was both shocked and irritated. How I relaxed was none of his business. If I knew — which I didn't — I certainly wasn't going to tell him.

"Well, I've got work to do and time and tide wait for no man," I said, using one of Mama's favorite quotes. I started back to the house.

"Mrs. Miller?" He was jogging to keep up — we Yoders are world-class walkers, especially when we're provoked.

"What is it?"

"Have you given any more thought to wearing one of my braces?"

I gave it a quick thought. "Yes, I've given it some thought."

"And?"

"Well —"

"Before you say another word, Mrs. Miller, I have some good news for you. I want to tell you that I've changed my mind and decided to go on your popular ALPO plan."

"You have?" That was indeed good news, now that Susannah was likely to quit so that she could fling herself full-time into Melvin's arms.

"Oh, yes. And I'm going to shovel out your barn just like you suggested. Provided that Pulitzer guy snaps my picture."

"I'm sure Angus will be happy to do so."

"So?"

"Is that a needle pulling thread?" I asked with remarkable kindness, considering my mood.

"So, are you going to reciprocate and wear one of my braces?"

He had at last worn my resistance down to a mere nub. "Yes!" I nearly screamed. "I'll wear one of your braces."

"You'll be happy you did," he said, falling a little behind. "It will improve your posture a great deal. You tend to slouch, you know. But one of my braces will straighten you right up. It'll make your bosoms appear larger as well."

"Well, I never!"

I slouched away so fast he ate my dust.

CHAPTER TEN

GREAT-GRANDMA BLOUGH'S UPSIDE-DOWN CARAMEL APPLE PIE

("Messy on the plate,
but clean on the tongue.")

INGREDIENTS

Crust
> 2 ready-made pie crusts to fit deep 9-inch pan

Caramel
> $1/2$ cup firmly packed dark brown sugar
> $1/2$ cup finely chopped pecans
> $1/4$ cup melted butter (or full fat margarine)
> 1 teaspoon warm honey

Filling
> 6-8 baking apples, peeled, cored, and sliced
> $1/2$ cup white sugar
> 1 tablespoon cornstarch
> $1/2$ teaspoon ground cinnamon
> $1/4$ teaspoon ground nutmeg

1 tablespoon butter
1 teaspoon fresh lemon juice

DIRECTIONS

Preheat oven to 400° F. Combine caramel ingredients in the bottom of a deep dish pie pan. Place one of the pie crusts in the pan, on top of the caramel mixture. Allow the crust to extend over the rim of the pan.

Arrange apple slices in the pan. Sprinkle with sugar, cornstarch, cinnamon and nutmeg. Dot evenly with thin slices of butter. Sprinkle with lemon juice.

Cover pie with top crust, trim, and crimp edge. Poke holes with fork to vent. Bake at 400° F for 15 minutes, then reduce heat to 325° F. Bake an additional 20–30 minutes. Remove from oven and cool. Approximately one-half hour before serving time return to oven for a few minutes to loosen caramel. (This may also be done by placing the pie in a microwave oven for 30 seconds or so.) Invert pie on a large plate and serve caramel side up.

Serves eight English,
or three Mennonite-Amish.

CHAPTER ELEVEN

The next two days were relatively peaceful. Every morning after breakfast my guests scattered like roaches at sunlight (not that I would know, mind you). The enigmatic Dixons, the lovely Ms. Pearson, and tiresome Terry Slock roamed the countryside, Amish spotting. After the first day they no longer moved as a pack, but spread out like true hunters, the Dixons in their station wagon dubbed the Dixonmobile, and Shirley and Terry in their rented cars.

They were every bit as devoted as bird-watchers. Armed with binoculars and cameras and notebooks, they tracked every buggy spotted, photographed every bonnet. In the evenings they compared notes, and, depending on their level of civility, either implored me to arrange an official Amish visit, or berated me for not having done so — not that it was my fault.

Freni flatly refused to have her home opened as a museum for curious English eyes. "Let them stare at me in the kitchen here while they help me do the dishes," she said. The truth be told, Freni looks down the considerable length of her nose at the

Amish in Lancaster County who not only allow, but promote home visits by English.

Dr. Brack appeared to be indifferent to the Amish. At least he never talked about them. He made frequent short trips to undisclosed places but, much to my satisfaction, discovered the joys of a good rocker. Perhaps someday I will be as fortunate.

Susannah I never saw. After spending two hours on her makeup she swirled right out the front door and into Melvin's waiting arms. She didn't even say good-bye, much less thank me. I caught a glimpse of fifteen feet of flowing fabric, and that was it. Well, that and a lingering stench of perfume so strong that I used up half a can of Lysol trying to mask it.

My point is that had I not had the awesome responsibility of a murder investigation thrust upon my broad but thin shoulders, it would have been a relaxing two days. After all, Aaron was out of town and I was free of the connubial duties that had taken an inordinate amount of time lately — although my Pooky Bear assures me that five times a day is the norm.

It was, however, impossible to ignore Freni's numerous complaints. She was like a Sunday school teacher chaperoning a class trip to Pittsburgh. There was something wrong everywhere she turned. Chief among Freni's complaints were the children. Although I had made it quite clear to the Dixons on that first day that they were never to leave their children unattended, they continued to do so.

"Buck up," I said to Freni. "We'll charge them day care and I'll split it with you, fifty-fifty."

Freni's brows bristled over baleful eyes. "All or nothing, Magdalena."

"Easy come, easy go," I said, and capitulated.

But even with a good chunk of change as an incentive Freni found it impossible to manage three rapscallions and cook a good meal.

"Well, there's more than one way to skin a cat," I said. I was not, of course, referring to her meals. "Why don't you ask Barbara to help with the kids."

"Which Barbara?"

"Your daughter-in-law."

The considerable nose aimed straight for the ceiling. "She doesn't know the first thing about children, Magdalena. She's never had any."

"I know, but she was one herself. And she had little brothers and sisters."

"*Ach,* Matilda the milk cow has a little

sister. Would you ask her to help?"

In the end Freni reluctantly agreed to my idea. As much as she despised and maligned her only daughter-in-law, she realized that she would never be a grandmother without the woman's participation. Barbara, unfortunately, had been sterile for years, but recently a minor surgical procedure — with the bishop's permission — had tipped the odds in favor of fertility. (Not that the poor woman, already in her late thirties, had many such years to look forward to.) At any rate, it was as if Freni believed that by exposing her daughter-in-law to the Dixon children, that Barbara might actually "catch" pregnancy.

"Twins would be nice," Freni muttered, as we watched the urchins tie up her daughter-in-law. "It would make up for lost time."

"Boys, girls, or one of each?"

"*Ach*, Magdalena, how you talk! Girls, of course. Boys bring nothing but trouble. Boys . . ." her voice trailed off sadly.

"Marry girls?"

"A son is a son till he takes a wife," she said fiercely, "but a daughter's a daughter the rest of her life."

I wondered for the millionth time what Mama would have thought of Aaron. She had known him as a youngster, of course, since he lived across the road, but she had never met Aaron the man. It pains me to say this, but Mama would probably not have approved of Aaron — or any man that I chose. Before she died she had her hat set on snagging Peter Kurtz, a devout young man who not only attended Beechy Grove Mennonite Church regularly, but who had plans for the ministry. Mama would roll over in her grave if she knew that Peter had not only left the Mennonite fold, but was now a rabbi in Tel Aviv.

The phone rang. Now, my faith frowns on delving into the paranormal, but there have been several occasions when I've been thinking of someone and the phone rings, and I pick it up only to find the object of my thoughts on the other end. But I assure you that I am not so far into the world that I get premonitions from overseas, and certainly not from Heaven. My caller was neither Mama nor Rabbi Kurtz, but my very own Pooky Bear from Minnesota.

"Aaron! I was just thinking about you." The kitchen phone has a long cord and I maneuvered as far away from Freni as possible. The woman has the ears of a fox, and can hear a mouse belch at fifty paces.

"Magdalena, I'm afraid I have some bad news."

That's just what the sheriff told me the day Mama and Papa died. That was the understatement of my lifetime. Bad news is finding out that a check bounced (mine never do!) or that your car has just gone through another set of brakes (my old car was a certified brake-eater). But learning that the only link to your past has been turned into mush inside the Allegheny tunnel is not bad news. It's catastrophic.

"Go ahead, I'm sitting down." I was, too, and had braced myself by wedging into a corner.

My Pooky Bear had the audacity to chuckle. "It's not that bad, sugarpeep. It's just that it's taking longer to tie up loose ends here than I expected. I don't think I can make it home before the end of the week. But I'll be bringing back that surprise, I promise."

What I am about to say is highly confidential, but for some strange reason I felt like laughing. Maybe even cheering. It was like Friday afternoon at school and the teacher announced there would be no homework for the weekend. Of course it didn't make any sense to me. I loved my Pooky Bear dearly, and each mile between us was a stab in the heart. Well, perhaps that is going too far, but you get what I mean. Anyway, I'm sure you can understand why I felt guilty for being elated that my husband's return home was delayed.

"See you when you get here," I said, hoping the cheer in my voice sounded like brave stoicism.

"That's my girl," Aaron said, the pride in his voice evident. "Your stiff upper lip could support the British Empire." I'm sure he meant that as a compliment.

"Ta ta and all that," I said.

"Magdalena? Don't you miss me anymore?" he asked, taking a sudden emotional turn.

"Why, of course, Aaron. I'm just trying to make the best of it."

But I felt like a liar when I got off the phone.

I certainly didn't feel like talking to the reporter from the *National Intruder*. Of course the man didn't announce himself as such, but I can smell a member of the *puke*razzi (Aaron's word, not mine) a mile away. Over the years I have had my share of run-ins with this species, and believe you me, they can tell some doozies. Take that pregnant rock star who has been in the news a lot lately — she was *not* impregnated by Michelangelo's DNA scraped from the ceiling of the Sistine Chapel. Who in their right mind would believe that? I have it directly from the Swiss doctor, a former guest of mine, who performed this test tube operation that the father is Hannibal, and that the DNA he left behind was found perfectly preserved in a Swiss glacier.

"They're not here," I said curtly to a man at the door.

He had the audacity to grin. "Of course not. You expecting them back soon?"

"Actually, they checked out about an hour ago." I honestly had no idea who he was talking about, but it certainly wasn't any of my current guests. None of them were famous enough to warrant an in-person visit from the *National Intruder*.

"You rented them rooms?"

"The best."

"How much did you charge? And where did they get the money?"

I told him my top rate for celebrities and added that it was none of his business where they got their money. Frankly, it isn't my business, either, unless the money is nefariously earned at my inn.

"They slept in beds?" he asked stupidly.

"No, they slept standing on their heads."

He jotted that down, the grin growing. "What did they eat?"

"Plastic. Anything plastic they could lay their hands on."

He snickered. "I suppose they were green?"

"Hot pink with sequins. Well, that is, all of them, but one. He was orange and black."

That part was perfectly true. I did have guests like that once. How was I to know that the Amazing Zebrina Brothers were a trio of itinerant magicians, and that Cleo, the fourth member of their party, was a full-grown Bengal tiger? Susannah, of course, knew, which is why she intercepted their application and made the arrangements herself. During the Amazing Zebrina Brothers' weeklong stay she dated all four of them. Well, she didn't exactly date the tiger, but she got so close to him that I actually feared for Shnookums's life. The mangy mutt wouldn't even have been a mouthful. Still — and it surprises me to say this — it was a rather pleasant week. The Brothers were both amusing and amazing, and as for Cleo the tiger, he was far better behaved than the Dixon children.

"Pink, orange, black." The man from the *National Intruder* wrote it all down.

"Is that all then?" I asked pleasantly. Who says I can't turn the other cheek?

"Yeah." He started to walk away, but turned abruptly after three steps. "Here." He slapped an envelope in my hand.

I stared at the envelope. "What's this for?"

"Give it to the old man. Mr. Miller. This story is too hokey even for us, but hey, I've got a grandpa. I know what it's like."

I slapped the envelope back into his hand. "What?"

"You know, the old man. The one who called and said he saw some illegal Mexicans swimming in your pond."

"Oh, that's not my pond," I said carelessly. "And they were aliens from outer space, not —"

"So you saw it, too?"

Too late. I was trapped. Mama had warned me about my big mouth before, but she had never uttered a word about the treacherousness of the *National Intruder*. And there was absolutely nothing I could do. My tongue was like a barbed hook. No matter which way I twisted and turned, it was only going to get worse.

Suddenly, from behind every tree and bush on my property, popped a paparazzi. Bulbs flashed, videotape whirled, and laptops clacked. And for a long time I just stood there with my mouth wide open. It wasn't until the Dixon children, who had tired of tying up Barbara Hostetler, wandered into the front yard to find out what all the fuss was about, that I found my voice.

"Are these alien children?" a reporter from *Slime* magazine asked. The nasty woman prodded the tiniest Dixon tyke with her pencil. Caitlin yelped, and some long dormant maternal feeling stirred within my meager bosom.

"They may be monsters," I said, "but they're mine. Touch them again and I'll sue you so fast you won't even have time to sit down in court."

Granted, those were not the words of a good Mennonite, but rest assured, I paid dearly for them. Days later I saw my face, mouth wide open, plastered across the cover of every scandal sheet carried by the Bedford supermarket in which I shop. Without exception the images of the Dixon children were superimposed on my photo. Some of the adulterations were very clear, and in one picture little Caitlin appears to be clinging to my skirt.

AMISH WOMAN GIVES BIRTH TO ALIEN TRIPLETS, the best of the headlines read. As for the worst — well, those are fillings in my mouth, *not* computer chips. I am not, nor have I ever been, an android.

★ ★ ★

All in all, both guests and family took the publicity pretty well. The Dixons appeared satisfied to learn that none of their children's names had been mentioned in the rags. Susannah was too preoccupied with Melvin to even care. Freni made me promise that if I did ever have triplets, I'd share the secret with her daughter-in-law. Only Aaron, who saw the same covers up in Minnesota, had the nerve to raise a fuss.

"It was not a publicity stunt," I repeated patiently. "You know I have more people on my waiting list than I know what to do with."

"But it's in every paper, Magdalena. Are you sure you didn't do or say *something* to get this kind of attention?"

That did it. That hiked my hackles just about as high as they'd ever been. If my Pooky Bear didn't believe me when I said I was telling the truth, then what was the point of it all?

"You have some nerve," I said, without raising my voice, "considering it's the old coot's fault to begin with!"

"Make sense, Magdalena."

"Pops," I hissed. "It was your precious Pops who called the paparazzi."

He had the audacity to snort with derision. "Pops? Why would he do something as stupid as that?"

"Because it was your Pops who saw the flying saucer land, that's why!"

The silence that followed was longer than your average wait in a doctor's office. And at long-distance prices, too.

"Are you sure?" he asked finally.

I tried willing myself to be calm, I really did. For all the good it did, I may as well have willed the sun to reverse its course. Now, I'm not claiming this as an excuse, mind you, but if I recall correctly, Grandma Yoder had a bit of a temper. So, perhaps — just maybe — it is possible that I received a mutated gene from her. Perhaps the pacifist blood that courses through the veins of my kin is not the same as my blood. Perhaps I am hematologically challenged. How else can I explain what I did next?

"Don't you ever hang up on me again," Aaron growled when I picked up on the tenth ring. "You slammed that receiver down so hard I'm surprised it's still working."

"I beg your pardon! This is my phone."

"So, it's come to that, has it?"

I honestly had no idea what he was talking about. "Make sense, Aaron."

"Sooner or later it had to rear its ugly head."

"Huh?" Why were men so obsessed with sex?

"This property thing," Aaron said. "I knew it would be an issue after all."

"I still haven't the slightest idea what you mean."

"Of course you do. I came into this marriage a virtual pauper and you — well, you're rolling in it."

"What's mine is yours," I snapped. "And vice versa."

"Sure. You share your thriving business with me, and I share my dotty daddy with you. That makes perfect sense."

"I'm not complaining," I said. "Besides, you get to share Susannah. That evens things up a bit."

I was being very generous and he knew it. A wise, mature man would have been grateful enough to keep his mouth shut.

"Don't condescend to me, Magdalena. You know it irritates you to have Pops around."

"It does not." It's okay to lie to save a marriage. It's not in the Bible in so many words, but it's implied. Somewhere.

"Yeah, right. Well, there are some things you can't understand because you're a woman."

"Such as?"

"Such as how a man might find it emasculating to rely on his wife for charity."

"We're talking in circles, Aaron, and I don't want to fight anymore. You're the most precious thing to me in the entire world. You're my" — I struggled to get the word out — "Romeo."

Coming from me that was as emotional an image as a bus full of nuns holding babies as it plummeted off a cliff. A reasonable man would have given me something back.

"Romeo ran around in tights," Aaron said. "The emasculation continues."

I decided to give him another chance. "I love you, Pooky Bear."

After one of his interminable pauses he sighed. "Yeah, me too."

"You — you man!" I shrieked, and slammed the phone down again.

Mere seconds later a car pulled into my driveway and someone rudely honked. I prayed for a charitable tongue.

CHAPTER TWELVE

My heart sank when I saw that it was Zelda. No doubt she had come to enlist my help in getting her studmuffin back. Well, she was going to be disappointed. I had caught a glimpse of my sister the day before when she sailed into the PennDutch to retrieve a few bolts of her clothing, and let me assure you of this, she was happy. I haven't seen her shine like that since Mama rubbed her with Vicks when she had a chest cold. So you see, there was no way I was going to help Zelda come between my sister and happiness. Especially if that happiness could be found outside the PennDutch Inn.

"I'm sorry, dear," I said gently, having chosen to totally ignore the rude honking, "but it's out of the question. Blood is thicker than water."

"That's because you have a well," Zelda said dryly. "You'd be surprised at what comes out of the taps in Hernia."

"Still, I'm not going to help you get Melvin back."

She shook her head so hard a few strands of short dark hair popped up through the inch of restraining grease.

"I don't want Melvin back. That's not why I'm here. It's about Enos."

"Enos Mast?" I don't believe in hocus-pocus premonitions, or any of that nonsense, but every hair on my arms was standing at attention.

"Last night he was shot and nearly killed. A .22-caliber bullet hit him in the head, fracturing his skull. The bullet stopped just short of entering his brain, but there was some bleeding, and he's still unconscious. We took him to Bedford County Memorial Hospital, but he's been airlifted to Trauma Care Center in Pittsburgh."

"Oh my." I sat down on the top step of my front porch.

"Harvey Zook found the Mast horse and buggy wandering around on top of Stucky Ridge."

"What was Harvey doing up on Stucky Ridge at night?"

As if I didn't know. He was courting, of course. Stucky Ridge is the highest point around and offers splendid views of Hernia by day, and on exceptionally clear nights, even the lights of greater Bedford can be seen twinkling seductively. There is only a gravel lane leading to the top of the ridge, and at the crest it splits, the right fork veering off to a picnic area, and the left to the historic Settler's Cemetery. It is not a heavily frequented area, but some families drive up the ridge during daylight hours to visit their dead or eat picnic lunches. At night it's a different place entirely. God versus gonads, my irreverent, but much experienced, sister used to say.

Because Hernia has yet to become the den of iniquity that some say Bedford has become, Melvin and Zelda used to spend an inordinate amount of their time rousting the osculating occupants of buggies and cars that line the picnic overlook each night. Rumor has it that these nocturnal patrols are what finally inspired Melvin and Zelda to become more than just working partners. Again, my source is my sister, who still has two unpaid loitering citations to back up her words.

At any rate, I knew Harvey, a Mennonite, and I knew his intended even better — Catherine Blough is my double first cousin once removed, and generally acknowledged to be the prettiest girl in all of Hernia. Physical beauty is, of course, in the eye of the beholder, and totally unimportant in the eyes of the good Lord, proving that cousin Catherine either wears blinders on her dates, or is a Godly girl. I know it is wrong to even say this, but Harvey is the ugliest boy to be born in Hernia since its founding. This is neither here nor there, and I wouldn't have even mentioned Harvey's milk-curdling looks, except that it irks me that a kid like Harvey can get a beautiful girl like my cousin, but I went virtually dateless between college and the first time Aaron asked me out. Okay, there was that one bizarre evening with Jumbo Jim, the fried chicken king, but surely it doesn't count. He was from Baltimore, for crying out loud, and everyone knows it takes *two* dates with a Marylander to equal one with a Pennsylvania man.

Zelda rolled her eyes at me under the lids the color of bruised plums. "You know darn well what Harvey was doing up on the Ridge, but Melvin said it's important to tell you that Harvey didn't find the horse and buggy in the picnic area. They were over in Settler's Cemetery."

I gasped and glanced at the long, low mountain, which was just barely visible above the top of my barn. Mama and Papa, both descendants of Hernia's original settlers, had the final privilege of being buried up there. Mama, who managed to die a virgin after bearing two children, would not have approved of smooching and groping anywhere near her grave. It was a wonder

Stucky Ridge was still standing. I would not have been surprised to learn that a Mama-induced earthquake had rendered the mountain as flat as one of Freni's pancakes.

"Shame on Harvey Zook," I said, on Mama's behalf. "If one can't respect the dead, then —"

"Harvey was not making out in Settler's Cemetery, if that's what you mean," Zelda said with embarrassing bluntness. "He was making out in the picnic grove just like everyone else. But he heard what sounded like a loud pop and drove over to check it out. He thought it might be some of those hooligans from Bedford — you know, the ones who knocked over some of the headstones last year? Remember?"

How could I forget? The oldest headstones in Settler's Cemetery date back to the 1700s. Fortunately these stones were not bothered. An encroaching copse of oak trees has all but obliterated the original cemetery. Those markers not hidden by saplings and under growth have been tilted to rakish angles by thickening roots of mature trees. For as long as I can remember, none of the ancient stones have been perpendicular to the ground.

The "new wing," as Susannah calls it, is that portion of the cemetery occupied by folks whose children or grandchildren are still alive. Seedlings are plucked from the ground before they can turn into saplings. The headstones are larger and more elaborate than their predecessors, and until last year, all decidedly upright. Last Halloween night that was all changed by a gang of Bedford boys wielding bats. When they were through having fun the newer stones had been flattened, knocked off their marble and granite pedestals.

The section in which my parents' graves are found fared the worst. All the stones were toppled, except for one. Mama's stone had clearly been desecrated — the bats had chipped the smooth marble edges — but it had remained standing. Apparently Mama had stopped turning in her grave long enough to stand guard over it. By the sheer force of her will she kept the marker bearing her name on it from budging. Why Mama didn't do the same for Papa's stone is anybody's guess. However, the rumor that Mama didn't die in that horrible wreck, but went into hiding along with JFK and Elvis, and has resurfaced as the leader of the Bedford Bad Boys, is pure poppycock.

"So what was Enos Mast doing in Settler's Cemetery after dark, and who shot him?"

Zelda shrugged. "I was the officer on call, but like I said, Enos was unconscious, and Harvey was very evasive. So, those are the details Melvin wants you to find out. He says it's undoubtedly related to the Japanese woman you ran over with your car."

I gave her a pleasant stare. "I did *not* run over her."

"Whatever you say." Bruised plum and egg white were all I could see of her eyes.

"Making faces is childish, dear," I said gently. "Besides, we're supposed to be on the same side here. Melvin is counting on us to work together."

"Yeah, yeah." Zelda sauntered back to Hernia's only cruiser, got in, started it, but didn't close the door. "Hey, Magdalena," she called over the noise of the engine. "Did I tell you that Melvin and I might be getting back together?"

"*What?*"

Zelda slammed the car into reverse and pressed the pedal to the metal, as if it were a go-cart. The tires spun and screamed, and so did I when Zelda's open door smacked my mailbox, the one Great-grandpa Yoder hand-forged. The car spun a full one hundred and eighty degrees, but apparently neither door nor driver were severely damaged. The tires spun and screamed again and

Zelda zoomed off, leaving a trail of exhaust.

"You'll pay for that!" I shouted.

But when I examined the box a few seconds later, except for a couple of scratches in the black paint, there was nothing wrong with it that I could see. I always knew Great-grandpa was a craftsman and had produced many durable things, but I wouldn't be surprised if Mama's will had something to do with the mailbox's survival.

I found homely Harvey Zook whiling away the last days of summer watching cartoons on television. We never had a TV, but nonetheless, Susannah got away with idleness when she was in high school. Not me. "Lazy hands are the devil's playground," Mama said ad nauseam, and made sure that the devil didn't delight in my digits. Not only did I have to work at Yoder's Corner Market after school and during vacations, but I had enough chores at home to stagger a Conestoga wagon full of pioneer women.

"You should be ashamed of yourself, watching that mindless drivel on TV," I said instructively to Harvey.

"Huh?" He stared at me with bleary eyes. His parents weren't home, and there was no sign of his two younger brothers. Quite possibly I'd caught the boy napping, in which case the devil was in seventh heaven. So to speak.

"You should try reading a book," I said kindly.

"I read a book."

"Oh? *Beach Music* by Pat Conroy?" I asked hopefully.

He shrugged. "I read the book back in ninth grade, Miss Yoder. There was a raft in it and some kid named Huck."

"I'm Mrs. Miller now, remember? May I come in?"

"I'm not supposed to have company when my parents aren't home."

I smiled patiently. "I'm not company. I've known you since you were in diapers — in fact, I changed one of them at a church picnic. And you're dating my cousin, for pete's sake."

"So?" In all fairness, there was no nastiness in his voice. Just a healthy teenage mixture of insouciance and lethargy.

I did not survive Susannah's teenage years without picking up a few tips here and there. I casually extracted a ten dollar bill from my purse and fanned my face.

"It's getting hot today, isn't it, Harvey?" The screen door opened slowly.

"Turn off the television, dear, if you don't mind. I need to ask you some questions."

He shuffled over to the couch and picked up the remote. "Are they about last night? Because if they are, my mom says I'm not supposed to answer them."

"I'm not a reporter, Harvey. I'm helping the police ask some questions because I know the area. Now be a dear and turn off the set." Some bizarre green creatures, half turtle and half human, were catapulting across the giant screen. The noise was deafening.

Frankly, and I should be ashamed of myself for saying this, but except for his coloring, Harvey was a dead ringer for one of those mutated reptiles.

"Ah, this is my favorite show."

I fanned faster.

He reluctantly clicked the remote.

"Mind if I sit?" I asked, and then immediately regretted it. I hadn't seen such a collage of crushed potato chips, spilled dip, and melted chocolate candy since the aftermath of one of Susannah's slumber parties.

"Be my guest," Harvey said, and had the cheek to grin.

"On second thought, I've been sitting all day. Now, Harvey —"

Thanks to the loud volume of the TV I hadn't heard Harvey's mother return. My first clue was the loud slam of the screen door.

"Magdalena! What are you doing here?"

"I need to ask Harvey a few questions —"

"Oh, no you don't," said Salina Zook, grabbing my arm.

She tried forcibly steering me toward the door, but I politely resisted by digging my heels into the soiled shag carpet, and clamping my free hand over the back of the food-encrusted sofa. I knew I could last only a few seconds, despite the fact that my fingers were practically glued to the fabric by the remains of a half-eaten Snickers bar.

Salina is a good six inches shorter than me, but all muscle. In high school she arm wrestled and beat every boy in Hernia High who challenged her except for Stubby Jenkins. Stubby's secret, he confided to me later, was that he'd gone to bed the night before with a large garlic clove crammed between his gums and teeth. Stubby panted to demonstrate, and even though three days had gone by, I nearly passed out. Ever since then I have had a love/hate relationship with shrimp scampi, and find Susannah's garlic-flavored bubble gum intolerable.

At any rate, Salina Zook was as close as our school came to having a bully. Although she had mellowed over the years, and was in fact president of the Mennonite Women's

Sewing Circle, she still exuded authority — the kind that could be backed up if necessary. As usual, the Good Lord knew what he was doing. People seldom made fun of Salina's children in her presence.

"I'm here on police business," I wailed.

"That's nonsense." She tugged harder.

"Call Melvin and ask him."

"Don't be ridiculous. You can't stand the man and you know it."

I felt the couch slipping from my grip and did my best Stubby imitation. Unfortunately oatmeal ions are not very pungent and Salina didn't flinch.

"Been there, Magdalena. Done that."

"Excuse me?"

She wrenched me loose. "How do you think I won all those times in high school? I would have had a perfect record, too, if Stubby hadn't found out my secret and tried it out on me the day I had a dentist appointment."

"Then ask Zelda Root!" I cried. "I'm practically a member of the Hernia police force."

"And little green men from Mars stay at your inn," she said cruelly.

"What?"

"I saw those magazines at the checkout stand of the Giant Eagle in Bedford. You were on the front page, sandwiched between that three-headed calf from India that sings rap music and Camilla Bowles Parker. Everyone in Bedford County thinks you're nuts. Are you, Magdalena?"

"Moo!" I bellowed in a British accent.

She let go of my arm. "Just be calm. All I'm asking you to do is leave."

I took a deep breath. "And all I'm asking you to do is to let me ask your son a few questions."

We regarded each other warily. No doubt I struck her as a loose cannon, liable to go off at any moment. On the other hand, I could see the muscles on her bare arms. Garlic might have helped her win all those wrestling matches, but it wasn't the only factor.

"Call Zelda."

She walked to the phone and dialed without breaking eye contact. She asked to speak to Zelda, told her the situation, and then said "uh-huh" half a dozen times. By the time she hung up she seemed a trifle more relaxed.

"Well?" she asked.

I realized I was still clutching the ten dollar bill and stuffed it in my bra. Unfortunately I was wearing a beltless dress that day and the bill fell straight through to the floor.

I surreptitiously kicked it under the couch.

"Well what?"

"Your questions!"

I dove right in. "Did your son" — I turned to Harvey — "did you see any other vehicles at the Settler's Cemetery last night? I mean besides your car and the Mast buggy?"

Harvey shook his head. His eyes had finally cleared. He'd been watching the exchange between his mother and me with amusement. Apparently we were more entertaining than a whole team of terrapins.

"Did you see anyone flee the scene of the crime? Maybe on foot?"

He shook his head again.

"Would you please describe what you saw and heard up on Stucky Ridge," I said through gritted teeth. Who says I can't be patient?

"Well, Cathy and I" — he glanced at his mother and then down at his dirty bare feet — "were enjoying the view, and then Cathy asks if I made this certain noise" — he had the poor taste to chuckle — "and I said I didn't. I said I thought it came from outside. Then we heard it a couple of times more.

"Only there wasn't anybody up there enjoying the view that night but us, and so I said it had to come from the cemetery side

153

then. I wanted to see if I could scare Cathy, see? There's this story about —"

"About a couple parked in a car at night in a deserted place and they hear this scratching at one of the car doors, and they drive off in terror, only to discover later than there is a prosthetic hook dangling from the door handle?"

His eyes were not only clear, but wide. "How'd you know?"

"I was a teenager myself, dear. That story is a classic. Cemeteries, overlooks, deserted country roads — it probably gets told every night during the summer."

The truth is I heard that story up in the hayloft of my father's barn. But thanks to Mama, I didn't get to hear it until this summer when Aaron and I got caught in the barn by heavy rains. Did I mention that the occasion was my wedding, and there were fifty guests up in that hayloft with us trying to escape floodwaters? Hearing the hook story under those conditions was probably not the same.

Harvey looked at me with a modicum of respect. "Yes, ma'am. Anyway, we drove around to the cemetery, and like I said, we didn't see anybody but that one horse and buggy. And of course the two guys in it that had been shot."

Chapter Thirteen

"*Two* guys?"

"Yes, ma'am. The one was bleeding horrible — Cathy puked, I almost did. The other didn't seem so bad off. Anyway, Cathy and I don't know much about life-saving things, so we decided the best thing we could do is go for help." He paused. "Actually, I asked Cathy if she wanted to stay with the guys until I got back, but she was too scared. And she doesn't know how to drive a stick shift."

"You did just fine, Harvey," Salina said. She gave me a challenging look, which I ignored.

"Did you know these boys? The ones in the buggy?"

"Nope. Amish kids. They all look alike to me." He laughed hollowly.

It would be a waste of breath to remind him that his great-grandparents had been Amish. The same was true of Catherine Blough.

"One boy was Enos Mast," I said. "He's in Bedford County Memorial Hospital now, in a coma. But he's the only boy listed in the police report. What happened to the other?"

He shrugged. "Zelda — I mean, Officer Root, drove me back up there in the squad car. Cathy stayed behind. The Bedford paramedics were on our tail the whole way. When we got there, we found just the one guy."

I asked for permission to use the phone, and was given it reluctantly. Salina hovered nearby as I gingerly picked up the smudged receiver and called the station. Melvin answered. I could hear the same turtle cartoon playing in the background.

"Turn off the TV, Melvin, I've got a question."

He sighed, but turned it off. "I'm allowed two official breaks, you know. And a half-hour lunch."

"Can the excuses. I want to know why there weren't two Amish boys listed as victims on that report Zelda showed me."

"Because there weren't."

"That's not a reason, Melvin. Why weren't they listed?"

"I mean, Yoder, there weren't two boys involved. Just the one. Enos Mast."

"But Harvey Zook —"

"Did Harvey tell you he was drinking?"

I glanced at Harvey. "No he didn't."

"The kid couldn't have walked a straight line if it had been painted on his shoes. It was a wonder he and the Blough girl made it down from Stucky Ridge in one piece. But when we gave him the breathalyzer test it came well below the legal limit."

"Pot," I said. Trust me, I only know about such things because of my clientele. It may shock you to learn that many of the rich and famous are cannabis connoisseurs. Of course if I catch them at it, they get the bottom of my shoe, whether they've inhaled or not.

"What?"

"The road up Stucky Ridge is full of *pot* holes," I said, trying to be discreet.

There was a long pause during which my nose began to itch. I rubbed the receiver against my shnoz, which was a big mistake.

"Melvin, are you there?"

"You're not making a bit of sense, Yoder."

"You're the pot calling the kettle black," I said, trying one more time. But it was no use. Melvin's shoe size surpassed his IQ in the eighth grade.

"I don't have time for riddles, Yoder," he snapped. "My point is, the kid was seeing double, even though he wasn't drunk. But there was only one victim in the buggy, I can assure you. Zelda checked the buggy and the area thoroughly. No sign of another kid."

"Uh-huh." I was staring balefully at Harvey for having supplied me with a possible breakthrough clue that didn't hold up in the light of sobriety.

Harvey was staring back. In his own way, he was daring me not to tell his mother his choice of refreshments the night before.

"You making any progress on your end?" Melvin asked, almost casually. I could hear the TV on again, although the volume was lower.

"I'll have this case solved for you by the end of the week," I said and hung up.

"Everything all right?" Salina asked, still inches away.

For some strange reason — call it intuition if you want — I decided to start playing the game as close to my meager chest as possible. I would hold off on trump until the rook was played.

I smiled. "Everything is hunky-dory, dear."

Salina's sigh of relief could have blown out a candle at thirty paces. Thank the Good Lord she was no longer into arm wrestling on a daily basis.

"Come back any time," she said, escorting me to the door. "See you at Mennonite Women's Sewing Circle?"

"What are we sewing this month? Layette

158

sets for Afghanistan?" We Mennonites, as you probably know, make a concerted effort to relieve the suffering of others. Our sewing group has, in the past ten years, produced over thirty-thousand baby bundles for disadvantaged infants here and abroad.

"This month it's Somalia," she said, as if we'd been having a casual conversation all along.

I was adjusting my rearview mirror, about to start backing our of her driveway when Harvey rapped on the passenger window. I leaned over and rolled it down.

"You owe me," I said.

"I know. Thanks. That's what I came out to tell you."

"Don't think you're getting off the hook. You need to tell her. Before Melvin or Zelda does."

"I know. I promised them I would."

"See that you do."

He cleared his throat nervously. "About what I owe you . . . I want to pay you back."

I smiled graciously. "Mose could use a little help cleaning out the barn. How about tomorrow morning? Make that ten?"

He winced. "What I meant was, I have some information that you might want?"

I glared at him. "I do not, and have never smoked pot."

He laughed and then caught himself. "It's about the boy. The other one in the buggy."

"What about him?"

"I know who he is."

"But you said —"

"I didn't want to be a rat, Mrs. Miller. He begged us not to tell anyone that he was even there, but then Cathy got excited and let it slip. But she didn't know his name. I do."

Never look a gift horse in the mouth, Mama used to say, although she had no idea what that meant. This time she was right.

"What is his name?" I asked gently.

"If I tell you, will you keep it to yourself?"

"I won't blab it," I said. "But I do intend to track him down. It's the best chance we have of finding the person or persons who shot Enos."

He nodded. "Yeah, Enos."

"You knew Enos?"

His homely visage was vastly improved by a smile, even a rueful one. "That crack in there about all Amish kids looking alike — I didn't mean it. We play ball with them sometimes. Hunt and fish. That kind of thing."

It was hard to imagine Harvey not tied to the tube, but of course I was too polite to say so. I bit my tongue and nodded.

"The kid you want is Samuel Kauffman," he said.

"You sure?"

"Positive. I know him pretty well. His parents let me fish on his farm — they've got some huge bass, but it's the channel catfish I go after. Some of them are three feet long."

"What happened to Samuel?"

"He got shot, too. But just in one shoulder. He was hurting real bad but he could still walk. But he was really scared. I mean, like *really*."

"You would be, too, if you got shot." I have, in fact, been shot at, and thus had the authority for my pronouncement. And even though the incident involving me happened some months ago, I can still hear those bullets whizzing by my ears.

"Yeah. But Samuel was afraid that the killer would come back to finish him off, and he wouldn't go with us to get help. He made us promise not to tell and then ran into the trees."

"The cemetery grove?"

"No, down the mountain. Maybe I shouldn't be saying this, but I think he was headed home."

I thanked Harvey for his help and made him promise to stop smoking marijuana. I didn't care, I said, if half the kids in Hernia High were into it these days, and if even a few of the Amish kids chose to get high as well. It was against the law and wrong, and if what I could extrapolate from some of my guests was an accurate picture, it eventually made one as dumb as a post.

"You're a bright boy," I said kindly, "but not so bright that you can afford to lose any brain cells. And quit watching all that mindless television and pick up a good book."

"Yes, ma'am," he said with only a hint of mockery in his voice.

"And tell your mama," I added sternly, "because she *will* find out."

I drove off thinking about the time Mama caught me drinking. One of my friends, Lucille Benderhaus, had recently moved from Bedford to Hernia and I had been invited to spend the night with her. We ordered in pizza, and much to my astonishment Lucille produced a beer. A *single* can to share between us. Up until that point not a drop of alcohol had passed these lips, but that night I yielded to temptation and had my first sip. I thought of it as a spiritual inoculation, you see. One small sip for woman, one giant leap for perpetual sobriety. Just one taste, and I would cheat the Devil.

Believe me, I would have stopped after

that first sip, but it was so awful that I just had to sample it again to be sure that my taste buds weren't playing tricks on me. Surely nothing that tasted like that was meant for human consumption. If so, the urine samples I handed the nurse during my annual physicals had marketability.

The second sip was horrible, but was it as awful as the first? I needed a third sip to decide. It was inconclusive. The fourth sip demanded a fifth as a tiebreaker, and by then the can of malt mash was manageable. By the eighth sip I was feeling positively merry.

I giggled when the doorbell rang.

"Is that you, pizza boy?" I said fumbling with the front door latch. Lucille had taken an inopportune time to use the bathroom. "Did you bring your cute pair of buns back with you?" I yanked the stubborn door open.

"Magdalena Portulacca Yoder!" There was a cute bun there all right, but it was on top of Mama's head, covered by a little white prayer bonnet.

"Mama! I thought you —"

"Here's your pajamas," Mama said thrusting them at me. "Going off to a sleep-over and leaving them behind! I can't imagine such a thing."

"Sorry, Mama." I belched. "Oops, sorry again!"

A few seconds later Mama's nose was twitching like the back end of a cat in heat. *"Gut Himmel!"* she gasped, "what is that terrible smell?"

"Pizza," I lied, compounding my sin. "Lucille and I were eating pizza. Medium crust, sausage, pepperoni, green olives, onions, extra cheese, but no anchovies. Did you know that the word anchovy is not Italian, but is originally from the Spanish word *anchova?*"

"Ach, you're lying," Mama said and leaned forward to get a better whiff.

"No, I'm not. It's in the dictionary. We looked it up."

"I'm not talking about fish," Mama snapped. "You're trying to hide something by lying."

"What makes you think that?" I asked carelessly.

"You always talk too much when you lie, Magdalena." Then her face went ricotta white. *"Ach!* You've been seduced by the Devil!"

I took her literally and was momentarily confused and flattered. Then it sunk in and I shamefully covered my offending breath.

"It's only beer, Mama. And I just had a few sips."

"The wage of sin is death," Mama said sternly, quoting from the Book of Romans.

"Jesus drank," I argued foolishly. "He even turned water into wine."

"Grape juice. That was grape juice."

"I don't think so, Mama. Back then everyone drank wine. It was the beverage of choice."

Mama's fingers closed around my wrist in a steely grip. "Stop that foolish prattle right now."

"The Disciples drank, Mama. John the Baptist drank. Even Mary —"

"Get behind me, Satan!" she hissed and yanked me out of the doorway and down the walk to her car. I felt like I was six years old.

"But I'm twenty-six!" I wailed. "And I left my purse behind."

"You're never too old for a good spanking," Mama said, and she was dead serious. I couldn't sit down for three days. But perhaps she did know best. The beer I shared at Lucille's was my first and last.

For Harvey's sake, I hoped that Salina Zook took a different approach. The boy needed to learn that marijuana was not going to solve any important issues in his life. Spanking was certainly not going to accomplish that. Mama, on the other hand, died believing that a hickory switch had saved me from a life on Skid Row, when in reality it was my taste buds that had spared me.

CHAPTER FOURTEEN

My first stop was the Hernia Police Station to see Melvin. He was on the phone when I walked in. Mercifully, the horrid little black-and-white TV that Melvin watches was turned off. Zelda was at her desk, staring at Melvin. Susannah was nowhere to be seen.

"Hey," I said to Zelda excitedly. "I just got a tip."

Zelda pointed with her chin in Melvin's direction. "Bad news. The Mast kid just died."

I sat down on a dirty white patio chair, the only furniture available to visitors at the station. "Oh my."

"It's a real shame, ain't it? Him just a boy like that."

Melvin hung up. He looked solemn. I don't mean to be facetious, but for once both eyes were in alignment.

"That was the sheriff. The Mast kid never stood a prayer," he said. "He was shot at close range in the face, you know. Maybe it's best this way."

For once I didn't argue. "The other boy —"

"There was no other boy," Melvin

snapped. "I've made that crystal clear."

"But you haven't," I said calmly. "Yes, I know, Harvey Zook has a history of drinking, but he's positive about this boy. He knows him personally. His name is Samuel Kauffman."

Melvin and Zelda exchanged glances.

"There was so much blood," Zelda said, shaking her head. "It was everywhere. I thought the blood on the seat beside him was his. How was I supposed to know?"

"You weren't, dear, and no one is blaming you."

"Speak for yourself." Melvin straightened a jumbo paper clip, inserted it between his leg and the cast, and commenced to scratch.

I wasted a frown on the man. "What matters now," I said, "is that we find the Kauffman boy and help him."

Melvin stood up. Much to my amazement, his eyes were still in sync.

"Where do the Kauffmans live? Eicher Road isn't it?"

"Zweibacher Road. But, Melvin, let me go up there."

His left eye began to waver. "Why? You already spoke to Annie Kauffman, remember? As I recall, you didn't get anywhere."

To my credit, I kept my cool. The old

Magdalena would have taken umbrage, possibly even said something sarcastic. But I was a married woman now, and as such, a pillar in my community. The tart-tongued Magdalena of yesteryear really was a thing of the past.

"I'll get somewhere this time," I said. "I promise. And anyway, you need to be careful of your leg."

"Damn my leg, Yoder. This is a job that needs to be done right." He started hobbling toward the door.

"It's Miller," I snapped, "and don't you use that 'D' word in front of me."

Zelda zipped around me and blocked the exit before I could as much as blink. Apparently all that grease on her head made for good aerodynamics.

"I'll go up there, Mel," she said.

"You?"

"Sure, me. I know Annie Kauffman — I bought eggs from her last Easter. I'll find her boy. I'll bring him back this time."

"You're a million laughs, Zelda," he said cruelly. "But like I just said, this is a job that needs to be done right. A big job. This isn't Rita's scarecrow we're out to recover, but a witness. No, this job needs to be handled by a professional."

"But I —"

"Face it, Zelda, you're a twit."

Zelda not only shrank from his rebuke, she burst into tears. Sad to say, one of the most creative paint jobs I'd ever seen was reduced to muddy rivulets in a matter of seconds. The poor woman needed to consult with Susannah who, due to self-induced economic need, perfected a makeup routine that renders her facial creations virtually indestructible. Her makeup jobs last for days, sometimes even weeks. Tammy Faye, I am told, spent a mere fifteen minutes with my sister, and ever since has been a much happier and wealthier woman.

At any rate, I was on my feet, my tongue honed sharper than a samurai's sword. "You apologize this minute, you miserable, miscreant, malodorous mantis."

"Who, me?"

I gave Melvin a look that, if maintained for just fifteen minutes, could melt the polar ice caps, thereby obliterating New York, Miami, and points in between. Fortunately, Melvin melted within my specified minute.

"Yeah, okay, I'm sorry."

"It's all right," Zelda said. She was clearly still in love with Melvin.

"Now sit," I said to Melvin.

"The hell I will! Yoder —"

I glared again, forcing him back to his chair. Then I turned to Zelda.

"You run along home, dear," I said kindly, "and scrub that face. You look like someone fire-bombed a Sherwin-Williams store. *I'll* go out to the Kauffman farm."

Zelda gratefully fled to fix her face.

I drove straight from the police station to the Kauffman farm. That is to say, I went there directly. I certainly didn't drive in a straight line.

My part of Pennsylvania is a series of long, low ridges. Mountains, we call them, and they all have names, but my guests from Denver and points west laugh at that. Most of our mountains — the tops at least — are forest-covered, but the lower slopes and the wide valleys between have been cleared and that's where our farms lie.

Buffalo Mountain separates the incorporated Village of Hernia from the Kauffman farm, and Zweibacher Road is the cut across the mountain nearest the Zook residence. It is by necessity a winding road, and for about a third of the way up the mountain it follows a stream we locals call Slave Creek.

This stream and its intriguing name do not appear on any maps, but legend has it that on several occasions runaway slaves, escaping from Maryland, stopped there to refresh themselves and get their bearings. One legend goes so far as to claim that the name Hernia is an African name bestowed on the area by one of these fugitives from injustice. That legend, I know, is not true.

Hernia was named by my great-great-great grandfather Christian Yoder, one of the first white settlers. He was clearing his land one day and foolishly tried to lift a rock that was too heavy for him. That rock, I am told, is one of the cornerstones of the Beechy Grove Mennonite Church, although I have never seen it, and I am a life-long member.

At any rate, it is hard to be objective about one's native surroundings. That said, Bear Mountain, the Slave Creek portion in particular, offers the prettiest scenery anywhere in the United States of America. Slave Creek isn't grand and pretentious like Niagara Falls, and Bear Mountain isn't excessively high like those much-touted Rockies. They are just plain pretty — prettier even than Stucky Ridge where my ancestors are buried.

So I should not have been surprised to find Terry Slock, with his flair for the dramatic, clad like a Tyrolean in lederhosen and knee socks hiking along Zweibacher

Road. Instead, he was dressed just like an Amish man — black pants, blue shirt, suspenders. Even a straw hat. He certainly hadn't dressed like that at breakfast.

When Terry saw that it was me he waved furiously. Reluctantly I pulled over and rolled down my window partway.

"Mrs. Miller," he panted, "I just saw a grizzly bear."

"What?"

Without asking my permission, he tried to open the passenger door. He was out of luck. The doors on my new car lock automatically whenever I put the gear into "drive."

"It was huge, and it was coming right at me."

I politely covered my smile with my hand. "That wasn't a grizzly bear, but a black bear. Chances are it was just as afraid of you as you were of him. Anyway, they're not very common around here, so consider yourself lucky."

"Oh." He seemed almost disappointed.

"Where's your car?" I asked pleasantly. He was, after all, sweating like a Mennonite bride on her wedding night, and the leather seats of my BMW had yet to be defiled by even a single stain.

"I left it back at your inn. I thought I

would get a better feel for the area by walking."

"Well, you're certainly —"

Something snorted in the woods and a terrified Terry nearly ripped the handle off my door trying to open it. Fortunately, the window was cracked only a few inches, otherwise he might have dived right on through.

"Mrs. Miller!" he screamed.

"All right, dear," I said, reluctantly unlocking the door, "but don't lean back until that sweat on your back has had a chance to dry." To be on the safe side I cranked up the air conditioner.

"What are you doing here anyway?" I asked, once he was safely ensconced and was breathing at a near normal rate. "Aren't you supposed to be learning how to bake pies?"

"Oh, that. No offense, Mrs. Miller, but your cook is — well — she's — uh —"

"Bossy?"

"Yeah, that'll work. I didn't sift my flour with other dry ingredients before I started to add the shortening. Well, you would have thought that I'd committed a capital crime."

"Did you at least cut the shortening into the flour with a knife until you had pea-size pieces?"

"They were more like walnuts, but they smooshed together nicely anyway when I rolled it out. Mrs. Hostetler didn't think so, however. She wanted me to start all over again, so I just left."

I sighed, perhaps a touch impatiently. There was going to be heck to pay when I got home. "Where did you get the duds?" I asked, displaying my knack for the vernacular. "Didn't I explain that the Amish might think you're mocking them?"

He grinned. "Pretty cool, aren't they? I went to Miller's Feed Store. Just like you said, they didn't have any ready-made stuff, but they did have these bolts of cloth, and this nice old lady offered to sew these for me."

"Was her name Abigail Cobb?"

"I think so."

"Figures." Abigail is a Presbyterian, for pete's sake, but she zips on over to Miller's Feed Store every time she sees a tourist headed that way and tries to sell them a bit of Amish culture. The woman is the craft maven of central Pennsylvania. She doesn't own a shop, but operates out of her home, hawking the culture of kitsch any way she can. Ceramic geese with bows around their necks, teddy bears in tutus, lute-playing angels, and two-dimensional garden ladies exposing their bloomers as they bend over to tend their blooms. Amish sensibilities don't even figure in her scheme of things.

We had chatted far too long. I had to find Samuel Kauffman and make sure he saw a doctor. I also needed to question him about his assailant. I couldn't very well do that with a nosy tourist along.

"Well, now that you know it wasn't a grizzly bear, I'm sure you wouldn't mind hopping out and letting me go on my merry way."

"You bet I do," he said and slid comfortably down into the seat. "A bear is a bear, if you ask me. Could you drop me off at the inn?"

"I could," I said graciously, "but I won't. I'm not headed that way."

"That's all right. I'll go whichever way you're headed."

I gave him one of my better frowns. Susannah says I could plant lima beans in my frown furrows, and who should know better than their most frequent recipient?

"I didn't invite you along, dear," I said.

He sat up. "Frankly, Mrs. Miller, I'm kind of nervous about walking back to the inn. This is the first time I've ever been in a woods. I certainly never expected to get attacked."

I rolled my eyes, but I assure you he was looking the other way. "You weren't attacked, dear," I said calmly. "Just whistle loudly or sing and you won't see hide nor hair of that bear again."

Terry Slock slid down in his seat again. It was no wonder, since he obviously lacked a backbone. "I can't do it."

"Then hum a mantra," I coaxed. "Remember that his bearness and your manness are part of the same oneness."

"You're making fun of me, aren't you?" he asked petulantly.

"Of course not, dear." Honest, I wasn't. I was just trying to get him out of my car peaceably.

"*Please* let me ride with you. Wherever you're going, I won't get in the way. I promise."

Against my better judgment I capitulated. He was a decent, albeit misguided man, and I couldn't very well abandon him to the wolves, so to speak.

"I'm going to be paying a visit to an Amish farm," I said. "Now I know I talked about taking all of you to see one, but this isn't the time. I have something private I want to discuss with the owners, so you'll have to wait in the car."

That seemed fine to him and we rode in

agreeable silence for a few short minutes.

"I've been thinking about converting," he said suddenly.

"I beg your pardon?"

"I've been giving it a lot of thought, and I'd like to become Amish. Do you think they'll have me?"

Much to my credit I snorted only once, and it was out of surprise, not derision. *"Why?"*

"I really dig their lifestyle — back to the earth, mother nature, peace." His posture improved as he became excited. "They're really with it environmentally."

"They're not trying to be with it, dear," I said kindly, "their aim is to be away from it. They strive to remove themselves from the temptations of the world, and that's much harder than you think. They don't watch television or movies. Could you handle that?"

"There's been nothing good on the tube since 1960 anyway," he said without the need to reflect. "But horses, buggies, and barn-raising parties — wow! You know, that could be so cool. I bet I'd be pretty good at all that stuff. Okay, so I grew up in Hollywood and all, but I know Harrison Ford personally, *and* I've seen *Witness* six times. I know what I'm getting into."

"Do you, now? They don't live this way in order to have fun, dear."

"But they do have fun, right?"

"Yes," I said hesitantly.

"I'm great at that!"

"How are you at humility? That's very important to them."

"I can be as humble as the best of them," he said proudly.

"It's a very close-knit community," I said, "and not only do they submit themselves to the will of God, but to the rules of the community as well. Could you do that?"

"No problem."

"You sure?"

His face colored, contrasting nicely with the brim of his hat. "Hey, I know what you're getting at and that's not fair. I was just a kid then. Anyway, community is what I'm after. It's a manifestation of the Oneness I've been talking about. By converting I'd be merging my Meness with their Theirness. Actually, it gives me goose bumps just to talk about it."

I sighed. "I'm afraid their idea of the Oneness and your Meness are not going to get along."

"What do you mean?" he challenged.

I cast about for a concrete example. "Well, they pray a lot."

"So do I! Ommmmmmmmmmmmm."

I waited a decent length of time for him to add an "amen." When he didn't, I jumped right back in anyway.

"Why don't you start your own little group?" I asked gently. "You could make your own rules then. You could create your own charming outfits and drive around in buggies — although you might consider using cars. Metal horseshoes actually do a lot of damage to the highways. The state tolerates it because the damage is offset by the revenue tourism brings in. But since your group would be concerned with ecology, you certainly wouldn't want to do anything wasteful, even if the cost is recovered in the end.

"Say, I've got an idea — your sect could use electric cars. The kind with rechargeable batteries. After all, Pennsylvania has plenty of hydroelectric energy to recharge those batteries. You could even make the use of electricity a religious requirement. You'd be the first sect ever to do so. You'd be on the cutting edge of a new religion — a way of life. And of course you personally would be the one to set the standards, to decide what's really in. You'd be the guru." I paused just long enough to let him nibble at the bait.

180

"And you know," I continued brightly, "by being an electrically based organization, you'd be free to watch TV and movies, something the poor Amish aren't."

He humphed. "Movies maybe, but no TV. At least none of those biting sitcoms that are on today. They don't make them like they used to."

"Indeed." Although it is against my principles to watch television, I have upon rare occasions enjoyed episodes of *Green Acres* in syndication. I am quite sure that there is nothing being produced these days that compares with that delightful show.

"Of course we'd still farm," he said. "That's the only way to ensure organic food. We'd have to have horses for that, right?"

"Maybe John Deere will come up with an electric combine," I said encouragingly.

Terry's face was glowing with the light of revelation. "What would we call ourselves?"

We had driven out of the woods and were surrounded by cornfields. The summer rains had been evenly spaced, and the corn was tall, the ears long and full. The darkening tassels hinted at a bumper crop, winter fodder for dairy herds our local Amish raised. If ever there was a sign of God's goodness, this was it.

Then it hit me. "You could call yourselves Children of the Corn," I said enthusiastically.

For some reason quite beyond me, he was deeply offended. "Very funny, Mrs. Miller. I didn't expect you to stoop to ridicule."

I hastened to assure him that I had not. "I'm sure it would be a very popular group. Lot's of folks would join."

"Like who?"

"Well, the 4-H Club for starters. And Shirley Pearson — maybe even the Dixons — but I doubt that Dr. Brack will cooperate. Not unless you make wearing his back braces a religious requirement." I chuckled appropriately at my joke.

Terry was no longer glowing, but glowering. "Shirley doesn't have a spiritual bone in her body," he growled.

"What do you mean?" I asked indignantly. Of my current guests she was my favorite, although I must say that little Caitlin was beginning to capture my heart.

"*Ms.* Pearson," he sneered, "is only interested in making money. Do you know why she's really here?"

"Why?"

"To buy up the Amish farms."

"What?"

"Yeah, you heard me right. She let that

slip the first day here. Silver Spoon Foods is on a buying spree, it seems. Their goal is to have all their food grown on their own farms. That way they can control cost better, and turn a larger profit. At least that's what their investors think. And as you know, Mrs. Miller, even though it's kind of hilly here, the land in these valleys is very good."

"It's the best," I bragged.

"Ms. Pearson said she'd never seen fields with yields so high."

It was all so perfect. Shirley could buy the Miller farm and spare me from having a Wal-Mart right across the road.

"My father-in-law will sell!"

"Yeah? Well, she figures her corporation will need at least ten farms to make the investment pay off."

"The Amish will never sell," I said sadly. "This land has been in their families for generations."

Terry laughed cynically. "Oh, they'll sell if the price is right, and these investors have a lot of money to back their offers."

More good news. "Who says our economy is in a slump?" I asked cheerfully.

"It's not our economy that's the issue here. It's *their* economy."

"Pardon me?"

"The Japanese."

"What do the Japanese have to do with this?"

"Didn't you know that Silver Spoon Foods is the American Division of Kakogawa Foods?"

"I most certainly did not! But that's impossible — the Japanese would never have a woman in such a high position."

He smiled. "Oh, yeah? Pretty clever, isn't it. Anyway, my point is that Ms. Pearson is here on a working vacation. Her interest in Amish culture is all pretense. She has no interest in religion."

"There's always the Dixons," I said in a daze.

He groaned. "The Dixons are philistines."

"They are?" I was sure they'd put down "American" on their applications. Japanese, Philistines . . . we were turning into quite an international gathering.

"Oh, yeah. Just because he's an award-winning photographer and she's a famous children's book writer doesn't mean that they have class. The Dixons are even bigger phonies than Ms. Pearson. Did you know that neither of them has read Franz Kafka, and they actually like Ayn Rand?"

"Could we do the book reviews some other time, dear?" I said kindly. "I'm getting a migraine."

"Fine, but that's not all."

I ignored the bait and he mercifully allowed me to drive that last mile in silence. My head was no longer throbbing, only pulsating, when I turned into the Kauffman driveway. I parked under a large, shady sugar maple close to the road. Terry Slock would have to wait for me as far from the Kauffman house as possible.

"You stay put," I directed him. "Don't even think about getting out."

"Will we be here long?"

"As long as it takes."

I walked slowly up the lane to the house. The first half of summer had been abnormally cool, but it now seemed bent on going out with a bang. The last two weeks had been stifling by Pennsylvania standards, but at least they had been dry. Today the humidity level was so high I would have been surprised, but not shocked, to see fish swimming along in the air at eye level. It was the type of day that could see a thunderstorm pop up at any minute.

As I plodded along, I took careful note of my surroundings. The Kauffman farm appeared deserted. Their buggy horse was not in the front paddock, nor was the buggy parked on the lawn. The work horses were not in sight, either, although it was possible that Eli Kauffman, Annie's husband, was working them elsewhere on the farm.

In the west pasture I could see at least thirty head of dairy cows, all of which would need milking that evening. If indeed the family was absent, they would be back by dusk to begin the milking unless — I caught my breath — they had made arrangements for friends or neighbors to come in and milk for them.

Perhaps the Kauffmans were so terrified by this assault on their son that they had fled the county, or the country even. After all, there were thriving Amish settlements in Ontario, Canada, and even in such far-flung places as Belize and Paraguay. Better the jungles of Belize or the pampas of Paraguay than the barrel of a gun in Hernia.

Then I noticed the chickens. A flock of Annie's prized free-ranging hens were taking a dirt bath in the shade of a pin oak on the east side of the house. The rooster and several more hens were lounging about beneath an apple tree midway between the house and the barn. From the direction of the distant chicken house I heard the faint, but satisfied, cackle of a hen who had just laid an egg.

There was something wrong with this scene. Our area abounds with chicken and egg-eating varmints. Although most of the critters — raccoons, foxes, opossums, owls — strike at night, some, like the hawk, hunt only during the day. Our most common and dangerous predators, however, hunt day or night. This is not a native species I refer to, but the packs of abandoned, semiwild dogs that roam our roads. Feral dogs kill not only lambs, but adult sheep. Chickens are just puppy-play for them. Annie would sooner dance the Macarena naked in downtown Hernia than leave her chickens loose unattended, even if only to visit a neighbor just down the road.

"At least someone is home," I crowed triumphantly over my shoulder.

Not that Terry had reason to give a hoot. He had no idea that I was an amateur — albeit semiofficial — detective, and that I had any reason to suspect that the Kauffmans might be hiding. My sleuthing powers would just have to go unappreciated.

Anyway, Terry was no doubt engrossed in the details of the new sect he was about to create. Of course it was vain of me, possibly even idolatrous, but I found myself hoping that if his new denomination had saints, he would see fit to name me as one. After all, I had given him numerous helpful suggestions, including a charming name for the group. I could picture it clearly — Saint Magdalena, and if there was a chapel erected in my honor — St. Magdalena of the Cornfields.

When I was almost to the house I turned and waved beatifically in Terry's direction.

The car was empty.

CHAPTER FIFTEEN

HERNIA CORN FRITTER CUTLETS

INGREDIENTS

5 raw ears fresh sweet corn
1 small onion, minced
$1/2$ medium green bell pepper, diced
2 large eggs, separated
3 tablespoons milk
2 tablespoons all-purpose flour
$1/2$ teaspoon salt
$1/4$ teaspoon black pepper
Bacon grease (although any cooking
    oil will do)

DIRECTIONS

Grate the corn off the cobs into a medium bowl. Add minced onion and diced green pepper.

In a medium bowl, beat the egg whites until they begin to peak and set aside. In a small bowl, beat the egg yolks and add to vegetables. Add milk, flour, salt and pepper and mix thoroughly. Fold in egg whites.

Drop by tablespoonfuls on to a hot, greased griddle, or frying pan. Flatten with a spatula. Fry until nicely brown on both sides, turning carefully. Serve with a dollop of sour cream.

Makes four servings.

CHAPTER SIXTEEN

I raced back to the car, madder than a hen at an Easter egg hunt. Terry Slock was not lying down on the seat, napping, like I'd hoped. The car was indeed empty. I spun around in all directions looking for him, but he was nowhere to be seen. My head resumed throbbing.

Then I heard it, splashing against the trunk of the sugar maple.

"Slock!" I hissed.

A moment later he came out from cover sheepishly. "I had to whiz."

"Behind a tree! Get back into that car," I ordered, "or you'll be walking back to the inn. That bear will be mighty hungry by then if he hasn't found anything else to eat."

Terry was obedient, but not humbled. He was certainly not trustworthy. If only I had a pair of handcuffs I could lock him to the wheel. But oh, no — stingy, stubborn Melvin had not seen fit to give me any of the paraphernalia that went with my job. Yet if memory served me right, the last time he and Susannah were dating, he gave her a brand-new pair. She must have used them a lot, too, because when I saw the cuffs a few weeks ago, dangling from her purse, they were a bit scuffed. Who knew my sister had a flair for law enforcement?

I trudged back up the lane to the house and knocked on the door. I knocked softly at first, in deference to my headache, but when no one answered I pounded with my fist. As long as I was going to have a headache, Annie Kauffman might as well also. Still no answer. I tried the screen door. It was hooked.

Hot as it was, I hoofed it around to the back of the house and tried that door. It was locked as well.

"Annie! I know you're in there!"

Silence.

I peered into the relatively cool darkness of the house. Annie was no Freni. Sure, Annie had a wounded boy on her hands, but that was no excuse for the mess I saw. Dirty dishes piled up on the kitchen counter was one thing, but there were dust bunnies on the floor large enough to make a real mama rabbit proud.

Freni would have been appalled. When not cooking, that woman is never without a feather duster in her hands. Trust me, her last movement will have nothing to do with her heart or her lungs. That feather duster will flick out one last time before falling

192

from her lifeless fingers to the floor. From dust to dust while dusting is her personal creed.

"You can't not be home and have both screen doors hooked from the inside!" I yelled.

Annie not only couldn't, but wouldn't, argue against that logic, and the dusty silence prevailed. I turned and just as I stepped off the porch I heard a woman's voice. The sound was coming from the open window of a second-floor bedroom.

I stepped back from the house and cupped my hands. "Aha! So you are home, Annie! And Samuel is, too, isn't he?"

No comment from the window.

"Well, I know he is, and I know he's been hurt — shot in the shoulder. And if you don't get him a doctor, the wound could get infected. Especially in this hot weather. It might even develop gangrene, you know. And from there it's just a hop, skip, and a jump to amputation. Is that what you want for your son, Annie? A life with just one arm?"

Of course Annie didn't want that, and it was probably mean of me to suggest that she did, but when the chips are down and all else has failed, trot out the guilt. Mama would have been proud of me. We Amish and Mennonites are masters of the art — making Baptists and Jews pale by comparison — and my mother was undisputed guilt champion of Bedford County. It wasn't until her untimely death, squished between a milk tanker and a truck full of state-of-the-art running shoes, that I realized four of the Ten Commandments actually had a positive spin to them.

Either Annie was adopted, or the bearer of a muted guilt gene, because she didn't as much as peep in protest. That, of course, made me feel guilty. The poor woman was obviously so upset that she couldn't even find her tongue.

"He could always get a hook to replace his arm," I shouted, "but the cows won't like it at milking time!"

Annie's lips were sealed tighter than a clam at low tide.

It was time to take a more drastic measure. I suppose I could have found some sharp implement in the barn and cut through the screen in the back door, but even as Melvin's unofficial representative, that was going too far. Much better to pretend to leave, double-back, and climb up the rose trellis that reached to just below the upstairs bedroom window. After all, Annie, unlike most Amish women, had a black thumb for gardening. The climbing rose-bush for which the trellis was intended had long since gone to that big compost heap in the sky, and all that remained was a thorny stump an inch in diameter.

As I'm sure I've already made perfectly clear, I am not a heavy women. I may be tall, but it's an economy shell that covers this generous frame. So, what happened next was not my fault, but the Kauffmans'. Halfway up the latticework ladder, it pulled loose from the house and like a giant sling-shot, catapulted me through the air.

It was my first truly airborne experience, and as such, a major disappointment. I would have much preferred the cramped seats and mediocre food my guests claim the airlines foist on them. My flight lasted only a second or two, and I did not have a smooth landing.

However, I suppose I should be grateful that I landed on a chicken. While it must have been horrible for the bird, it cushioned my fall, and provided little Lizzie Kauffman with another drumstick for her supper. That is not to say that I walked away unscathed. One of my own drumsticks was sprained, albeit lightly, and my back felt as if it had been used as a practice ring for sumo wres-tlers.

"You don't fool me," I moaned, shaking my fist feebly at the furtive fugitives. "I know you're up there" — I gasped with pain — "and I'll be back. But for your sake, not mine! Don't think for a moment that who-ever shot Samuel in the shoulder is going to leave it like that. If you want to keep your family safe, Annie, you need the protection of the law."

I realize now that it was a stupid thing for me to say! Telling Annie to trust Melvin Stoltzfus with the lives of her loved ones was like asking Susannah to chaperone a slumber party for Sunday school girls. I would have been better off telling Annie to dispose of her worldly goods and flee in the general direction of Paraguay on the next available Valuejet flight out of Pittsburgh. At least then she might have respected me.

If I hadn't known that Annie Kauffman was a God-fearing woman who lived her faith, I might have concluded that the sound I next heard coming from the bedroom window was a snort of derision. Instead, I chalked it up to my imagination, and then, barely able to straighten my back, hobbled bravely back to my car.

By the time I got there I was dripping with sweat. My back ached and my foot burned. Quite frankly, I was more than a little bit annoyed with Annie Kauffman, and quite possibly annoyed with myself. I certainly was in no mood to be tolerant of Terry Slock's idiosyncrasies.

"You slovenly slacker!" I nearly screamed when I saw him clipping his toenails, *inside* my car. The parings, I am disgusted to say, were scattered everywhere.

"Huh?"

I pointed to his bare feet, which were not even the least little bit attractive. "That should be done behind closed doors. Don't they have manners out in Hollywood?"

It was, of course, a rhetorical question. B.R., one of Hollywood's biggest stars, was a guest of mine last summer. In the short week she was here, the poor innocent people of Hernia got to see more of her body than most married folks see of their spouses in a lifetime. They also got to hear words that even Susannah didn't know, not to mention her sailor friends. Did you know that it is possible to pierce — well, never you mind. Suffice it to say it is impractical if you're a nursing mother, which by the way B.R. was at the time.

"Wow," Terry said, "I didn't think nail-trimming was such a big deal."

"Even filing one's fingernails in public is disgusting," I said for his education.

And I'm sure you agree. If only Edna Naffziger did. Every Sunday morning she sits in the pew directly in front of mine, shamelessly filing her nails while Reverend Schrock drones on with one of his interminable sermons. I know, that's an awful thing to say about my minister, but it's true. His sermons not only lack fire, they are a free (if one ignores the offering plate) substitute for melatonin.

At any rate, each and every Sunday morning Edna and the good Reverend go about their respective business, as complacent as cud-chewing cows. At least, when the service is over, Reverend Schrock has only left behind a sea of nodding heads, whereas vain Edna has covered the pew and the floor at her feet with a coating of nail powder. This simply isn't fair to Old Man Schwartzentruber, our custodian, who has to clean up Edna's discarded body parts.

"It's more than disgusting," I added. "It's downright vile."

Terry had the temerity to grin. "I bet Mr. Yoder gets a kick out of you."

"That's Mr. *Miller*," I snapped, "and what he does is none of your business."

"Yes, ma'am."

He was still grinning, which irritated me to no end. I like people to cringe those few times I actually lose my temper.

"Stop it this minute!"

The smiled slowly faded.

I swallowed enough irritation to make me gain a few pounds. "Now be a dear and drive for me. I threw my back out."

He grinned. "Oh, boy."

I gave him one of my sternest looks. "This is a brand-new car, buster. Treat it like a baby."

"Will do," he said gleefully and scooted over to the driver's seat, leaving a pile of parings behind on the floor. I made him scoot back and shake off the passenger-side mat.

Properly chastened, his manners seemed to improve. "Shall I pick the feathers off your back, too?" he asked politely when he was done.

We were halfway home when the storm, which must have been building up all day, broke. It was a downpour for the record books I'm sure. Papa would have called it a frog-strangler, and Mama would have blamed Papa for not having built and stocked a navigable ark.

Visibility vanished in a matter of seconds, and even Terry, whose eyes are much younger than mine, found it impossible to see the road. Left with no alternative, he slowed to a stop, after pulling over on what we hoped was the shoulder of Zweibacher Road.

"Man, it never rains like this in Southern California," he said. There was admiration in his voice.

"*Ach,* this is nothing," I said proudly. "Just a little drizzle. We see this at least once a week."

"I want to go home," he wailed in a little girl's voice.

I stared at him. "Say that again."

"I want to go home!"

Terry's lips had not moved. Either Terry was a much better ventriloquist than an actor or — I whirled. There, huddled in the backseat like a pair of lost puppies were little Lizzie and her English friend, Mary.

Trust me, it is perfectly proper to scream when faced with a startling discovery. It was, however, very rude of the little girls to keep screaming so long, and there certainly was no excuse for Terry's shrieks.

Finally we all settled down enough to carry on a rudimentary conversation, albeit one punctuated by gasps and the occasional shriek from Terry.

"What on earth are you two doing in my car?" I puffed.

"We wanted to run away," Lizzie sobbed.

"Why?"

"So the bad people don't get us," Mary whimpered. Then her eyes widened and her chin began to tremble. "You have an awfully big nose, Mrs. Miller. Are you a witch?"

"Why, I never!" I huffed.

Lizzie stopped sobbing and regarded me solemnly. "You're a *real* witch? My mama says there is no such thing."

Mary nodded vigorously. "Oh, but there are. And there's even a picture of this witch in my fairytale book. She lives in a gingerbread house and eats little children."

"I most certainly do not!" I huffed and puffed. "I live in a farmhouse, just like you."

"And she rides a broomstick," Mary said. In a just world, her nose would have been growing faster than Pinocchio's.

"Cool," Terry said.

I glared at him.

"Then why does she have a car?" Lizzie asked.

"My broom is in the shop for repairs, dear," I said, and frowned so deeply I could actually feel the furrows on my forehead meet.

The girls screamed.

I wish I could claim that it was my terrifying visage that prompted their outburst, but someone with a nose as long as mine cannot take risks with unnecessary lies. The truth is that Terry had parked my brand-new BMW just in front of the little bridge that spans Slave Creek and we were caught in a flash flood. It was as simple as that.

Whereas one second all four wheels of my car were in contact with the ground, the next second we were bobbing about like a fishing cork on Miller's Pond when the wind is high. Almost immediately we began bumping into things; young trees or saplings, I suppose. Maybe the tops of a couple of rocks. The rain was still streaming down too hard to see anything, and our collective breaths had completely fogged up the windows. Even Susannah, on her hottest dates, had never had that much privacy.

"Do something!" I screamed at Terry. "Do you know how much this car cost?"

Of course there was nothing he could do. The poor man was spinning the steering wheel around like a kid in a toy car, the kind you feed quarters to in front of the supermarket. My car was no more responsive.

"We're going to die!" the girls wailed in unison.

"Not by the hair on my chinny chin chin," I said resolutely.

It was a poor choice of words, and they wailed louder.

I began to regret that I had not stocked the car with earplugs. What good were three maps of Pennsylvania, two maps of Ohio and West Virginia, and half a roll of old, stale Certs breath mints in a floating car? Noah had at least been given sufficient warning.

Despair and prayer go together, Mama always said, and she was absolutely right. Had my car been a luxury-size model, and my limbs not quite so long, I would have gotten down on my knees to beg for deliverance. But, the Lord hears the prayers of His faithful even when they're securely strapped in, and in this case He chose to answer them as well. Abruptly the rain stopped. The ensuing silence was practically deafening. Unfortunately it didn't last very long.

"Are we dead now?" little Lizzie asked.

"Don't be silly," Mary the sophisticate said. "The car's still turning around in circles. Besides, in Heaven you have Jesus and the angels, and in Hell you have the Devil. We just have a man with stinky feet who can't drive very well and a skinny old witch."

I was on the verge of asking the girl to stick out her finger so I could see if she was plump enough to eat when the spinning, like the rain, stopped abruptly. I discreetly extracted a wad of facial tissue from my less than ample bosom and wiped the foggy windshield.

Slave Creek was no more, but Slave Lake seemed to be all around us. I wiped a spot on the passenger-side window and peered through the streaks. We were definitely surrounded by water.

CHAPTER SEVENTEEN

"We are perched on top of a rock like Noah's ark on Mount Ararat," I announced. "What do we do now?"

Terry had no tissues to extract from his bosom, and was not in possession of a handkerchief, but he had removed his T-shirt and was wiping the windows on his side of the car. His view appeared to be much the same as mine.

"I took swimming at UCLA," he said, and began to remove his jeans.

"Put your clothes back on, for Heaven's sake! There are little ones present." Presumably Terry had the same equipment as Aaron, and if that was indeed the case, the sight of him naked would traumatize the girls for life. And there is no trusting boxer shorts, believe you me. There is no telling who, or what, is going to stick its little head out that front vent.

Terry sighed but obediently zipped up. "I was hoping you'd stop me. I flunked that swimming class."

"So what are we going to do?" I wailed, feeling suddenly very helpless.

"We could roll down the window and let a

dove out," Lizzie suggested helpfully. "When he flies back with an olive branch, that's when we know the water's gone down all the way."

I thanked her for the biblical tip. "Next time you stow away bring a dove with you," I added kindly.

"Looks like we're screwed," Terry said.

I would have slapped him for that kind of talk, had he not immediately realized his error and obligingly slapped himself.

"Witches cast spells," Mary said thoughtfully. "Can you cast a spell, Mrs. Miller, and make the water dry up?"

"Hocus-pocus," I said. "Mumbo-jumbo. Jambalaya, crawfish pie, and fillet gumbo."

"Wow!" Mary exclaimed. "It's working!"

I peered out my window. If the waters were abating, they were doing so at an infinitesimal rate. I have hair-clogged drains at the inn that drain faster than that.

Who knows how long we would have remained stranded had not Jacob Zook, a Mennonite farmer, appeared on the scene with his tractor. Jacob has the personality of a hibernating woodchuck, but he is one of the kindest men I have ever met, and is a wizard at mechanics. At some risk to both limb and tractor, Jacob managed to pull us loose from the rock and up on the slowly emerging creek bank.

My knees were shaking when I got out of the car, and not because I had just survived a near-death experience, either. It shames me to say it, but all I could think about was the condition of my car. When I saw that it was unscratched, except for one small ding on the rear bumper, I literally threw myself on the ground and thanked the Good Lord for His mercy. Then I gently complained to my Maker about the ding on the bumper. I know, that might sound ungrateful to some, but when a car costs that much, every dent is like a stab in the heart, every ding a punch in the stomach. On the other hand, I could have lent my old car to Thelma and Louise and never noticed the difference when I got it back.

Just to be on the safe side, I finished my prayer with a veritable onslaught of thanksgiving. After all, it was possible the Good Lord had provided the flash flood as a lesson to me on perspective, and I didn't want to risk another lesson. Perhaps it is paranoid of me, but I have always suspected that there is a troublesome angel up there whispering into God's ear that Magdalena is a slow learner.

But form must not be confused with function, and there was still the question of whether or not the car was operable. Jacob, as it turned out, was a genius with machines. He fiddled with the engine until it started, and after a few feats of magic had that thing purring smoother than a snoozing kitten. Needless to say I thanked him profusely, although I remained standing. Then Terry thanked him, albeit a little less profusely, and even the girls praised him for his expertise. The poor man was the color of a pomegranate before we were through.

"Are you the Good Samaritan?" Lizzie asked, causing him to turn an even darker shade.

"*Ach,* no. Just a farmer."

"Mrs. Miller is a witch," Mary said proudly.

"Just for a *few* days every month, dear," I corrected her.

Jacob went through several more color changes, but he seemed loath to leave. Even after we were back in my car, he stood stock still in front of it, as if rooted in the mud. Much too late I noticed that there was an expectant look on his face.

"Thanks again!" I called gaily.

"Yes, thanks," Terry said and put the car into Drive.

The engine raced, but the car wouldn't budge.

"Darn," I said, which is as bad as I swear — even on my witch days. "We must be stuck in the mud."

Terry gallantly rolled down his window. "We seem to be stuck," he said to Jacob. "Would you mind giving us a tow?"

Jacob with the woodchuck personality grinned slowly. "Oh, you ain't stuck, mister. I still got you hooked up to my winch cable."

Terry flashed him a Hollywood smile. "Would you mind unhooking us?"

"Oh, but I would."

"I beg your pardon?"

"Of course I'd be happy to oblige, just as soon as you pay me my rescuing fee."

I couldn't believe my ears. Sometimes — perhaps due to their large size — my ears pick up snitches of distant conversation. How else can I explain the time I distinctly heard Aaron say that I was his *favorite* wife?

"The funniest thing just happened," I said, and chuckled soothingly, "but I thought I heard you say something about a rescuing fee."

The hibernating woodchuck hiccuped and smiled broadly. "That's right, you did. That's thirty dollars for making the call, a hundred and thirty dollars for towing you out of the stream, and thirty dollars for unhooking my winch cable. That generally covers my expenses back. Plus, of course, eleven dollars and forty cents tax. Your total is two-oh-one and forty cents. Will that be cash, check, or credit card?"

"*What?*" Ignoring my bruised and battered body I struggled from the car.

Jacob took an involuntary step backward, but otherwise stood his ground. "I don't take American Express, though. Just Visa and MasterCard."

He was serious, too. For the first time I noticed the credit card imprinting machine bolted to the engine block of his tractor.

"You should be ashamed of yourself, Jacob Zook! And you a good Mennonite."

He shrugged. "It's not much of a living, Magdalena. Only five or six cars each year get caught by the creek. I still have to put my corn in. 'Course ninety-three was a good year. Twenty-one cars in all — the wife and I took us a trip to Cancun the next winter. It was the first vacation my little Emma had ever been on."

I paid with a check.

We drove straight back to the Kauffman farm. The second we turned into the driveway the front door of the farmhouse flew open and out came Annie, her arms flapping like the wings of a giant crow.

Terry was barely able to stop the car before Lizzie jumped out and ran shrieking with joy into the arms of her mother. The two Kauffman females embraced ecstatically.

"What a touching sight," I muttered.

"She ain't even afraid of getting whipped," Mary said. "Imagine that!"

I made a mental note to meet Mary's parents as soon as things settled down a bit.

"Out you go, dear," I said kindly. "Hurry it up."

Mary reluctantly unbuckled her seat belt and slid halfway out. "I don't think you're the wicked kind of witch, but you sure are bossy."

"Touché," Terry said.

I glared at him and then turned to smile warmly at Annie who, still clutching Lizzie, was approaching the car.

"Gut Himmel!" Annie said breathlessly. "My little Lizzie says you saved her life."

"I did no such thing!"

"She did so, Mama. Mary, you tell her."

Mary nodded vigorously. "Mrs. Miller is a good witch. She said a magic spell and the water went down."

Amish, and we Mennonite as well, do not believe in witches or magic of any kind. It is, in fact, an anathema to us, and by extension, so is the secular celebration of Hal-

211

loween. Some liberal Mennonites have moderated their stance and do allow their children to go begging for treats on October 31, but Mama was not one of them — not until Susannah came along, at any rate. I had to watch as many of my classmates gorged themselves on candy the next day. My sister, born ten years later, not only got to canvass Hernia for candy, but Mama made her the most adorable little outfits; fairy princess, Snow White, and even a mermaid costume with a sequined tail that Susannah dragged along behind her on a roller skate. But even my precious sibling was forbidden to dress like a witch.

I could feel Annie Kauffman's bright-eyed gaze scrutinizing me.

"I am not a witch," I said stoutly, "and you should be ashamed, Annie, for filling these little girls' heads with all that witchy nonsense."

"Me?"

They say the best defense is offense, and I can be very offensive if I put my mind to it. "All this witch talk is a sin, Annie. What would your bishop say if he knew your little Lizzie believed in witches? What else do you believe in, Annie? Little green men from outer space?"

"Why I —"

"How is Samuel doing?" I had decided to let her off the hook. She was under enough stress.

"I don't know what you're talking about — I mean, well —"

"It's imperative that I speak to him, Annie. It could save his life."

Poor Annie looked like a raccoon caught raiding the hen house. It wasn't just her guilt, but the dark circles of fatigue around her eyes.

"*Ach,* my Samuel is in the house," she said quietly. "Come see for yourself."

The upstairs bedroom in which Samuel lay was beastly hot. Annie had closed the windows when the storm began, and they were still closed.

The room was simply furnished, as are all Amish bedrooms. There were three beds in the room, evidence of Samuel's older brothers, now married; a simple chest of drawers with an oil lamp on top; and on the floor a large, braided rug. There was no closet. As in most Amish homes, the clothes were hung on wall pegs. The only decorative elements were the rug, a quilt on each bed, and a picture calendar, the only type of wall art generally permitted in Amish homes. This month's scene was a bright red

Japanese *tori* bridge with flowering pink cherry trees in the foreground.

Eli, young Samuel's father, was sitting at the floor of his son's bed. I had always thought that Eli was a tall man, but this was the first time I had ever seen him close up and without his hat. Sitting, at least, he looked much shorter than I had remembered. His dark brown hair was cut in the traditional bowl style, and like his graying beard, was unkempt. He looked up when I entered.

"Hello, Eli," I said. "Hello, Samuel."

Eli stood up. "He can't hear you. He has a fever."

"He's unconscious?" I gasped. "And you've been keeping him here?"

"*Ach,* what else could we do? Someone wants our Samuel dead."

I laid what I hoped was a reassuring hand on his arm. This was no time to worry about propriety.

"Eli, your Samuel might die if he doesn't see a doctor. We have to get him into Bedford."

He nodded. His faded blue-gray eyes were brimming with tears.

"But it cannot be done. An Amish boy, wounded by a gunshot — the man who shot the boys would find him in the hospital.

Like they will find Enos."

"Enos is dead."

Annie's hands flew to her face. "*Gut Himmel!* Enos was such a sweet boy — he never hurt anyone. Now you say he is dead. My Samuel could be dead, too!"

Eli put a rough hand on his wife's back in a rare gesture of Amish affection. "You see why we cannot take him to the hospital?" he said to me.

"I see," I said sadly. Then something Eli had said sunk in and I caught my breath. "Did Samuel tell you who the man was who shot them?"

"No."

"But he said it was a man?"

"No."

I swallowed my irritation which, I am happy to say, was fat-free. "But you just said —"

"Samuel didn't tell us anything," Annie said, dipping a cloth in a basin of water and touching it to her son's head. "He didn't want to get us involved."

I waved my arms to take in the room. "But you are involved! And if you don't get your son medical attention real soon, you might be involved in his death."

It may sound like a horrible thing to say, but they needed shaking up. I didn't, however, expect them to turn the color of hot-house mushrooms.

"We will pray," Eli said stubbornly. "But no hospital."

"Enos died from complications," I explained patiently. "There was no second attempt on his life."

"But you cannot guarantee my Samuel's safety," Annie cried.

"Don't worry," I said. "We'll take him in my car. Nobody will know. We'll register him under another name. I'll speak to the Bedford County Sheriff. We'll keep it all hush-hush. I promise."

"His name is Samuel Kauffman," Eli said almost fiercely. "Another name would be a lie."

It was time to trot my knowledge of the scriptures. I chose a quote from Jesus himself, as recorded in the book of Matthew.

" 'I am sending you out like sheep among wolves. Therefore be as shrewd as snakes and as innocent as doves.' You definitely have the dove part down pat, Eli. For your son's sake, work on the snake."

Eli frowned. " 'Thou shalt not lie.' It says so in the Bible. It's the ninth commandment."

I smiled patiently. "Why yes, that is one of the traditional translations, dear. But the

New International Version has a much different translation. In it the ninth commandment tells us not to bear false witness against our neighbors, which gives it an entirely different meaning. Samuel is not your neighbor, and this is not a court case."

Eli took an eternity to respond. Perhaps he was waiting for Mama to stop turning in her grave. The day I switched from reading one version of the Bible to another was the day our relationship hit its all-time low. You would have thought that I'd gone out and built a golden calf by her reaction. Strangely enough, but not surprisingly, when eight years later Susannah announced that she was going to be a Buddhist, Mama barely blinked. Of course Susannah never became a Buddhist and Mama was dead by the time Susannah did the truly unfathomable and became a Presbyterian. Still, Mama turns over rhythmically in her grave every time I deviate in the slightest from her approved way of doing things, but manages to snooze right through my sister's blatant blunders.

"*Ach*," poor Eli said at last, "you are tempting me, Magdalena."

I ignored the flattery. "How about the sixth commandment? 'Thou shalt not kill.' It says that even in your German version, doesn't it?"

"*Ach!* What are you saying, Magdalena?"

"Well, you can't leave him here, Eli. You know that. And if we take him to the hospital and register him under his own name — well, you know what could happen then. And you would have been a party to it, Eli. Your own son's death."

They were harsh words, but true. Someone had to make him face up to reality.

Eli stared at me. I felt him looking into my soul, searching for something worth trusting.

"Eli, you have my word that your Samuel will be safe if we move him to Bedford. That is what you want, isn't?"

"Yah," he said, teetering in his resolve.

Annie had been standing beside her husband, listening quietly. "Magdalena saved our little Lizzie's life."

I flashed her a grateful smile. Now wasn't the time to correct her.

Eli glanced at his son and back at me. "Yah, *gut.* Take him to the hospital in Bedford. It is the only thing to do. But maybe it is better if Annie and I stay here."

"Good thinking," I said. "Try to carry on your lives just as normally as possible. I'll keep you constantly informed. I'll come straight back from the hospital and tell you what the doctor says."

Annie shook her head. "You might be seen, Magdalena. Better you should call at little Mary's house. They have a phone."

It was not an unusual request for an Amish woman. While the Amish do not have telephones in their homes, there is nothing in their tradition that prevents them from using non-Amish phones in an emergency situation.

I took down the number. "You can trust these people?"

Eli and Annie exchanged glances.

"Yah, they are good people," he said, "but maybe it is better to be like the snake. We will tell them we are expecting an important phone call from a relative. That will be enough for them."

"I see," I said, and smiled conspiratorially.

"*Ach,* but it's true," Annie protested needlessly. "My mama was a Yoder, Magdalena. A second cousin to your father. Just look at my nose. It's almost as big as yours."

Frankly, it had a long way to go, but this was no time to make her feel inadequate. Because of my back I couldn't help them carry Samuel to the car, but I distracted the little girls while Terry, who was delighted to be conscripted, participated in this life-saving mission.

"Wow," he said over and over again on the way to the hospital, "this is so cool. Harrison is going to be so jealous."

"Don't you say a word to anyone," I chided. "We don't know who to trust. Although Harry is probably okay. He has yet to break any of his promises to me."

"*You* know Harrison Ford? The actor who starred in the movie *Witness*?"

I looked down the length of my considerable nose. "How do you think he did his research?"

"Wow! Cool!"

From the backseat Samuel moaned.

CHAPTER EIGHTEEN

Dr. Rosenkrantz was a competent, if unpleasant man. He had his underlings hook Samuel up to so many tubes, the poor boy resembled a bagpipe. But Doc knew his business, and in less time than it takes Susannah to steal from the offering plate, Samuel, now known as Thomas Arnold, began to recover. Within the hour his temperature dropped to near normal and he began to drift in and out of consciousness. I phoned the good news back to the Kauffmans.

"Thomas is on the mend," I said joyfully to Annie.

"Who?"

"Thomas!" I hissed. "Thomas Arnold in Bedford."

"Make sense, Magdalena. I don't know any Thomas Arnold in Bedford."

"Is that the man who runs the fresh fruit stand on Route 96?" Eli asked on the extension.

"Yah," Annie chirped, "that's the one. And he's a real cherry pie if you ask me."

While Annie is fluent in English, she is idiomatically challenged. Still, I knew who she meant.

"The expression is fruitcake, Annie, and you're talking about Thomas Amstutz. He's a different Thomas. This Thomas is the fruit of your loins."

"*Ach*," they cried in unison. "*That* Thomas!"

"Yes, *that* Thomas. Anyway, he's going to be just fine."

"When will he be released?" Eli asked anxiously.

"Yah, when?"

"Good heavens," I said, "not for several days, I should think. Even then, he must stay at the fruit stand until we have a buyer."

"*Ach*, so it isn't our Thomas after all," Annie wailed. "It's the cherry pie man."

"Is his fruit stand for sale, Magdalena?" Eli asked. To be sure, he sounded disappointed, but Eli is a practical man, with a knack for making a dollar.

Call me a quitter, but I despaired of speaking in code. "Your son Samuel is fine," I practically screamed into the phone. Fortunately it was a slow day at Bedford County Hospital and the corridor was empty except for Terry, who had been sworn to secrecy, and Nurse Dudley. The latter, I know from personal experience, is either stone deaf, or a prototype masochist.

My call button, not to mention my screams, never once went answered. At any rate, I had been observing Nurse Dudley, and true to form, she wasn't the least bit interested in her new patient.

Before I left I talked with the Bedford County Sheriff for the third time. It was agreed that the hospital staff would call me at the PennDutch as soon as Samuel, alias Thomas, was strong enough to be interviewed. I could have first crack at him on Melvin's behalf.

"We still can't get over how he broke his leg," the sheriff said, laughing. "Is it true he once shipped his cousin in Philadelphia a gallon of ice cream by UPS?"

"He shipped the ice cream to his cousin in Scranton," I sniffed, and pointed my shnoz skyward. I am told that I do a fair imitation of your average Parisian when asked for directions.

"Betcha he won't be milking any more bulls," the deputy said and nudged his boss. They both laughed.

Melvin might have more faults than the State of California, but hey, he's a Hernia boy born and bred — make that *in*bred. And a lapsed Mennonite to boot. *I* just barely had a right to criticize him; but the sheriff, and most certainly the deputy, did not.

"Police Chief Melvin Stoltzfus is the finest man I've ever met," I snapped, and then buried my nose in a hankie so they wouldn't see it grow.

As was my right, I presided over dinner that night at the inn like a five-foot-ten-inch Queen Victoria. I sat bolt upright like the old gal, too, thanks to a chance encounter with Dr. Brack in the parlor. Two hundred and sixty-five dollars later, including tax, I was the proud owner of a Brack's Back Brace. Due to my injury, which had become more painful as the day progressed, I dispensed with his offer of a free trial period and plonked the money down on the spot. And let me tell you this, the fool thing actually works. One minute I was in agonizing pain, and the next I was singing Brack's praises.

You, like some of my guests, may wonder why it is necessary to have a sit-down supper every evening with everyone in attendance. Well, I'll tell you. It's because American table manners disappeared along with the Edsel and the advent of the first frozen entrée. Today entire families eat on the run, stuffing fast food into their faces with their fingers of all things. The proper use of cutlery is a forgotten art. Virtually no one remembers how to use a table knife correctly; I have actually seen folks cut their food using the sides of their forks!

And believe you me, the rich and famous are not exempt from boorish behavior. One popular movie star chewed with her mouth open so wide I could see the inside view of her recent tummy-tuck. Another Hollywood figure, who shall also remain nameless, didn't even stoop to lick his fingers after eating chicken, but instead ran them through his hair. Later that evening he got too close to a candle and his grease-soaked coiffure burst into flames. On his next visit he wore such an atrocious wig that poor Shnookums, Susannah's pitiful pooch, fell in love with the hairpiece and attempted to do what comes naturally — at least in the animal world. It was not a successful mating.

At any rate, my dining room table is built of solid oak and it stretches almost two-thirds of the length of the room. It was built by my great-grandfather Jacob "The Strong" Yoder from a tree that occupied the site of the original farmhouse. This table can seat twenty people comfortably, twenty-six in a pinch. Incidentally, Jacob "The Strong" and his wife, Magdalena, had sixteen children, forty-seven grandchildren, and one hundred eighty-nine great-grandchildren. The figures for great-great grandchildren keep changing, but sad to say, it looks as if Susannah and I will never add to that number.

Contrary to some of the tabloid rumors, my guests are not forced to eat their food directly off the table. It is true, however, that I do not use tablecloths. What is the point, after all, when five minutes into the meal the linens resemble Rorschach tests? And anyway, a nice rough surface, studded with splinters, is a most effective way to ensure that elbows are kept off the table (although a long-handled fork with sharpened prongs will do the trick as well).

Of course I always sit at the head of the table, and as a symbolic second in command, Susannah is accorded the foot. Most of the time, sad to say, it is a footless table, and on those special occasions when the foot is present, she is more likely to be playing footsie under the table, than helping me with my hostess duties.

This particular evening my foot was in the arms of Melvin. In her place was Bradley, the oldest of the Dixon children. His sisters, Marissa and Caitlin, flanked him.

Normally I would not have put up with such nonsense. Children at a dinner table, indeed! But normally I would not have had children to contend with, and what else was I to do? Children had to eat, I supposed, but these three couldn't very well eat in the kitchen. Not after the day Freni had trying to teach the English how to bake a decent pie. There was nothing left to do but plunk the urchins down at the far end of the table and hope that any food that got flung was deflected by the guests seated immediately in front of me.

Terry Slock was absent from the table. The poor man was just too tuckered to tackle tucker. An assault by a fierce bear, raging floodwaters, and a daring rescue mission had left him too pooped to pop. His words, not mine.

But speaking of Pops, my father-in-law, God bless his soul, had accepted a supper invitation with the Amos Augsburgers, an Amish couple who live on the other side of town. With any luck, the opportunity would arise for me to speak to Shirley Pearson about his farm. Such a conversation would be impossible with Pops present. The old coot was dead set against selling the homestead, even if it was the only way he could afford to check himself into a nursing home.

The rest were there, however. Dr. Brack, dressed in formal attire, was seated to my left, and Angus Dixon, clad insolently in an open-necked pink polyester shirt and black slacks, was on my right. To his right was Shirley Pearson, resplendent in her version of Amish evening wear. I must say, in all sincerity, that her floor-length, navy broadcloth gown with contrasting apron was rather fetching.

On Dr. Brack's left was Dorothy Dixon. Like her husband, she'd opted for casual. While I have nothing against casual clothes — I myself do not "dress" for dinner — a yellow halter top with purple polka dots and black spandex pants that start below the navel, are simply not acceptable. Perhaps I first cracked that evening's can of worms by telling her just that.

"You'll have to change, honey," I said kindly.

Dorothy appeared taken aback. "I'm a writer. We're supposed to be eccentric."

I pointed politely to serene Shirley. "That's eccentric. But you" — I shook my head — "even Rahab the Harlot wouldn't be caught dead in clothes like those."

To her credit, Dorothy changed, but it was hardly a change for the better. The scarlet dress she slipped into was so short that if it hadn't been for her scarlet unmentionables, there would have been nothing left to the imagination.

"And you call yourself a mother," I muttered.

She wasn't supposed to hear that; unfortunately she did. Susannah claims my private mutterings are actually louder than my speaking voice. This is, of course, not true. And I have no idea how it is that Reverend Shrock heard me criticize his sermon last Sunday when I was seated in the last row. The truth be known, I'm glad he did. I am sure that when the Good Lord told us to tithe one-tenth of our possessions, he meant *after* Uncle Sam had taken his share. A just and logical God would never insist that we tithe for Uncle Sam as well.

"I'm a damned good mother," she growled.

I growled back. "I will not permit swearing in my establishment, especially not in front of children."

The woman was without shame. "My children have heard it all before," she said. "They're only words — inanimate objects. They only have a bad meaning if one chooses to attach it to them."

"That's nonsense," I said.

"Is it? A dam holds back water, right? You wouldn't object if I used damn in that context, would you."

"That's different."

"No it's not. It all boils down to seman-tics."

"I don't think so, dear."

"What are you, anti-semantic?"

"Some of my best friends are Jewish," I said, hotly offended.

"Please, could we say grace?" Dr. Brack begged. "I'm starving."

"Grace, grace!" the children chanted. Not that the urchins had waited to begin — the serving bowls of children's food Freni had placed before them had all but been licked clean. The little ones were, however, obviously quite starved for religious instruc-tion and they appeared to love it when I prayed.

"Amen," I said when I was through.

"Amen," they chorused.

I passed a platter of pan-fried pork chops. "How was your day?" I inquired pleasantly of Angus Dixon.

He grimaced. "I spent it baking pies with Mrs. Hostetler. What do you think?"

"That bad, huh?" I plopped some parsley potatoes on my plate before passing them on.

"When are we going to meet the Amish you talked about?"

"Mrs. Hostetler *is* Amish, dear."

"Not her. Younger Amish" — he gestured

at his children who were busy flipping peas with their knives — "ones with children."

"Oh, soon," I promised. "Maybe tomorrow."

"Of course they'll be farmers," Shirley said. It was a question, not a statement.

"That's the only kind we grow around here." I laughed politely at my little joke.

"Ones with big farms. I mean, I'm interested in large-scale farming."

I gave her a charming smile. "I'm so glad you brought that up, dear. I've been meaning to talk to you about my father-in-law's farm. It's for sale, you know. Some of the best farmland in Bedford County. I'm sure the Chinese you work for will approve."

Angus speared a potato piece. "Chinese? I thought you worked for Silver Spoon Foods?"

Shirley nodded. She looked super in her getup, but wearing a prayer bonnet was carrying the thing too far. Amish and more conservative Mennonites wear out of obedience to the book of 1 Corinthians, chapter eleven, verse six. As a young girl I covered my head, but when Mama died I stopped. Verses seven through ten of the same chapter were just too hard to swallow. Shirley, I'm sure, would never swallow them, either.

"I do," Shirley said. "Silver Spoon Foods is the international division of Kakogawa Foods. My employers are Japanese."

"Oh."

"Would you like to see the property?" I asked hopefully. "I could give you a quick tour after dinner — if it isn't too dark by then. Or we could do it first thing in the morning."

"How many acres?" she asked practically.

"Eighty-seven," I said. "All of it prime stuff."

"It's not listed, is it? I didn't see a sign of any kind, and I've been on the lookout for that kind of thing."

"Oh, that's Pops for you. He's selling it himself you see, and he keeps meaning —"

I was rudely interrupted by a hard tap on my left shoulder. It was, of course, Freni Hostetler. No one else I know would dare interrupt me when I am presiding over my guests at the table.

"Yes?" I hissed.

"Phone, Magdalena. Didn't you hear it?"

Of course I heard it. I don't have a phone in the dining room — no one should. But I do have a phone in the kitchen, and I'm afraid it is audible, even though the kitchen is properly separated from the dining room by a heavy, swinging door.

"What's the matter with you, Freni? You know I don't take calls during dinner."

"*Ach,* but this is different."

"Tell Melvin I'll call him back in an hour. Tell him if he gets bored, he should try arranging a bag of M&M's in alphabetical order." I know, it wasn't the Christian thing to say, but it had been a long day.

"It isn't Melvin. It's Aaron."

"*My* Aaron? But he knows it's dinnertime." And indeed he did. Dinner at six sharp every evening, whether we were hungry or not. Tight schedules rank next to cleanliness on the godliness scale.

Freni glanced at the group, who were, of course, all staring at us just as intently as the congregation had that Sunday my sister Susannah, having given Presbyterianism a mad fling, set a tentative toe back inside the sanctuary of Beechy Grove Mennonite Church.

"I think he's been crying," Freni whispered. Alas, Freni whispers louder than I mutter.

My dinner guests' ears perked up just as pertly as the parishoners' ears had when the organist played her first chord, and Shnookums, who'd been smuggled into church, thanks to Susannah's otherwise empty bra, began to howl.

I sprinted to the phone, nearly knocking the swinging door off its hinges. "Aaron?"

"Magdalena! Thank God you're there."

Freni was right. He did sound sort of husky.

"It's dinnertime, Pooky Bear," I said brightly. "Where else would I be?"

"Are you sitting down?"

"Yes." It wasn't a lie since I'm sure he didn't mean it literally.

"Magdalena, this is going to be the hardest thing I've ever done in my life."

I racked my brain for clues. Ah, but of course! My Pooky Bear had been gone for three days, and had only packed for two.

"Be sure to separate the whites and the colors. That navy plaid shirt of yours with white stripes belongs in the color pile. Those tan slacks are kind of iffy. The navy might make them blotchy. But since they're polyester and not likely to bleed, I'd wash them with whites."

There was a moment of awed silence. My Pooky Bear knew I was a woman of many talents, he just didn't know I could read minds. Well, he'd learn. I've said it before, and I'll say it again, the female brain, if allowed to develop naturally, is capable of astounding feats of intuition. Any open-minded person will agree that a hunch from a woman is worth two facts from a man.

"I'm not talking about my damned laundry."

"Aaron!"

"Sorry, Mags, but this is really important. I don't want to waste time with your guessing games."

I pulled up a kitchen chair. "What is it, dear?"

He sucked in his breath sharply. "I'm married."

"Of course you are, dear. I was there, remember?"

"No, I mean *married*."

I blushed. "I know, dear. I was there for that, too. Frankly, it wasn't quite what I expected but —"

"Mags! Listen to me. What I'm tried to say is that I was married before I married you."

Chapter Nineteen

Why don't kitchen chairs come equipped with seat belts? If I hadn't chosen to sit right up against the corner, with a wall penning me in on either side, I would have slumped to the floor.

"You were married before? You mean, I'm your *second* wife?"

"Not exactly, Mags."

I gasped. "You were married twice before?"

"Huh? No, that's not what I mean."

Two times, three times, how much worse could it get? Pretty darn much worse, from what I understood. Susannah has a friend who's been married nine times, and she's not even in show business.

A visiting African head of state once told me that he found our monogamy laws rather silly. "You Americans find polygamy abhorrent," he said. "Yet you practice a form of it — serial monogamy." He was right. Apparently more so than I knew at the time.

"How many wives *have* you had?"

"Just one."

"*What?*"

"Just Deirdre. That's what I'm trying to tell you. And she's still my wife."

"Deirdre? What kind of a name is that for a Mennonite?" The mind can take interesting turns when its main conduits have been clogged by shock.

"She isn't Mennonite."

"Amish?"

"She isn't anything."

"She has to be something!"

"Deirdre was raised Catholic, I think."

"You *think?*"

"All right, so she was. But it's not important. We don't talk about religion that much."

"This is all a joke, Aaron, isn't it? You've gotten together with some old army buddies of yours, and they've convinced you to play a practical joke. Well, this one isn't funny, Aaron. Tell them it isn't working."

"Damn it, Mags, I told you this was going to be hard, didn't I?"

"Aaron —"

"This isn't a joke, Magdalena. I met Deirdre up here in Minnesota after I got out of the army. She gave me my first haircut after I got back from Vietnam. Of course that was 1970, and long hair was in. Deirdre told me to go away and not come back until I had something I could afford to cut.

"So, I did. I mean, I stayed away for a whole year. When I went back to the shop, she was still there. We got married in August of '71."

"August? *We* were married in August, Aaron."

"Different dates," he said dryly. "Do you want to hear the rest of it, or not?"

"By all means."

"We were married for eleven years and then something went wrong. I don't know what it was — just say we fell out of love. We went our separate ways, but we never divorced. She actually filed for one, but when the papers came, neither of us wanted to go through with it."

"Divorce is a sin," I said stupidly. Whose side was I on anyway?

"At any rate, we all but lost touch — even though we were living in the same city. Minneapolis is a big city, you know."

"So I've heard."

"Then when Pops fell and broke his hip last year, and I moved back to Hernia, I didn't even think about Deirdre."

"Of course not, you met me."

"That's right, I met you. Then you and I got married — but, as it happened, I was already married."

I intentionally slammed my head into the

wall. It didn't clear my cerebral circuits, but it did affirm that I was indeed awake, and not just dreaming the whole thing. The nightmare was real.

"Let me get this straight," I said calmly. "You married me when you already had a wife?"

"Yeah, that's what I've been trying to tell you. You've made this damn hard for me, Mags."

"Me? Hard?" I'll admit, I was no longer quite so calm. To her credit, Freni closed the kitchen door again as soon as she saw that I was still in one piece.

"This never would have happened, Magdalena, if you hadn't pushed me into marriage."

"I did no such thing! You proposed, Aaron Daniel Miller. You proposed on our way home from Ohio last February."

"Maybe I did, but you were expecting it. In fact, your behavior demanded it."

"I didn't twist your arm, buster. But I wish I had, you sap-sucking, lily-livered swamp snake! I wish I had twisted it off into a bloody stump." The rational side of me fought to keep control of my remaining faculties. "But that isn't the important thing —"

"The important thing is that I am still legally married to Deirdre, and that our

Hernia marriage is null and void."

I banged my head again. "You married her in Hernia, too?"

"Deirdre and I were married in Minneapolis. I was talking about you and I. Since Deirdre and I never divorced, our marriage is still legal. It's *our* marriage — yours and mine — that is null and void."

"Null and void? Don't be silly, dear. I may have been innocent, but I wasn't that innocent."

Aaron sighed. "It was the best sex I'd ever had, I'll grant you that."

It all clicked then. It all came together at once, like the offering plates at the end of the Doxology.

"It may have been great sex for you," I screamed, "but it was adultery! I am an adulteress!"

"Don't be so hard on yourself, Mags."

"You're an adulterer, too, Aaron!"

"Well, that's taking the negative view."

"What other view could there possibly be? Read your Bible, Aaron!"

He sighed again. "I was hoping you'd be more enlightened, Mags."

I tried strangling the receiver but it didn't satisfy my English desire to kill. "What do we do now, Aaron?" I asked through clenched teeth.

"That's why I'm calling, Mags. I want to do the honorable thing."

"Dumping Deirdre is not going to be easy, dear."

There was a long, pregnant pause, in which Deirdre might possibly have gotten pregnant. "Uh — Mags, what I've been trying to say the whole time is that I still love Deirdre. I want the marriage to work now."

My pause was decidedly barren. "What did you say?"

"Don't you see! I owe it all to you. After we got married — our ceremony, I mean — I got to thinking about my life with Deirdre. I came back up here to see if there was any hope for her and I."

"And?"

"I'm in love with her, Mags. I think I always have been. And you reminded me of her, Mags. You made me remember the good times she and I shared together. I'll always owe you that."

I screamed so loud that David Bowie heard me on his compound on Bali. He told me that the next time I saw him. Claimed I owed him for two lightbulbs and a champagne glass.

Freni put me to bed. She rubbed Vicks on my chest, wrapped my neck with a strip of flannel, and tucked a hot water bottle under my feet — never mind that the afternoon's downpour had done little to ameliorate the heat, and the air-conditioning in my back bedroom leaves something to be desired. She was, of course, just expressing her love the only way she knew how. At least she didn't force-feed me the remains of her largely uneaten dinner. The castor oil she finally got past my lips was all the supper I needed.

I woke up sporadically, remembered my horrible conversation with Aaron, and almost immediately fell back into a shock-induced sleep. I remember feeling unbearably hot at one point, but whether it was a freshly refilled hot water bottle, a menopausal hot flash, or my dream that Aaron was burning in Hell, I can't say for sure. Perhaps all three. It was just after ten a.m. when I came to a sleep-satiated start. Someone was sitting on my bed, patting my leg.

"Oh no, you don't!" I screamed. "We're not even married, remember?"

"*Ach!*"

I opened my eyes. "Freni?"

Freni slid to the floor. "Yah, you were having a bad dream, Magdalena.

"You mean all that stuff about Aaron wasn't true?"

Freni's eyes rolled. It was a desperate, not an insolent gesture.

"Freni! What is it?"

Freni was frantic. "*Ach,* it wasn't all a dream, Magdalena, but there are other kettles in the sea."

"What?"

"The fish called the pot black and it broke the camel's back," she said. "But you'll be all right, you'll see. It's always darkest when there's a bun in the oven."

"I'm pregnant?" I screeched.

"*Ach,* how should I know?"

I sat up in bed. My head pounded as if I'd just come off a bender — not that I would know, mind you. But I've observed Susannah enough times to know the symptoms.

"Freni, did Aaron call last night during dinner and tell me that he'd been married before? That he was *still* married to her?"

"Yah." Her bottom lip quivered.

"So I *am* an adulteress," I wailed.

"Yah, but it wasn't your fault," Freni said in her most soothing voice, the one she uses to coax soufflés from the oven. "It was Aaron Miller's fault. And the Millers have always been," she lapsed into Pennsylvania Dutch, "*anner Satt Leit.*" The "other sort of people."

"Miller." The word sounded foreign on my tongue, never mind that Susannah and I have Millers on both sides of the family. "May I never hear that word again."

"Amen," Freni said loyally. "Now you are back to being a Yoder. Just like you always were."

"Not quite," I said, hanging my head in shame.

Freni blushed. "*Ach*, that! Nothing is perfect, Magdalena. Anyway, now you know what it is all about."

"Much ado about nothing, if you ask me."

"Speak for yourself," my elderly kinswoman said. "Like they say, some of the best lunches in life are free." She said something else, too, but I put my hands over my ears and kept them there until she was done.

"What will I tell everyone, Freni? How can I face the shame?"

Freni drew herself up to her full five feet two inches. "You will tell them the truth, Magdalena. Everyone knows the kind of woman you are. No one will believe for a second that you did anything wrong."

I caught my breath, pointing to the ceiling. "Except for Pops."

"*Ach*, the man should talk. It was him who raised Aaron Junior."

"Melvin will get a huge kick out of this, you can count on that."

"Melvin, schmelvin, let him talk. The more *he* talks, the more everyone else will feel sorry for you. You want to make it easy on yourself? You call Melvin right now and tell him the whole story. By dinnertime the whole town will think you're a saint. Like Lot's wife or something."

"Lot's wife was turned into a pillar of salt for the sin of disobeying God, and bigamy is a sin," I said, forgetting for a moment that most of the characters in the Bible were, in fact, bigamists, if not polygamists. "Stand back. I'm liable to be turned into a white chunk of sodium before your very eyes."

"*Ach,*" said Freni, "you always did look good in white."

I reached out and clasped her hand. My own mama could not have been half as supportive. Even dead, Mama was no doubt judging me for a sin I had committed unwittingly. If I didn't hurry up and change the subject she would start turning in her grave again. The last time she reached a full spin the folks out in L.A. reported a 6.2 earthquake.

"So, what else is new?" I said, willing my features into the approximation of a smile.

"Nothing — *ach,* just one small thing, but

I wasn't going to bother you with it until you were feeling better."

"Bother away."

She frowned. "A lady has been calling the desk phone ever since I got here this morning. Five times now, maybe six."

"What does she want?"

"Flowers."

"What?"

"Each time a different flower. Orchids, roses, daisies — even a lotus. That is a flower, isn't it?"

"Yes, sort of like a water lily, I think. Exactly what else does she say?"

"*Ach,* I don't remember, Magdalena. She asks for the flowers, and when I tell her we don't sell them, she hangs up."

"That's very strange," I said.

Freni smiled. "*Ach,* but not as strange as the time Susannah got a call from the Pope."

"And Susannah had the nerve to pretend she was Mother Teresa! Who would have thought the phone companies could cross wires like that?"

Freni retucked a hospital corner that had come loose. "So, you will be all right then?"

I smiled bravely. "Right as rain."

"Good. Then I'll get you your breakfast."

"Bacon with still a little play left in it, two

eggs poached medium, and some cinnamon toast will be nice," I said. "Oh, and some hot chocolate — with extra marshmallows."

Now that I was no longer married, and would certainly never marry again, there was no reason to hang on to my figure. I'd read some place that the taste buds start to go at age sixty, or thereabouts. I had a lot of eating to do if I was going to catch up with my contemporaries in the next fifteen years. As soon as I got a chance I'd drive in to Bedford, buy a size 24W dress at Dancing Joe's Dress Barn, and proceed to fill it out.

"No bacon, Magdalena. No eggs either until the chickens lay again. Those English are eating us out of house and home."

"They're paying guests," I reminded her gently. "What do we have in the larder?"

"Scrapple," she said brightly.

I wrinkled my nose. Scrapple is a mixture of cornmeal and ground animal parts that can't make it to the plate in their normal guise. The stuff is shaped into a loaf, sliced, and fried, and often served with syrup. My people think it's a delicacy. Since only a Germanic stomach can tolerate scrapple, I have often entertained the idea that I was adopted. Local legend has it that the late Duke and Duchess of Windsor toured Hernia in the forties and, according to at

247

least one rumormonger, abandoned an unwanted royal baby. Freni insists, however, that any resemblance between me and the late Duchess of Windsor is purely coincidental.

"Well," Feni said, with a gleam in her beady eyes, "since you were in no condition to eat your dessert last night, I saved it for you."

"What is it?" I could barely remember anything about the evening. Becoming an adulteress takes a lot out of one's system.

"Gingerbread. From scratch. I made it just in case none of the pies turned out."

"Did any turn out?"

Freni pursed her lips. "Mrs. Dixon's pie wasn't too bad. It wasn't too good either, but everyone seemed to think so. They barely touched my gingerbread."

"Does that gingerbread come with warm lemon sauce?"

"*Ach*, what else?"

I would have clasped Freni gratefully to my bosom, had it not been for the Vicks smeared on my chest. Freni's gingerbread is the best in the world, and my second favorite food, after her homemade cinnamon rolls. Filling that size 24W dress was going to take less time than I thought. Perhaps I had aimed my sights too low.

CHAPTER TWENTY

BIGAMIST'S BREAKFAST GINGERBREAD

INGREDIENTS

1 3/4 cups sifted all-purpose flour
1 teaspoon ground ginger
1/2 teaspoon cinnamon
1/2 teaspoon baking soda
1/4 teaspoon ground cloves
1/4 teaspoon salt
1/4 cup shortening
1 large egg
1/2 cup white sugar
3/4 cup buttermilk
1/2 cup dark molasses

DIRECTIONS

Preheat oven to 350°F.

In a large bowl, sift dry ingredients together and set aside. Cream the shortening and sugar in a large bowl. Beat in egg. Slowly add sifted dry ingredients, alternating with small amounts of buttermilk and molasses until all ingredients have been combined. Beat well. Bake in a 9-x9-inch greased loaf pan for 25 minutes. Serve warm with homemade lemon sauce.

LEMON SAUCE

$1/2$ cup white sugar
3 tablespoons cornstarch
Pinch of salt
2 cups boiling water
$1/4$ cup butter
1 lemon, grated rind and juice (seeds removed)

In a medium saucepan, thoroughly mix sugar, cornstarch, and salt. Add boiling water gradually, stirring constantly. Bring to low boil and cook 6–8 minutes, stirring frequently. Add butter and stir until melted and combined with sauce. Add lemon juice and grated rind. Stir and serve over generous squares of warm gingerbread.

Note: If recovering from a traumatic revelation, do not bother to count calories.

CHAPTER TWENTY-ONE

One should be allowed to finish one's breakfast in peace. "There is no peace for the wicked," Mama often said, and I guess she was right. You would have thought it was National Bother Bigamists Day.

When the phone rang on my personal line, I reluctantly picked up. Only three people, Aaron, Susannah, and Melvin Stoltzfus are apt to be on the other end, and I wasn't in the mood to speak to any of them that day. Still, a phone unanswered is a potential problem waiting to be nipped in the bud.

"Hello?" At least that's what I intended to say. The gingerbread may have distorted it a little.

"Magdalena?"

I swallowed. "I am *not* buying any, thank you very much! I never, ever buy from phone solicitors. In fact, you tell your supervisor —"

"Magdalena, stop screeching this minute. I am not a phone solicitor. It's me, Elizabeth."

Elizabeth is as common a name among Mennonites and Amish as Jennifer, or even

Caitlin, is among the English. It could have been any of a hundred acquaintances. Grandma Yoder was an Elizabeth, for crying out loud. If it was her, I certainly didn't want to talk. Even while she was alive, Grandma Yoder was intimidating.

"You have dialed in error," I said in my most mechanical voice. "Please check the number you wish to reach —"

"You aren't fooling anyone, Magdalena, with that fake phone voice. I always said you sounded like a goose in a thunderstorm, and you haven't changed a bit."

"You're so kind," I said, "but I haven't the slightest idea who you are."

"We are not amused, Magdalena."

"Neither am I, toots," I said getting tough. "Identify yourself, or I'm hanging up."

"*Ach,* it's Lilibet, of course."

I knew who it was then. Elizabeth Augsburger was the only Amish woman I knew who went by that nickname. Lizzie, Elizabeth, even Betty — but Lilibet? You would think she was the Queen of England by the way she carried on. It was most un-Amish of her. Everything about her was. Maybe it was she who the Duke and Duchess of Windsor abandoned as a baby. That would explain her inordinate fondness

252

of dogs and horses and her use of the royal "we."

"Why are you calling, Lilibet? You don't even own a phone."

"*Ach,* somebody had to call, so I walked into Miller's Feed Store. You owe me, Magdalena."

"I'll put a quarter in the mail."

"Very funny, Magdalena. You haven't the slightest idea why I'm calling, do you?"

"Miller's is having a special sale and you didn't want me to miss out?"

"It's your father-in-law, Magdalena. Aaron Senior is very upset. He barely slept a wink last night."

"How would you know, dear?"

"He and my Amos were up half the night talking, that's why. The other half I heard him crying."

"What? Pops spent the night at your place?"

"As if you didn't know. That poor man."

"Just because I didn't believe his story about a flying saucer landing in the pond. Do you believe in flying saucers, Lilibet?"

Of course she didn't. We are a practical people, with Bible-based beliefs. And there is absolutely no mention of flying saucers in the Bible, the Book of Ezekiel notwithstanding.

She gave a little gasp. "What on earth are you talking about, Magdalena?"

"Little green men from Mars. Illegal aliens whose children we *definitely* don't want in our schools."

"*Ach,* you never could think straighter than a row of English fence poles. It's no wonder you did what you did. A mad dog wouldn't be so mean."

If there's one thing I hate, it's being called mean. I really do try to see the good in everyone. Hadn't I been proving it by helping Melvin out in his time of need? And Pops — how many women these days would put up with their father-in-law moving in the day after their wedding?

"Tell the old coot, I'm sorry," I said.

There was a pregnant silence during which the population of Bangladesh doubled, as did the number of Elvis sightings in Fargo, North Dakota.

"I'll tell him," she said at last, "but I am disappointed in you, Magdalena. You don't seem to feel the least little bit of shame."

"Shame? For what?"

"Jesus forgave that adulteress, Magdalena, but the crowd was ready to throw stones. And there are lots of stones around Hernia."

My ears were burning, but it was embarrassment, not shame. There is a difference, you know. The bee in Lilibet's bonnet had nothing to do with Martians. I laid back against my pillows and pondered the possibilities. It could only be one thing, but surely the Amish-Mennonite grapevine couldn't be that fast, not when half the grapes didn't own telephones and relied on horses and buggies to get around.

"Before you lob a boulder at me, at least spell out the charges," I said bravely.

"Kicking an elderly man out on the street would be enough," Lilibet snapped, "but to do so in order to carry on an affair is just —"

"Affair?"

"Don't you take that innocent tone with me, Magdalena. I've seen those loud, brassy outfits you wear into town. Multicolor floral prints!"

I ignored her fashion observation. Surely it wasn't possible to have an affair and not know it. I know, there were times — with Aaron — when I was a mite distracted, but I never got so lost in my menu-planning that I didn't know what was going on.

"Who am I having this affair with?" I asked calmly.

"*Ach,* you have less shame than a dog in heat. Next you'll be saying that this affair was the back doctor's idea."

"Back doctor?"

"He was here trying to sell me one of those braces, you know. Magdalena, you could do better in the looks department — as long as you're going to cheat, I mean."

Whether it was my looks, or Wilmar Brack's that went lacking, it wasn't clear. But it was finally as plain as dandruff on Aaron's collars that there was a plot underfoot to disgrace me.

"Did *he* say I was having an affair with him?"

"*Ach,* I wouldn't have such a conversation with a stranger," she said, temporarily forgetting her high-blown ways and lapsing into Dutch.

"Even Jesus knew who his accusers were," I said.

During the ensuing pause the British learned to cook and the number of Elvis sightings in Butte, Montana, tripled.

"Aaron Senior," she whispered. "He said you and the doctor were carrying on like — like —"

"Dogs in heat?"

"Yah. He said that poor Aaron Junior couldn't take it anymore and had to go back to Minnesota just to keep from going crazy. Aaron Senior said that Aaron would not be divorcing you — since it's wrong — but that the marriage was essentially over. He

256

warned me that you would deny everything. That you would pin everything on Aaron. He said I mustn't believe a word you say."

I smelled cover-up just as definitively as I smelled gas whenever Aaron — my *ex*-Pooky Bear — ate cabbage. Pops was already off to his dinner with the Augsburgers when Aaron called. Therefore, it was not a case of him misconstruing our conversation. He had been primed beforehand, and planted at the Augsburgers to purposefully spread lies about me. It was a very clever move on Aaron's part, turning me into the Whore of Babylon while he lollygagged around in Minnesota with his real wife.

Turn the other cheek, the Bible says, but it also says that the truth will set us free. Since I can never remember which is my good side, I did the only thing I could and told Lilibet the truth.

In the silence following that revelation the French learned good manners and Elvis was spotted riding a Harley-Davidson through the streets of Nome, Alaska.

"You poor dear," she said finally.

It was as much of an apology as she was going to freely give. If I wanted more, I was going to have to work for it.

"My heart is broken," I wailed, which was true. "I will never be able to hold my head up in Hernia again." That was probably not quite so true. I have broad shoulders and a strong neck, and I knew from past experience that most pain eventually passes — either that, or you die from it. Frankly, I am not the kind who dies easily.

"You poor, poor dear," Lilibet said, scraping the bottom of her sympathy well. "Of course there is nothing I could do to help."

"Then a cobbler can't fix shoes, dear."

"But —"

"You're at Miller's Feed Store, right?"

"Yes —"

"Share my story of woe with the next person you see. Share the whole story. Tell them how Aaron married me under false pretenses and then tried to smear my reputation. But make them promise they won't tell a single living soul."

"I always said you were a bright one, Magdalena. But how is it going to look for me? I believed" — she gasped — "oh my gracious, he's here!"

"Aaron?" I will admit, that despite everything, my heart was beating faster.

"Aaron Senior. I forgot that he was still at my house. He said he never wanted to go back to the PennDutch — to Jezebel's Inn, he called it. What am I going to do? He can't stay here, Magdalena. We already have eight mouths to feed."

I thought fast. "Tell the old coot that Jezebel has declared a cease-fire until ten-thirty tonight. That's when the next direct flight to Minneapolis leaves. Tell him that I'll even spring for the tickets, but how he gets to the airport is his problem. You might suggest that he call a cab from Bedford. It'll cost him an arm and an leg to get to Pittsburgh airport, but hey, that's what he gets for lying. Tell him that I'm only going to make the ticket offer once."

"I will. Thanks."

I was so shocked to hear the "T" word that I nearly blew it. "But you owe me," I said a microsecond before she hung up.

"Anything," she said carelessly.

"Throw another potato or two on the stove. I'm bringing some English guests to lunch."

Frankly, I was quite satisfied with the way I was holding up, not to mention the way I had handled things with Lilibet Augsburger. There had indeed been a seat available on the ten-thirty flight, and what's more, thanks to an airfare war, it was undoubtedly cheaper than Pops' ride to the airport was going to be. I wasn't gloating, mind you, and I certainly wasn't feeling like I'd extracted revenge, even though I knew that Pops hated snow and the *Farmer's Almanac* was predicting the worst winter in a hundred years for the Upper Midwest. It just felt good to be able to function in a situation that, just twenty-four hours earlier, I would have thought impossible to survive.

Something caught the corner of my eye and I sat up with a start. There, not more than a foot from the end of my bed stood little Caitlin, holding her sorry doll by one arm. Lord only knows how long the urchin had been standing there, grinning at me like a Cheshire cat.

"What on earth are you doing in here?"

She giggled. "Wan Oou wants to say good morning."

"Wan Oou needs to knock before she barges into someone else's bedroom."

Her laugh was an irritating mixture of joy and amusement. Mama wouldn't have put up with it for a second.

She laid the filthy doll on my bed. "Wan Oou thinks you're a funny lady, Mrs. Miller."

"I'm glad you think so, sweetie." Sarcasm was lost on the tyke, so I scowled appropriately. "Now scram, Wan Oou, and take your doll with you."

Apparently I was funnier than a barrel full of monkeys, and I had to clap my hands to get her attention. She stared at me, her pug features trying hopelessly to compose themselves, and then she burst into another fit of giggles so intense they were almost contagious.

"You could at least let me in on your joke," I wailed.

"My name is Caitlin, you silly-billy! Wan Oou is my dolly!"

Without further ado the tyke and her toy were shown the door.

I had just finished dressing, having devoured a huge chunk of gingerbread fairly floating in lemon sauce, when my private phone rang again. It is true, I frequently jump to conclusions — it is, after all, a form of exercise — but the male caller did sound like Aaron. Perhaps I should have allowed him to say something in addition to my name.

"You have a lot of nerve," I shrilled. "It's one thing to lie to me but to lie *about* me — that's utterly reprehensible, you two-timing, lily-livered weasel. And don't think your father is getting off easy. I just sent him packing to Minneapolis. You can expect him on the ten-thirty flight out of Pittsburgh. Come to think of it, you just saved me a call. And for the record, I'm paying for his flight." I gasped for breath.

"Since Papa died when I was three," Melvin Stoltzfus said with remarkable alacrity, "could you send Mama to Minneapolis instead?"

"Melvin!"

"It's first class, isn't it? Mama's gained a few pounds lately. She prefers a wider seat."

"They don't make them that wide, Melvin, and besides, I wasn't talking to you! I thought you were someone else."

"Oh." He sounded genuinely disappointed.

"What is it, Melvin?" I snapped.

"Ah, yes. There's been a complaint, Yoder. No, make that numerous complaints from outraged citizens. They all think it's highly inappropriate. But it's more than that. It's illegal."

Bless the little man, mantis mandibles and all, for calling me Yoder. It felt good to be called that again — not that Melvin had ever called me anything else, of course. Perhaps the man was prophetic in his persistent refusal to use my married name. Still, what right had he to call me with complaints of impropriety? Melvin had never been married, but despite his arthropodan looks and obnoxious personality, he had known enough women in the biblical sense to make an NBA star feel inadequate.

"I didn't know! And I will not wear a scarlet 'A' unless you do as well," I shouted.

Believe it or not I could hear his eyes rotating in their sockets. "You're nuts, Yoder. You know that?"

It was time to eat crow. But just one, baked in a nice flaky pastry crust and served with a giblet gravy. Melvin had never been married and always, at least in my eyes — and I mean this charitably — been a loser. Perhaps I had gloated a bit too much when I married Aaron. No doubt I was being punished, and deserved every bit of scorn Melvin threw my way. Still, it was hard not to defend myself.

"It's his fault, Melvin. He had me totally hoodwinked. I didn't even suspect he was married, but then again, why should I?"

"I thought you screened them," Melvin had the audacity to say. "Anyway, his marital status has nothing to do with it. It's his pushiness. Selma Eichleburger says he pushed his way right into her kitchen and stripped down to the waist before she had time to blink. She says she nearly fainted when she saw it."

"And you think I'm crazy?" I snapped. "It's not *above* his waist, dear. Even I knew that before I got married. And Selma is a widow yet!"

"He wears a truss, too?"

"What?"

"Seems he's bothered every housewife in Bedford County in the short time he's been here."

"He has an insatiable appetite for it," I wailed. There, I finally said it, even if it was to Melvin.

"He isn't licensed to sell that thing door to door, Yoder."

I gasped. "They give licenses for that?" At last the Commonwealth of Pennsylvania had followed the rest of the country you-know-where in a handbasket.

"A vendor's license is only a couple of bucks, you know. That's what I hate about these outsiders. Think they come in and just ignore the law, like we're some little one-horse town."

"He's no outsider," I said, temporarily forgetting that I was no longer obliged to defend Aaron. "He was born and raised right across the street from the PennDutch Inn. Went to Hernia High just like you and I. Who would have known?"

"Give me a break, Yoder. Your Dr. Brack

did not go to Hernia High. I have all the yearbooks —"

"Dr. Brack? Are you talking about Dr. Wilmar Brack?"

"Are you deaf, Yoder, or do you flap your gums for exercise?"

Of course not! I got all the exercise I needed jumping to conclusions.

"I'll have a stern talk with him," I said and hung up. The crow pie could wait.

CHAPTER TWENTY-TWO

I am a woman of my word. I found Dr. Brack in the parlor examining the back of his head in the parlor mirror with the help of a little mirror. A compact, Susannah calls them. I'm sure I startled him because he dropped the little mirror. But then, barely missing a beat, he kicked it sideways underneath Grandma Yoder's walnut burl Victorian sofa.

"Shame on you," I said, wagging my finger at him. "You've been caught red-handed."

"You may not understand this, Mrs. Miller, but it's important for a man in my position to look good. Next year I'll undoubtedly be up for the Nobel prize again, so, I was just checking to see if a hair transplant was in order. But of course it's not. Is it?" he asked, taking me by surprise.

"Of course not," I said kindly. "I'm sure those three hairs you've trained across it help cut down the glare substantially."

"Madame Curie used to love running her fingers through my hair." He sounded convincingly wistful, but I knew that Marie Curie died in 1934 when Wilmar Brack was nothing more than a gleam in his father's eye.

266

"It's not your vanity I was talking about, dear. It's the way you've been pestering everyone in the county to buy your braces. You're obviously a man of accomplishment and means, so why do you feel compelled to go door to door like the Fuller Brush man?"

He gently fingered the three lacquered strands. "It's the personal contact. It revitalizes me."

"You're a doctor, for pete's sake. Don't you have personal contact at work?"

He stared at me. "What's this all about? Have there been complaints about me?"

"Apparently tons. You aren't licensed to sell door to door and you push your way into people's houses. If you don't stop, you might find your belongings have been moved over to the Hernia jail. Trust me, it's not the kind of place you want to spend your vacation."

He stiffened. "I've been in jail before. There was that time in India with the Mahatma. We shared a cell for six months. Did you know that Gandhi married when he was only thirteen?"

I shook my head. I was as likely to get through to him as I was to Susannah. Some people are just born without a clue.

"You're intrusive," I said gently. "You get under people's skin like a polio vaccination."

"Ah, Jonas Salk! What a nice young man he was."

"And you're a braggart, dear."

I made no progress except to offend my guest to the point that he refused to go with the rest of the group to the Augsburgers for lunch. Perhaps he would have declined anyway, having already made his pitch to Lilibet and failed.

Freni was put out when I announced to her that I was taking the gang over to Lilibet's for lunch. Actually, that's putting it mildly. The woman flapped around the kitchen like a chicken with its head cut off. Of course I may have been partly to blame, springing it on her at the last minute, but it wasn't like I had much warning. Besides, I was going through a very difficult time, and should be cut some slack, especially by older and wiser cousins.

"What about my poached chicken salad?" Freni wailed.

"It's the best in the world," I said, and meant it. "I'm sure our guests wouldn't mind having it tomorrow for lunch."

Freni frowned fearsome furrows. "The walnuts will get soggy."

"Leave them out," I said patiently.

"I already put them in."

"Either take them out, or serve the salad tonight at dinner."

"I've got a roast planned."

"That's perfect. Your scrumptious chicken salad will be the appetizer."

"*Ach,* the English and their meals! Whoever heard of having dinner at night?"

"That's because they're not farmers, dear. They don't need high-calorie noontime meals so that they can have strength to plow the fields. They prefer to take the bulk of their calories at night. This bunch is actually rather easy to cook for, wouldn't you agree? I mean, at least we don't have any macro-vegetarians to contend with this time."

"This bunch is *meshuggah,*" she said. It's the only Yiddish that Freni knows, and it's thanks to one of our favorite guests, a great gal with a trademark proboscis and an outstanding set of pipes. The two women seemed to hit it off.

"You say that every time, dear, and frankly, that sounds a little proud to me. We are all a little crazy in our own way. Even you, dear."

"*Oy gevalt,*" Freni said and rolled her eyes. Apparently she and Babs were closer than I thought. So that was *them* in the kitchen singing tunes from *Funny Girl.* Who would have known that Freni could even carry a tune?

"This attitude of yours is not in the least bit Christian," I said sternly. "You should be ashamed of yourself, the pot calling the kettle black. You shouldn't even have bothered with those walnuts, dear. They probably think you're as nutty as a Christmas stolen, already."

"*Ach*, me? They should talk! That business woman snooping around our farms, making us ridiculous offers —"

"She has?" I cried in dismay. Shirley Pearson had said nothing further about having a look-see at the Miller farm. Of course now with Pops winging his way to Minnesota, it was no longer a matter of life and death. But it was still critical. I had had no time to rustle up Amish buyers for the place, and unless I wanted a Wal-Mart sitting in my lap, I was running out of time.

"Yah, but she isn't as crazy as that movie star."

"Former child television star," I corrected her.

"Whatever. He wears such ridiculous clothes, Magdalena. Everybody's laughing. Thelma Mishler asked me yesterday if he was a refugee from Bosnia. She thought maybe that was his national costume. Frieda Gingrich said she was sure he was a Mormon missionary and wanted to know why he didn't have a partner with him. Don't they always travel in pairs?"

"I think so."

"Well, I told them that this was the way people in California dressed, and they could hardly believe it. They said they felt sorry for him and wanted to donate some of their husbands' old clothes. Do you think he would wear our style of clothes? they wanted to know. I told them I would ask him, but I haven't seen him since he walked out of my pie-baking demonstrations. Is that crazy or what?"

"Let me ask him about the clothes," I said wearily. Terry Slock was not going to be happy to learn that Abigail Cobb's creations had failed miserably. The Amish had not even recognized them as resembling their own. The Children of the Corn were going to be the laughingstock of Bedford County.

"And he can't make a pie crust to save himself," Freni said, on a roll.

"Poor baking skills does not make one crazy, dear. And anyway, Dorothy Dixon bakes a decent pie, you said so yourself. So, at least one of our guests isn't crazy."

"*Ach,* but her husband. Whoever heard of a black room yet?"

"A what?"

"In the cellar. He said you gave him permission for his black room."

"Darkroom!"

"I just went down there to get a jar of huckleberry preserves, Magdalena, and he acted like I'd let the cows out of the barn. Is that crazy or what?"

I shrugged. "Apparently light ruins the film. It's a big no-no."

"Everyone who does evil hates the light," she said, quoting from the Gospel of John.

"What's that supposed to mean?"

"*Ach,* don't you read your Bible anymore, Magdalena?"

"Of course I do. But I want to know what you mean by that."

But she was walking away, shaking her head and muttering to herself. "Mark my words," was all I could make out.

The Augsburgers live on Augsburger Lane. This fact tickles me, because we Yoders have always lived on Hertzler Lane, and the Hertzlers live on Mast Drive, the Masts on Kauffman Road, and the Kauffmans on Zweibacher Road. As for the Zweibachers, they moved into town two generations ago, gave up the faith of their fathers altogether, and joined the First Methodist Church. There is no Yoder anything that I know of within a day's buggy drive of Hernia.

Amos Augsburger, like all good Amish men, is undoubtedly humble. As I've said before, I'm not so sure about Lilibet. The two-story frame house she presides over gleams white in the sun like the tip of a giant iceberg, emerging above a lush green sea. The long drive that leads up from the lane is the iceberg's wake. Only the flower borders, still vibrant this late in the summer, remind one that they are in the Pennsylvania countryside and not the north Atlantic.

Other Amish women maintain kitchen gardens near their back doors, but not our Lilibet. Her vegetable plot is located behind the barn, to spare visitors the sight of organic detritus. Ditto for her clotheslines. To spot bloomers blowing in the breeze, one had to hike around the back of the white chicken house, a smaller but more pungent iceberg. Lilibet's laundry might look clean, but you wouldn't want to bury your nose in her towels.

"Awesome," Terry said.

To avoid cluttering the Augsburger driveway with an unseemly number of cars,

I had gallantly chauffeured the two unmarrieds. The Dixons, cum urchins, were on their own.

Shirley paid no attention to the house and lawn. Her eyes were on the barn and the fields beyond.

"From here the corn looks a little stunted. What's his bushel yield per acre?"

"It's a much smaller crop than what the Miller farm produced in its day," I said, stretching the truth only slightly. Aaron Sr. primarily raised beef cattle.

"This place has good vibes, though," Terry said. "It reminds me of Sedona. And the placement of the house on the lawn is good fueng-shui. It would make a great retreat center."

"I saw it first," Shirley said. I was surprised by the fervor in her voice.

Apparently Terry was as well. "What?"

"You heard me," she said almost coldly. "This one is mine. I'm not just playing childish games here, Terrence. If it comes up to specs, I intend to make an offer."

"And I don't?"

"Why would you? You're not a businessman."

"I had a career in show business, lady."

"I'm talking about the real world, Terrence, not *Mama Wore Pearls*."

I clucked my tongue. "Children, please!"

"For your information," Terry shouted, ignoring me, "I had a major role in *The Young and the Spiteful*."

"That doesn't make you a businessman, Terrence. You don't know the first thing about profit margins. You just want to turn this place into some ex-hippie hangout."

"Ha, that's what you think! And I have so had business experience. I had investments, you know."

"Such as?" Shirley sneered. Frankly, I was shocked at her behavior.

"Such as — well, I even ran my own business there for a while."

"A Fortune 500 firm, I bet!"

"No, but it was successful. I produced my own films. Slock Studios."

"Children!" I shouted. They paid no attention.

"Oh, yeah? Name *one* film!"

"*Her Cup Runneth Over!*"

"Ha, just as I suspected, a porno film. You were in the business of selling sleaze."

In the rearview mirror I could see that Terry had turned a shade of red that clashed horribly with my car. Sudden, passionate flushes of blood to the face were not something I had taken into account when making my choice.

"It was a soft-core film," he said through clenched teeth. "And it wasn't nearly as sleazy as what you do with the Japanese."

"What?"

"You heard me. Doing business and making cozy nice-nice with the enemy. That's the definition of real sleaze, if you ask me."

"You're nuts!" she hissed.

"My daddy was killed by the Japanese. I never even got a chance to meet him!" Terry burst into tears.

I threw up my hands in exasperation. Fortunately we had just come to a stop. The Dixons in the station wagon were right behind us. They must have been engrossed in the scenery as well because Angus didn't stop in time.

It wasn't a very hard collision, because none of the airbags were deployed, but it was enough to make us rock a little in our seats. Nobody was hurt, so we all spilled out of the cars like ants from an opened cookie jar to see if there was any damage to my beamer. I had the most at stake, so I was the first one there. Fortunately there was no new damage, just that one little ding that had been a punch to my stomach.

The adult Dixons, I'm happy to report, were properly mortified. The urchins, on the other hand, were as incorrigible as ever. The mishap seemed to exhilarate them. The older two frolicked about like lambs in a spring pasture, bleating inanely. From seemingly out of nowhere several of Lilibet's children appeared and began frolicking with their English visitors. It was an ecumenical scene if I ever saw one.

For a few seconds it was actually charming. Then little Caitlin got into the act by squealing something nonsensical and doing a series of cartwheels on Lilibet's lawn. Call me old-fashioned if you will, but even a girl of five should keep her knees together whenever she wears a dress. Mama would have rapped my knuckles good for such unseemly behavior.

"Are you sure you're all right?" Dorothy asked.

"Fine as frog hair, dear." I glanced down at my bumper. "I'm just glad it wasn't any worse."

"Oh, don't worry about that," Angus said, whipping his wallet out of his back pocket. "Two hundred bucks should get that fixed, shouldn't it?"

"Yes, but —"

"Four hundred then, but I'll have to write a check. Dorothy, get your purse from the car."

She obediently trotted back to get it.

"Mr. Dixon, I have no intention of accepting your money," I said firmly.

He looked bewildered, like a doe caught in the headlights of your car. That has only happened to me once, but it was a horrible experience that I wouldn't wish on my worst enemy. Fortunately I was able to swerve and miss that poor deer, but in doing so I ran off the road and smack into a haystack on the Bontrager farm, nearly snuffing out the lives of two people.

Actually, I missed the people entirely, but if the truth be told, at the time I almost wished I hadn't. I mean, how was I to know that it was Susannah and Bobby Bontrager who were doing unspeakable things in that haystack? Nonetheless Papa grounded me for a week, even though I was twenty-eight at the time. Meanwhile Susannah and Bobby, neither of whom were hurt, were treated like royalty just because they'd had a frightening experience. I even had to do Susannah's chores for a week while she lolled about, supposedly recovering her wits — although just between you and me, she never found them.

At any rate, Angus Dixon suddenly seemed confused and very nervous. "Uh — well — it's such a hassle dealing with insurance companies, isn't it? If I could just pay you the damages directly, it will save us both a lot of time."

"You didn't do the ding, dear," I said, sounding a tad dingy myself. "God did. There are no new damages."

He breathed a sigh of relief that blew out Yvonne Roth's birthday candles two and half miles away. Miss Roth is Hernia's oldest citizen at ninety-nine, and while there weren't perhaps quite that many candles on her cake, there were a lot of them.

"You sure? I mean, we don't have to involve the police or anything?"

"Not unless you're a glutton for punishment. It would take Chief Stoltzfus hours just to write everything down, and it's time for lunch. But you," I said sweetly, turning to Dorothy, "cannot go into lunch looking like that. Didn't you at least bring the sweater I suggested?"

"I brought it," she said, sounding uncannily like Susannah. "I left it in the car."

"Then get it, dear, or our hosts are liable to think you're Delilah risen from the dead. Bare shoulders and tunnel tops are definite no-nos."

"It's called a tube top," she sniffed, "and you're just jealous because you couldn't wear one even if you wanted to."

"Well, I never!" She was wrong, of course. Her top was nothing more than a big sock with the toe cut out, and my socks never collapse.

I turned my back on her and waved to Lilibet who was calling to the children from the front porch of her glacial farmhouse. They all ignored her. She ignored me.

"Get inside this minute!"

One of the Augsburger kids glanced at his mother, and then chased after Marissa, who was screaming like a banshee from the pure pleasure of being eight years old and alive.

Lilibet ducked into the house and reappeared a moment later with a wooden paddle. "I will count to ten!" she shouted. *"Eens — zwee — drei — vier — fimf — sex — siwwe — acht"* — her voice grew louder and shriller, eclipsing even the banshee — *"nein — zehe!"*

Immediately the Augsburger urchins fell into line and trooped into the house. Much to my amazement the Dixon offspring followed suit.

"You see what a little discipline can do?" Shirley said over her shoulder.

"That's child abuse," Dorothy muttered.

"Relax," I said. "Mrs. Augsburger would

sooner dance naked on the Eiffel Tower than hit her children. That paddle is for taking pies out of the oven."

"But they didn't obey her until they saw the stick."

"The stick symbolizes dessert. If they hadn't obeyed then, there would be no dessert."

"That's still child abuse."

"Give me a break," Shirley said. "You bleeding heart liberals make me lose my appetite."

I was politer and merely rolled my eyes.

Lilibet finally turned her attention to us now that we were only feet away. "*Ach,* hurry up," she said. "The dinner's getting cold!"

We hurried. I introduced my guests and was pleasantly surprised at how gracious Lilibet could be. No doubt it was noblesse oblige.

"Welcome, welcome," she said as she ushered us into a spotless room. "I'm sorry for the mess, but we had a house guest we weren't expecting." She gave me a penetrating look.

I realized with a start that I had made no provisions to take Pops back to the inn so he could pack. For all I knew the old coot would be joining us for dinner. No doubt the two of us would spend the entire meal glaring at each other, and I, for one, would have no appetite. My goal of filling up the size 24W dress was going to be delayed.

CHAPTER TWENTY-THREE

True to character, Lilibet Augsburger put on a feed of royal proportions. In addition to a cold ham, there was meat loaf, fried chicken, chicken croquettes, mashed potatoes, baked honeyed yams, macaroni and cheese, green beans with bacon, buttered corn, stewed tomatoes, watermelon pickles, homemade bread and preserves, blackberry pie, chocolate cake, and hand-cranked ice cream. If she hadn't belonged to a tee-totaling faith, I'm sure she would have served us six kinds of wine.

Like the ill-mannered ragamuffins that they were, the Dixon children delayed dinner by running around and around the table screaming and otherwise inciting the Augsburger children into new levels of disobedience. At last Amos, who is six foot-four and weighs close to three hundred pounds, put his foot down. Literally. He claimed that stepping on Bradley Dixon's foot was an accident, but it did make the boy stop, and after a few tears and accusations, we were finally seated at the groaning table.

We were obliged to hold hands — something I frankly hate to do — while Amos intoned an interminable prayer in German. If Lilibet was worried about her food getting cold she should have cued her husband to opt for a shorter version, or else have had him say grace after the meal. The Good Lord can hear prayers said by full stomachs just as well, if not better, than those said by empty stomachs.

As luck would have it I was seated between little Caitlin Dixon and Obadiah Augsburger, a boy about Caitlin's age. The rationale was, I suppose, that my scary presence would ensure their good behavior, while their impish joie de vivre warmed the cockles of my heart. However, the only thing this seating arrangement ensured was sticky hands for me and the formulation of a new life rule — *never hold hands with a five-year-old.*

Much to my relief, however, Aaron Sr. was not present for grace, which according to traditional etiquette meant he most probably wouldn't be eating at all. I recklessly decided to confirm this.

"*Ach,* the man is a nutcase," Lilibet said in response to my question.

Massive Amos stroked his beard. He had sparse carrot-orange hair, but his beard was full and a deep, lustrous auburn. It looked eminently strokeable.

"Aaron is my friend."

"Yah, he is your friend," Lilibet said as she heaped baked yams on one of the children's plates, "but he's still a nutcase."

"Some of my best friends are nutcases," I said, eager to help the conversation along.

They looked at me and I looked down at my plate. After an eternity I looked up again. They were still looking at me.

"It's not my fault!" I wailed.

Lilibet dropped a drumstick on her youngest child's plate. "Yah, maybe so. *You* don't believe in flying saucers, do you, Magdalena?"

"Lilibet!" Amos had a voice that could have brought the walls of Jericho down immediately and saved the Children of Israel seven trips.

"Well, a fact is a fact, Amos," she said and speared a slice of ham for herself. Then turned to me. "You were right. That man believes in flying saucers, if you can imagine. That's what he's doing right now. Looking for a so-called machine from outer space."

My spine tingled. "Where?" I asked casually.

Amos cleared his throat. "I took him back

this morning, to his old place. Miller farm."

"The pond? By himself?"

"Yah. He has a little boat."

"But he's eighty-one years old, for pete's sake. He's supposed to be home packing, not poking around in a pond."

"Ach," Lilibet said, "I gave Aaron your message. He said he had to prove that he wasn't crazy first. Well, if you ask me —"

"We didn't ask," Amos said testily. He said something then in Pennsylvania Dutch. Mama and Papa often spoke to me in the dialect, but I will admit that my grasp of the language is rudimentary at best. At any rate, I understood Amos to say: "Don't hang your squirmy long johns in front of an Englishman's eyes."

Lilibet rolled her eyes, confirming — as I have often suspected — that she and I are distant cousins. "You talk like a noodle-head," she said in Dutch. She turned to me and smiled. "I spread those rumors at Miller's store just like you asked."

"What rumors?"

"That you and the back doctor are not" — she glanced at the children seated on either side of her — "well, enough said."

"But they're not rumors," I wailed. "They're the truth! And anyway, that's not what I asked you to say. You were supposed to tell them about Aaron. What he did to me."

She shook her head. "*Ach,* but who would believe such a thing? Everyone knows Aaron Junior is such a nice man. Now the back doctor — he has pestered everyone in Hernia. Nobody likes him. Trust me, Magdalena, they were much more interested in that story."

The good news is that I didn't actually leap across the table and strangle her with my bare hands. The bad news is that I wanted to, and might have, had there not been over a dozen pairs of eyes staring at me as intently as if I were an alien recovered from the bottom of Miller's pond. If Jimmy Carter was guilty of adultery in the Good Lord's eyes for lusting in his heart, then I was every bit as guilty of murder in my heart.

I suppose now I was going to have to wear a scarlet "M" along with the scarlet "A." In that case, the best thing to do would be to sell the PennDutch Inn and move to Massachusetts where I had a chance of blending in. Even Cain wasn't so clearly marked.

I stood up. "Lunch was delicious," I said through clenched teeth, though I had yet to pick up my fork.

Lilibet dropped her fork with a clatter.

"*Ach,* where are you going?"

"What's it to you?"

"I work my fingers to the bone doing you a favor — making a nice meal for you and the English — and this is how you repay me? You always did know how to make a scene, Magdalena."

"Thank you, and if you must know, I'm off to Miller's farm. There's a vindictive old man there in a rowboat looking for aliens at the bottom of a pond. Frankly, I'd rather be there."

"Why, I never!" Lilibet said. She turned to her husband. "Amos, say something."

"*Gut Himmel,*" Amos muttered into his auburn beard.

"I'll be back in two hours to pick you two up," I said to Shirley and Terry. I was too embarrassed to look at them, but I assumed they knew I meant them.

"Angus, do something," I heard Dorothy Dixon whisper. "She shouldn't be driving in that state."

I heard him push back his chair. "I'd be happy to drive you, Mrs. Miller."

"It's Yoder," I said, "not Miller. And no thanks, I don't need someone to drive me. I'll be just fine."

"But —"

"I'm not in a *state,*" I snapped.

"He was just trying to be helpful, Magdalena," Shirley Pearson said. "Why don't you be a good girl and sit back down?"

"*Girl?*"

"Please," Terry said, "can't we talk about this later? I'm starving."

"Yah, let's eat," Amos said. Either his stomach growled then or there was a dog under the table.

"Is that all you can think about?" I screamed. "Food?"

Lilibet picked up the platter of fried chicken again, and leaning across the table, thrust it at me. "You're nothing but skin and bones, Magdalena. It's no wonder your Aaron left you for greener pastures."

I snatched the platter of chicken from her and started for the door.

"Mama, she took all the chicken!" one of the little Augsburger girls wailed.

"*Ach,* my platter!"

"Ji!" Caitlin sobbed. "Ji!"

"I'll wash it and return it tomorrow," I said over my shoulder.

"You see?" Lilibet said. "What did I tell you? Always a scene."

It was quite a scene at Miller's pond. The old coot was standing in his rowboat in the middle of the pond, waving his arms and shouting.

"I found it. It's really here."

"What's it look like?" It was Jacob Zook, the man with the miracle tractor. He was standing on the bank, shading his eyes with his hands. He shifted from one foot to the other, and back again. I had never seen him so animated.

"I can't tell yet," Pops called. "There's too much algae. I've never seen the pond this scummy.

"But it's metal, I can tell that much just by banging on it with my oar. We need to get your winch hooked up to her and pull her in. I bet she's worth a million bucks. More to the Smithsonian."

Jacob grinned and scratched his head. He was going to wear himself out if he didn't watch it.

"I have to hand it to you, Aaron. I didn't think flying saucers really existed. You said I get half of what we recover, right?"

"That's right. Now I'm going to row back and get you so we can hook this thing up."

"Hot dog!" Jacob said in a gush of ecstasy. "My little Emma wants to go to Switzerland next summer and look up her roots. I reckon half a million will get us there, all right."

Pops laughed heartily. "With that kind of money you can bring back an Alp for a souvenir."

I sat down on the grass in the shade of a pin oak tree. It was the exact spot I was sitting in exactly a year ago, when I first met Aaron Jr. Only one year — I could hardly believe it. So much had changed in the intervening time.

The oak was maybe a little taller, the grass definitely was, now that there were no longer any cows to keep it short. The pond definitely had more scum. But some of the changes were much more profound than that — for one thing, I had changed. In such a short time I had gone from being a naïve, maiden lady, to a savvy matron, to a bitter adulteress who stole chicken from little girls.

At least it was good chicken. Lilibet Augsburger may put on airs, for an Amish woman, but she can fry up a chicken that would make the Colonel weep with envy. I bit into a plump breast that was crispy on the outside, but tender and juicy on the inside. There were three more just like it on the platter, plus a smattering of thighs and drumsticks. Just skin and bones indeed! By the time I licked that platter clean I would be well on my way to that size 24W dress.

Then we'd see who had the biggest laugh.

The men had to know that I was there, but they didn't acknowledge my presence. That was fine with me. Let them pretend I was invisible. I really didn't want to speak to the old coot anyway. I just wanted to make sure that he was all right. Yes, I was furious at him, but I didn't really wish him ill — well, a bad case of gout maybe. Certainly not death by drowning. If Aaron Sr. died before I could get him on the plane that night, then my ex–Pooky Bear would no doubt return to Hernia, if only to make arrangements to have his father's body shipped to Minnesota. I couldn't let that happen. If I looked into those Wedgwood blue eyes again, I would throw up. In fact, just the thought of them made me nauseated. I quickly put the chicken breast down and took a deep breath.

Where was I? Ah, yes, Aaron Sr. It was in my own best interest to make sure that the old geezer got safely on that plane to Minneapolis. Besides, he was just trying to be a protective parent, wasn't he? Maybe if Mama was alive, and I had been the deceiving, low-life scumbucket — no, Mama would willingly, if not eagerly, have picked up the first stone. "You make your bed, you lie in it," she said to me at least a thousand times.

When I was in the fourth grade, my teacher, Miss Enz, caught me passing a note to Darrel Stucky and thrashed me with a willow switch. The truth was, I hadn't written a note, but was just doing Esther Rickenbach a favor. Well, Mama refused to take my side. At supper that night she wouldn't even listen to my version of the story.

"Chew with your mouth closed, Magdalena," she said, when I tried to tell her about it.

"But, Mama —"

"Chew with your mouth closed, Magdalena."

I picked up the chicken, took a big bite, and chewed with my mouth wide open just to spite Mama. Two breasts and a drumstick later my mouth was still open, but for a different reason. The old coot and his accomplice were stripping to their skivvies.

"Pops, you put your clothes back on right now," I hollered.

Aaron Sr. smiled and waved. Being right made him magnanimous.

"It's here, Magdalena. I told you, didn't I? Jacob, tell her it's here."

Jacob waved, unabashed in his baggy boxers. "Yah, there's something here all right."

Then to my amazement Pops, who shuffles when he's on land, dove neatly into the water and disappeared from sight. Jacob followed him with only a slight splash. They both surfaced a few seconds later, thrashing and screaming. Apparently the water was a lot colder than they thought. Either that, or neither of them could swim.

I put the chicken aside, stuffed to the gills. If the men couldn't swim, they were out of luck. I was a decent swimmer in my youth, but thirty years and half a chicken were bound to make a difference. The best I could do was to find my car keys and hold them, ready to sprint to the car at the first sign of trouble.

Both men were expert swimmers. It took them about an hour to hook the cable to the flying saucer and winch it close enough to shore so that a preliminary inspection could be made. During that time about a dozen onlookers, besides myself, had gathered. Folks driving by on Hertzler Lane, either by automobile or buggy, couldn't help but notice the unusual proceedings. Even Freni, who had successfully picked the walnuts out of poached chicken salad, wandered over.

"*Ach*, they're like little boys," she said when she saw the two men, covered in slime, grinning from ear to ear.

At that point the flying saucer, also covered with slime, was halfway to shore. It is hard to describe the excitement that was building up in our little shore-bound band. The mixture of holiness and heresy was, frankly, rather stimulating.

"Of course there's no such thing as flying saucers," someone said in a high, girlish voice. "It's contrary to God's plan of salvation."

Our eyes shifted from the salvage operation to Nora Ediger. She is a plain woman with a broad jaw and a deficit bosom. She is also on the shady side of thirty and has never been married. Aaron Jr. once admitted that he was attracted to her.

"How is it contrary to God's plan?"

We turned to look at Dan Gindlesperger. For most of us it was more than just a passing glance. Dan is, after all, one of Hernia's few eligible bachelors old enough to have been weaned before the Clinton years. He is also an ex-Mennonite, but has fallen so completely through the ranks that he teaches philosophy at Bedford County Community College. Even the Presbyterian church has been unable to hold him, and there are rumors that he is an agnostic.

Nora was game. "Because there was only one Jesus," she said. "How could Jesus have died on the cross here on earth to save us from our sins, and died on another planet as well?"

Dan smiled. "Maybe the aliens didn't fall from grace. Maybe they weren't in need of a plan of salvation."

Several people gasped, Freni among them. "That's nonsense," Nora said, her voice rising to an almost inaudible pitch. "That would mean they were sinless. Besides the Trinity, only angels are sinless. Are you saying that aliens are angels?"

Several people laughed, I among them. "Now that's silly," Dan said with irritating calmness. "Even you don't believe angels are sinless. The biggest sinner of them all was originally an angel. Lucifer was his name. I believe you call him Satan."

Nora, bless her heart, stood her ground. "Genesis gives us a detailed account of the Creation, but it doesn't say anything about aliens. Did God make them before or after he made man?"

Dan shrugged with annoying nonchalance. "What difference does it make? The creation story in Genesis is a metaphor anyway —"

I'm not saying that it was God who intervened, but the loud curse that came from Aaron Sr. certainly grabbed our attention. The debate was suddenly of no importance.

CHAPTER TWENTY-FOUR

"What did he say?" Freni demanded.

"He said it's a 1988 Ford Festiva," I said, omitting the offending words.

"*Ach*, a car?" She sounded disappointed.

I think we all were, even Nora. At least there was the possibility of dead bodies to look forward to. I know that sounds grizzly — like we don't have enough to keep us entertained in Hernia — but hey, that's just human nature. At least I don't rubberneck when I drive by an accident, like Susannah does. She once got whiplash from trying to do her makeup, drive, and accident-watch all at the same time. Believe it or not, her insurance company actually paid her benefits until they discovered that Susannah had caused the accident by changing her blouse.

Much to our collective disappointment there was nothing more to see. Just an old, waterlogged Festiva, covered with slime. As near as we could determine, the exterior of the car was gray, the interior brown. There was nothing in the glove compartment, in fact, nothing in the car that didn't come attached from the factory, except for the key. That was in the ignition.

"Maybe the driver tried to swim to shore and drowned," Nora said hopefully.

We all nodded.

"Drag the pound with your tow hook," Dan directed.

With nothing to show for their effort except a junked car, the old coot and his accomplice readily agreed. There would be glory in dredging up a decomposing body, if not vindication. A corpse would mean that the incident had happened recently, and would explain the mysterious nocturnal lights.

The pin oak tree was not large enough to shade a dozen people, and some of our number were beginning to swelter. After all, with the exception of Dan Gindlesperger we were all God-fearing folks, which meant we were modestly dressed. I know the Good Lord gave us brains for a reason, and so I quite expected to see a few people take off their shoes and socks and wade sedately up to their knees. What I didn't expect was a full-fledged, free-for-all water fight that began just seconds after Nora slipped on the slime and fell. Witnesses later claimed that Dan started it by tripping her.

"Someone needs to call the police," Freni said, who hadn't budged from her spot in the shade next to me.

"In the absence of Melvin I *am* the police," I said irritably. Strictly speaking, it wasn't true, of course. But I was Melvin's "legs," and every bit as capable as he.

"Then do something."

I needed no further urging. I am not bossy, as Susannah claims, but I was gifted with certain undeniable leadership qualities. And as any good Christian knows, it is a sin to hide one's talents under a bushel basket.

"Get out of that stinking pond this minute," I ordered the drenching duo. "And you," I shouted at Jacob and Pops, who were still sloshing around the stranded Festiva, "put some clothes back on, for pity sake."

I hope you won't find this offensive, but there isn't enough cold water in the world to shrink a Miller man down to a modest size. Several of the women, and at least one of the men, couldn't take their eyes off my bogus father-in-law.

Not only did Aaron Sr. ignore my order, he headed my way clad only in his underpants. "That's not my car, Magdalena. You've lived across the road from me your entire life, and you know I've never driven a Festiva."

"You're right." To my credit, I refrained from saying "so?"

Perhaps Pops was psychic. "So, that good-for-nothing Jacob Zook wants to charge me over two hundred dollars for pulling that piece of junk out of the pond. And he wasn't going to charge a thing when he thought it was a flying saucer!"

I pried my peepers from Pop's pants and pondered the problem. "Tell him you won't pay him the unhooking charge, dear. That will save you thirty bucks, and as long as that remains hooked up to Jacob's tractor, that's his problem. He'll have to haul it away and find a place to dump it."

Pops hemmed, hawed, and pawed at the ground with a bare foot. "I don't have the rest of the money, either. I'm flat broke."

"I'll take care of it," I heard myself say. Believe me, I wasn't being generous. It was in my own best interest to remove any stumbling blocks that might prevent Pops from catching his ten-thirty flight.

To protect Pop's modesty from the prying eyes of the curious, I had begun edging away from the throng and closer to the car. Pops padded along with me.

"Thanks, Magdalena. You're a real peach, you know that? I don't care what Aaron says. It's a funny thing about that car though — it doesn't have a license plate."

"Most abandoned cars don't. People can

be traced through their plates."

"They should stamp the owner's name on the car," he said vehemently. "Then I could have them arrested for dumping their car in my pond."

I sighed. "Let go of it, Pops. I said I would pay Jacob."

"They could use the same kind of machine they use to stamp the date on milk cartons."

I was gazing at the car when he said that, and the dark splotch on the inside of the windshield jumped out at me first. Pops does not get any credit for this.

"Is that an inspection sticker?" I asked.

He shrugged.

I trotted over. Indeed it was a sticker. It was almost the same green as the pond scum and would have been easy to overlook initially. But most of the algae had either sloughed off the windshield, or shriveled in the sun. The rectangular shape of the sticker was now quite distinctive.

"Well, I'll be dippy-doodled," I said.

"What?" Pops asked impatiently. Obviously he doesn't see very well.

"It's an inspection sticker, all right — a Pennsylvania sticker. This vehicle was inspected last month."

"And?"

"You were right, Pops. This isn't some old clunker that someone decided to dump. Just like you said, this car was hidden in the pond, and recently, too."

"I said that?"

"It was very clever of you to pretend you saw a flying saucer. Too bad we didn't pay attention to you sooner."

Pops beamed. "I was right, wasn't I? I did see something go into the pond."

"As right as rain, Pops. Now you go on home and pack. Remember, we leave for the airport at seven."

He looked suddenly miserable, small and shriveled like the dried algae — well, most of him at any rate. "Aaron made me say those things, Magdalena. I didn't want to, but he said I owed it to him because I was never much of a father. He said he wouldn't have gone off to fight in Vietnam if he hadn't been so angry at me."

"It doesn't make a difference, Pops. He's your son. You belong with him, not with me. I'm not" — I gulped, choking back the shame — "even your legal daughter-in-law."

"But Hernia is my home! I've never even been to Minnesota."

Trust me, there are few things more heartbreaking than to be arguing with an eighty-one-year-old man in his underwear who is feeling the angst of displacement.

I tried to smile reassuringly. "I'm sure you'll do just fine in Minneapolis, Pops. You're going to make it after all."

I paid Jacob Zook his pound of flesh but had him leave the car on the bank. His precursory dredging of the pond with a tow hook had yielded no bodies, but that didn't mean there wasn't foul play involved. The Festiva might well have been stolen. It was clearly a matter for the law to investigate. And by that I don't mean Melvin, but the big boys — the dreaded DMV.

Please understand that I had every reason to be hot, tired, and crabby by the time I got home. I also had to use my private facilities in the most urgent way. I most certainly didn't have the patience to deal with rude and intrusive members of the press.

"Go away," I said to the blonde who was sitting in a car in my driveway in the shade of one of my maples.

She opened her door and got out. She was quite young, barely more than a girl, which meant I probably couldn't outrun her.

"It's not here anyway," I said. "It's across the road by my neighbor's pond."

She pretended to be confused, and did a good job of it. "Are you the owner of the PennDutch Inn?"

"It has nothing to do with me or my inn," I snapped. That was true in its own way, since Pops would be leaving the inn that evening for the very last time.

She had one of those puttylike faces set with two huge, brown eyes. It was enough to make a puppy jealous.

"I'm here about an alien —"

"I told you, it's over by the pond, and it's crammed full of aliens. All of them slime green."

"What?"

"Beat it, toots. Scram, before I call the cops."

She pretended to be scared, which I thought was really rather decent of her. Perhaps it was something new they were teaching in journalism school these days. So many reporters from the old school try to stare you down — one gal from the *Post-Gazette*, a heavy smoker, tried to intimidate me by putting her face just inches from mine and puffing like a chimney. Fortunately I was wearing a pair of garden-aerating sandals at the time — you know, the kind with cleats mean enough to make a football player weep with envy. It took only one false step from me, and Miss Obnoxious from Pittsburgh had to be carried from the yard.

I went inside to take a nice cool shower and change into my traveling clothes. Call me compassionate if you must, but Pops clearly didn't have two nickels to rub together, and no Bedford cabby was going to give the old geezer a ride to the airport on the strength of his good looks. So, I would sacrifice my evening and drive him there myself. Besides, that was the only way I could be sure he actually made it on to the plane. The new Pittsburgh International Airport is a veritable city of shops, restaurants, and immaculate rest rooms. With just the right doleful look, Pops might well receive enough dole to live in the airport indefinitely. While this would be no skin off my teeth, it wouldn't skin Aaron's dentures, either. No, my pseudo-pops-in-law belonged in Minnesota, at his son's side, where he could drive his offspring stark raving nuts.

True, I wasn't going to step one foot on the plane, but one should always look their best when they venture more than five miles from their home community. This is especially true of airports. Just ask Susannah. She went to the airport without having bathed for a week and accidentally got swept up in a party of British tourists. She was halfway to London before she could convince anyone that she was an American.

It was only when Shnookums popped his head out of the nether reaches of her bosom and whined for his supper that she was able to make her case. No self-respecting Britisher would be caught dead with a dog that ugly.

After having worn Dr. Brack's brace all day, it actually felt good to climb back in it after my shower. While it was off I felt like a willow sapling that had broken loose from its stake. Perhaps it was because I was tired, emotionally and physically, but I felt like I *needed* that brace to prop me up. Since my bogus wedding I had relied on Aaron Jr. far too much for support, but painful as that was, it was good to have it stop.

I would make a special effort to thank the braggart doctor for insisting I try his contraption. A brace is a lot easier to care for than a man, and in general less aggravating. It doesn't leave dirty clothes lying around on the floor and it doesn't snore. What else could one possibly want from a constant companion?

Freni interrupted my reverie by rapping on my door. The woman has knuckles of steel.

"You have a visitor, Magdalena. In the parlor."

"Who?"

307

Please forgive me for saying this, but for just a second I hoped it was Aaron Jr., come crawling on his knees. I wouldn't have taken him back, mind you. I just wanted to see him beg.

Freni shrugged. "An English woman. She didn't give me her name."

"Young? Old? Blond? Brunette?"

"*Ach,*" she squawked, "they all look the same."

"You don't know who she is and you let her in?"

"She said it was a matter of life or death."

"And you believed her?"

I stormed out to the parlor, Freni on my heels. Just as I feared, it was the reporter with the soulful eyes. She was sitting in Grandma Yoder's favorite rocker, but she popped to her feet.

"You! How dare you talk my housekeeper into letting you in!" I raged.

Freni gasped, all but depleting the room of its oxygen. "*Housekeeper?* Is that all I am to you? That does it, Magdalena, I quit!"

"Freni —" Too late. She was out of there like a Christmas tree on the twenty-sixth of December. I turned to the girl. "Now see what you've done? You've gone and hurt an old woman's feelings just so you could get your scoop for that supermarket rag. Well, don't think you're getting away with it. There's a special place you-know-where for reporters like you."

The brown saucers didn't have the decency to blink. "I'm not a reporter."

"Autograph hunter then? Let me tell you, dear, you've picked an off week for autographs. Last week you could have had Bette, the week before Babs. Oh, and Mel was here in April," I added just to taunt her.

"I don't know what you're talking about. My name is Leona da Vinci and I'm a student at Temple University."

"Right, and I'm the Mona Lisa."

"That's her car, you know."

"I have a black belt," I said, assuming a pseudo-karate stance. "If you don't hightail it out of here, I'll let you have it."

The nice thing about that threat was that it was true. I have a hideous, black plastic belt I got with one of my dresses from Dancing Joe's Dress Barn, and since the Salvation Army had refused it in their last collection, Leona was welcome to help herself.

Da Vinci was invincible. "What have you done with Flower?" she demanded.

"There's a nice little rest home halfway between Bedford and Somerset," I said kindly. There is, after all, a special place in my heart for raving lunatics.

"I was with Flower the day she bought the Festiva. I know, they might all look the same to you, but it was hot and Flower dropped her lipstick on the driver's side. The stain never came out. I bet a lab could prove it was hers."

My brain has never quite worked fast enough to bless me with an epiphany, but this time it came very close. It was certainly less painful than the time I borrowed Susannah's curling iron without her permission and then accidentally dropped it in the bathtub.

"Aha! So you're the one who's been pestering Freni with those calls."

The brown eyes flashed. "I wasn't pestering her. I was trying to find my friend, Flower. I've been trying to locate her for three days. I was finally able to track her here." She took a bold step forward. "I know she's here, because the Festiva is hers."

I pushed Leona aside and sat in Grandma's rocker. I wasn't being rude, just practical. I do my best thinking in Grandma's chair. The warped slat second from the left helps keep my mind focused.

"You have a friend named Flower?" I know, it was redundant of me, but it takes the slat a moment or two to work.

"Her real name is Wang Mei Hua. Wang is her family name. Mei Hua means Beautiful Flower in Chinese. Sometimes she goes by other names though — like Rose, or Lily, or —"

She paused to catch her breath, but by then the slat had worked its magic.

"Like Lotus?" I asked.

"Yes."

"Did she have a small blue rose tattooed on her left wrist?"

"Yes! So she is here!"

I decided to break it to her slowly. "Not here, but I saw her in town. Tell me, how well do you know her?"

"Not very well — but well enough. You see, we're both graduate students at Temple University. We've just started sharing an apartment. Actually, we haven't even moved into it yet. That's why I'm here."

I shook my head. "It would be a four-hour commute, dear. Stick with the one you found in Philly."

I wouldn't have thought it possible, but the brown eyes widened further. "You're crazy, aren't you?"

"Why, I never!" I gasped.

"But that's okay," she said quickly.

"Flower is a little crazy, too."

I swallowed at least a thousand calories of irritation. "Tell me all about her, dear," I said wisely.

Leona pulled up a ladder-back chair and began.

CHAPTER TWENTY-FIVE

WORLD'S BEST CHICKEN SALAD

INGREDIENTS

1 whole stewing hen, plucked and cleaned* *or*

2 cups cubed cooked chicken

$1/2$ cup diced celery

$1/2$ cup chopped walnuts

$1/2$ cup mayonnaise

$1/4$ cup chunky bleu cheese salad dressing (this is the secret ingredient)

$1/4$ teaspoon salt

$1/4$ teaspoon onion salt

Pepper to taste

*For really moist and delicious chicken try the following: submerge whole chicken in large pot of rapidly boiling water. Return to full boil. Cover tightly and turn off heat. After one hour remove chicken. Allow to cool before removing meat from bones. Cube.

DIRECTIONS

Combine chicken cubes, celery, and walnuts in a medium glass bowl. In a small bowl, mix remaining ingredients and spoon over chicken. Toss thoroughly. Cover and allow to chill for at least two hours.

Chapter Twenty-six

"Flower gets these wild ideas, see. I mean we were both in this new restaurant called Freddy's Pajamas, or something like that, having lunch, and they're mopping the floor because some little girl dumped her milkshake. Flower comes over to my table and asks me if I'll be her witness if she slips and falls. I said I would, but I thought she was speaking hypothetically.

"Not Flower. She falls down right there and starts to moan and groan. The first thing you know, the manager comes over and starts making a fuss over Flower, and the next thing you know, Flower gets to eat there free for a week."

"I know a con woman when I smell one," I said, and sniffed the oxygen-starved room.

"Yeah, but it wasn't a major con. It's not like Flower threatened to sue or anything. She just wanted a place to eat."

"I'd be ashamed to stick my head in Freddy's Pajamas," I said sternly, "and so should you."

"Oh, but it worked, you see. And not only did Flower get to eat there for a week, I did, too. Then one day I was looking at this ad in the paper for an apartment, and it seemed just perfect, but when I called up the landlady said 'mature couples only.' That isn't legal, is it?"

"I haven't the slightest idea. But it's definitely sensible."

The brown eyes narrowed. "It's easy for you to say that because you're old."

"Now look here" — I caught myself — "did you get the apartment or not?"

"Oh, we got it, thanks to Flower. She got on the phone and told the landlady she was the Chinese Ambassador's daughter! Can you imagine that?"

"She's got nothing over my sister, dear. Susannah would have told your landlady she was the Chinese Ambassador herself. So tell me, how long was it after you met Flower that the two of you moved in together?"

"A week."

I sat bolt upright. Either the warped rung had pinched a nerve, or Grandma's ghost was prodding me.

"Let me get this straight, dear. You barely knew this woman, yet you decided to share an apartment with her. Isn't that a little risky?"

"Do you know how hard it is to get a reasonable apartment within walking distance of school? Besides, it was either room with Flower, or move into a graduate dorm. Flower spoke good English. She said she had me between a wok and a hard place."

I laughed pleasantly. "Still —"

"And do you know how many crazies there are out there? No offense, of course. I'm talking really *crazy*."

"Well —"

"Sure she's a foreigner, but she's a lot like me. We're both loners, you see. Flower likes to do her thing, and I like to do mine. We'll make great roommates because we won't be in each other's face." The brown eyes contracted to near-normal size. "I bet you never had to live with someone who gave you the creeps."

"Don't bet the farm, dear. So anyway, you agreed to rent this apartment —"

"We more than agreed. We paid the landlady first and last month's rent and, just because we're students, a damage deposit you wouldn't believe. I'm on a stipend, Ms. PennDutch. It nearly wiped me out."

"The name is Yoder, dear. You're standing in the PennDutch. Now tell me, why did Flower come to Hernia?"

Leona da Vinci smiled. It was a lovely smile, not unlike the Mona Lisa's.

"I thought that was a funny name, but

Flower didn't get the joke. Anyway, Flower said she had a business opportunity here. Some way she knew of making some fast money. She said we wouldn't have to worry about the rent for a long, long time."

That would have floored me, had I not been sitting. There were no businesses in Hernia except for Miller's Feed Store and Yoder's Corner Market, and they were not the sort of places to which the young came West seeking their fortunes. I told her the score.

"There's this place," she said, glancing around the room, "but it doesn't look like the kind of place to make a quick buck, unless — say, you don't suppose Flower — I mean, you're not what they call a madame, are you?"

I recoiled in horror. "Bite your tongue. I don't have a single drop of French blood."

"Naw," she said, answering her own question, "Flower made it sound like a whole lot of money, all at once. Maybe even thousands. Frankly, I don't think your girls would get that much."

I finally got the picture. In a strange sort of way I was flattered, although no doubt it was just another sign that my so-called marriage to Aaron had left me a fallen woman.

"I'm a good Christian woman who runs a

simple country inn," I said, trying to sound indignant. "But *if* I was who you thought I was, I would be able to pay better than you think."

She seemed neither impressed nor convinced. "There has got to be some kind of business opportunity around here. Flower might be a little crazy, but she has a good head on her shoulders."

For some reason Shirley Pearson's food company popped into my brain. "Are you sure Flower is Chinese, and not Japanese?"

"Positive. Flower hates the Japanese. Her grandfather was killed by the Japanese in the Sino-Japanese War."

"I beg your pardon?" There had been so many wars in my lifetime it was hard to keep track. Perhaps this one had taken place over the summer when I was busy with my wedding plans. In that case, I had a good reason for being so distracted.

"The Japanese invaded Manchuria in 1931, but what we call the Sino-Japanese War broke out in 1937 —"

I waved a hand. "I know all that. I was just testing you."

She smiled again. "I'm a history major."

"Is that so? And what was — is Flower's major?"

"Economics. But from what you just said,

Flower screwed up this time."

As you well know, I positively hate the "s" word, but I forced myself to laugh pleasantly nonetheless. Susannah tells me most people anymore don't even realize it's a vulgar word.

"Tell me, dear, what brings you here looking for Flower. Is there some sort of emergency?"

The brown eyes clouded. "You might say so. The landlady says her check is no good. If I don't come up with her half of the rent by Saturday, we're out of there."

I thought fast. I normally tithe one-tenth of my considerable income. Of course the bulk of this goes to Beechy Grove Mennonite Church, but there are some private charities to which I contribute from time to time. Granted, they usually have tax-exempt status, but there was no reason an exception couldn't be made. After all, I can't take it with me, and I was never going to have children — a very regular visitor had just confirmed that. And Susannah was already well provided for with a trust fund I'd set up the year before.

"I can lend you the money, dear."

She nearly fell off the ladder-back chair. "Excuse me?"

"It'll be strictly a loan, of course. But I

320

won't charge you any interest, and you can pay me back at your convenience."

"Miss Yoder, I — uh — don't know what to say."

"A simple thanks would be nice, dear."

"Thanks!"

"But not that simple."

She elaborated on her thanks and I graciously accepted her efforts. Then we briefly worked out some of the details of my loan.

At last I cleared my throat. "I have some very bad news for you, Leona."

She looked startled. "There's a catch to this loan stuff?"

I shook my head. "That's on the level. This is about your friend, Flower."

"What about her?"

I sighed. When it came down to it, there was only one way to say it.

"Your friend is dead."

I was relieved to see shock, not grief on her face, since I am far better at directing than I am comforting. I poured her a glass of lemonade and had her sit in the parlor's one easy chair.

"You stay right there, dear, while I make a few phone calls."

She nodded.

I was in for a few shocks of my own.

Melvin was actually pleasant to me.

"Hey, I'm glad you called," he said. "I was just about to call you."

I pinched myself. "Ouch!"

"You're always so funny, Miller." He laughed.

"It's Yoder now, Melvin, haven't you heard?" No doubt he'd heard at least a dozen versions.

"Oh that — well, I guess I did hear, but it doesn't matter one bit to me. I hope you believe that."

"Apparently I'm so naïve I still believe in the Tooth Fairy."

"Confidentially, so do I. Say, Yoder, how would feel about going on the *Jerry Springer Show*?"

"What? And air my dirty bloomers on national TV? I'd rather be stranded with you on a desert island."

"I guess I'll just have to tell them no," he said, still remarkably cheery. "I told them I was your manager."

"You *what?*"

"They were going to let me sit on stage with you. It would have been my fifteen minutes of fame."

"Get a life, Melvin! I didn't call you to discuss your personal goals. I have some very important information for you."

"And I have some for you, Yoder. Who should go first?"

"This is my dime, Melvin. This is about the young Chinese woman who was found dead at the intersection of North Main and Elm streets early Sunday morning."

"Still jumping to conclusions, are we, Yoder? We don't know that she was Chinese."

"Yes, we do. I have someone here who can identify her. The victim's name is — well, in English it means Flower."

His stunned silence was music to my ears.

"And that's not all, Melvin. This woman has identified the victim's car."

"She didn't have a car," he said triumphantly.

"Oh yes, she did. Jacob Zook pulled it out of Miller's Pond a little more than an hour ago."

The prolonged silence that followed was almost pathetic.

"And get this, Melvin, the key is still in the ignition."

"You should be ashamed of yourself, Yoder, for wanting to take a drive in a dead woman's car — hey, can I drive your BMW?"

"The day you grow a beard!" I said carelessly. "And I don't want to drive Flower's car. I mentioned the key because it might contain important fingerprints."

"Don't be silly, Yoder. We've got the victim's fingers. We don't need another set from the key."

"I'm talking about the murderer's prints!" I screamed. "He or she was the last one to touch the ignition key."

Either I could hear the laborious process of Melvin's brain at work, or the ceiling fan at the Hernia police station needed oiling.

"Good work, Yoder," he said, knocking my freshly clad socks off. "You hold tight, and I'll be right there."

"You can't drive, Melvin, remember? Your right leg is in a mammoth cast."

"I'll get Zelda, then. Or Susannah. But you don't move a muscle, get it?"

"Got it."

I hung up and did a silly little jig. It wasn't a real dance, mind you, since that is forbidden by my faith. And I certainly didn't mean to be disrespectful to the dead. But the pieces to Flower's murder were beginning to come together, and I had a gut feeling that before the day was over that jigsaw puzzle would be complete.

When my jig was over I called Pittsburgh International Airport and rescheduled Pops's flight.

★ ★ ★

It's not over until the fat lady sings, Mama always said. She meant that literally. It was her way of getting in the last word.

Dr. Wilmar Brack seemed determined to prevent Mama from singing. "Where do you keep the knives?" he asked when I walked into the kitchen.

I couldn't believe my eyes. Freni was barely out the door and already there was a man rifling through her drawers. And in broad daylight, too.

"What on earth are you doing?" I demanded. "Is nothing sacred anymore?"

"I'm trying to make myself a sandwich, that's what. I need something to spread the mustard with. Say, you wouldn't happen to have any pickles, would you?"

"The kitchen is not open to guests," I said, raising my voice only slightly.

"I didn't have lunch," he said and clattered among the cutlery.

"That was your choice, dear. You chose not to go to the Augsburgers."

"Ah," he said, picking up a bread and butter knife and wielding it like a scalpel. "My guest agreement clearly states that the PennDutch Inn will supply me with three meals a day and two light snacks if so desired. This" — he pointed to a loaf of bread and an open packet of bologna — "is a light snack. I still expect lunch."

"But it's almost supper," I snapped, and then realized with horror that there was nobody there to make the meal. My cooking skills are serviceable only if one has had their taste buds surgically removed. At least that's what Aaron said the first (and only time) I tried to cook a romantic dinner for the two of us.

"What is for supper?" Dr. Brack asked.

Then I remembered Freni's frustrated efforts for lunch. "The world's best chicken salad. You're going to love it."

"Maybe. I'm pretty picky about food. I'm what you might call a connoisseur. In fact, you might say I taught Julia Child everything she knows."

"You don't say?"

"Well, I did see some ripe tomatoes on the vines out back. And there are some cucumbers in the refrigerator. I could whip up a nice tangy gazpacho —"

"Whip away, dear," I said. "In the meantime I'll duck down to the cellar and retrieve a jar of Freni's delicious homemade pickles for you."

I will confess that I was feeling very proud of myself for having turned the tide of the conversation. The truth is, I really owed it all to Mama. "Make a man feel useful and he'll move mountains for you," she once said. Fortunately for Papa's back, she didn't mean that literally as well.

Freni's cache of home-canned goodies takes up most of the space not used by the furnace, but there is a small room behind the furnace which, in the old days, was the coal room. Papa gave it a thorough cleaning when we converted it to gas, and it was his intention of installing fluorescent light fixtures and using it as a wintertime workshop. I would never air dirty family linens in public, but if I were to do so, you might expect to see sheets of marital discord flapping on the line. Just because a couple stays married for thirty-five years, doesn't make them a pair of lovebirds in private.

Well, more than enough said. The point is that it was where Papa planned his private getaway that I had so graciously permitted Angus Dixon to set up his darkroom. Papa had already installed a water line — even a commode where he could read in peace. At any rate, while I was down there plucking pickles from the pantry, I thought I may as well pop into the darkroom and see what a Pulitzer prize–winning photographer does on his vacation.

Of course I ignored the homemade sign

that said DARKROOM — KEEP OUT. It is my establishment, after all. In fact, few things make me more aggravated than seeing a DO NOT DISTURB sign hanging from one of my guest room doors. If folks want privacy, they should stay home.

You may call me frugal if you like, but I see no point in putting a high-wattage lightbulb in a refurbished coal bin. Therefore it took my eyes a minute or two to adjust, and I wish they hadn't. The Bible tells us to pluck out our eyes if they cause us to sin. Fortunately it doesn't command us to pluck our peepers if someone else has sinned. Just judging from what I saw that afternoon, Angus Dixon was racking up his frequent-traveler miles on that wide and winding road that leads away from Heaven.

I slammed the door shut without turning off the light. Freni is right. It is true what the Bible said about sin loving darkness. I had never seen such filth. Hanging from wires strung across Papa's planned workshop were photos of women in various stages of undress. Some, and I shudder to say this, were as naked as the day they were born, and smiling about it.

But that wasn't the half of it. Hanging up there right along with the photos of these happy harlots, were photos of Amish children. Thank God the Amish children were fully clothed. I'm sure my ticker couldn't have taken it any other way. Nonetheless it made me furious just to see them up there with the trash, and I bolted up the basement stairs two steps at a time.

At the top of the stairs I ran smack into Melvin. Fortunately, I wasn't hurt, but the jar of pickles made a second trip to the bottom of the stairs. Dr. Brack was out of luck.

CHAPTER TWENTY-SEVEN

It was a toss-up as to who was madder, Melvin or me. I might have apologized for knocking him over, had he not started screaming at me from the get-go.

"Do you know how hard it is to drive a stick shift when you're wearing a cast?"

Having never broken anything made out of calcium, I couldn't say that I did. Besides, I had yet to drive a standard shift vehicle for more than a thousand feet. That, incidentally, was when Papa got his first gray hair. I kid you not. He left the house with a full head of wavy brown hair, anxious to teach me how to drive, and returned an hour later a broken man, whom Mama barely recognized.

"You said you'd have Zelda or Susannah drive you!"

"Zelda's mother needed her and Susannah — well, you know."

"You're going to have to get tougher with Susannah, dear. When she lived with me, I made sure she was up before lunch."

"I didn't come to talk about your sister, Yoder. I came about that damn key."

"You hush your mouth, Melvin, or I'll

wash it out with soap. And that's no empty threat. There's enough smut in this house already."

"Make me," Melvin muttered.

"I could make you from scratch — out of pie dough, because I wouldn't need a brain."

"Children, please," Dr. Brack said foolishly.

I glared at him, and I think one of Melvin's eyes made visual contact as well. At any rate, Dr. Brack grabbed the bread and bologna and scooted to the far corner of the kitchen.

"The key, Yoder!"

I must have stared blankly.

"I stopped at the pond first, Yoder, and there was no key. That means you took it, which undoubtedly means you got your greasy fingerprints smeared all over it. Now what the hell am I going to do?"

I lunged for the bottle of dish detergent by the sink. Oh, for a big chunk of lye soap like Grandma Yoder used to make. Melvin would lay off swearing for the rest of his life.

Alas, I didn't even have the pleasure of making Melvin gargle with Joy. Before I could get my hands on him, the door from the dining room swung open and in walked Terry Slock with little Caitlin on his shoulders. The child's head nearly hit the door-sill, causing visions of a lawsuit to dance through my head.

"Put her down at once!"

Terry grinned and slid her to the floor. "Whew! You were getting heavy anyway," he said to her. "I think you're turning into stone."

Caitlin giggled and came bounding to me. As usual she had that silly little doll with her.

"Ni how," she said, waving that doll practically in my face. "Ni how ma?"

"Speak proper English," I snapped. "You're too old for baby talk."

"It isn't baby talk," Dr. Brack said, his mouth full of sandwich.

"*What?*" I'd just as soon snap at him, as I would the child.

"What she said. It isn't baby talk. The little girl was speaking Mandarin Chinese. She asked how you were. Did I tell you that Pearl Buck was a dear friend of mine? As a matter of fact, it was I who suggested she write —"

The last piece of the jigsaw puzzle fell neatly into place. Unlike the game, however, this real-life puzzle did not resemble the picture on the box. Not the mental picture I'd painted, at any rate.

"This is all very interesting," Melvin said, "but you people are interrupting police business."

I gave Melvin a look that could freeze asphalt on a summer day. Then I took a deep breath and smiled warmly at Caitlin. She smiled back.

"I'm fine, dear," I said to her. "How is your dolly?"

"Wan Oou likes you," she said and giggled.

"Tell her I like her, too."

She said something to the doll in a singsong voice and then thrust the sorry thing at me. I reluctantly took and patted it, and returned it forthwith.

"Where are your mommy and daddy?" I asked the urchin gently.

She shrugged.

"I'm sitting for the kids," Terry said. "They had some things they wanted to do in town."

My blood ran cold. "Which town?"

"Bedford, I guess. They said they might be gone for a couple of hours. Don't worry, I'm good with kids."

"I'm counting on that," I said and bolted for the door.

I have a list of ten things I want to ask my Maker some day, and one of them has to do with why hospitals serve their evening meal at such an ungodly early hour. My uncharitable guess is that the staff are in a hurry to get home to fix their own meals, to be eaten at the regular time.

The front receptionist was unfamiliar to me, so I tried to read her name badge. It wasn't easy to do, because the woman was hunched over a magazine laboriously sounding out the difficult phrases like "six easy payments" and "a collector's piece you'll be proud to call your own." When I finally read her name I did a double take. Hillary Clinton. This woman was not the First Lady, I was pretty sure of that. She didn't look a day over twelve to me.

"Excuse me," I said politely. "Which room is Thomas Arnold in?"

She glanced up casually from her magazine. "Visiting hours don't resume until after supper. Come back at five."

I glanced at my watch. It was four thirty-two.

"This is an emergency," I snapped. "I have to see the patient now."

She treated me to a wide yawn. "He's not here."

"*What?*"

She looked down at her magazine. "I said he's not here."

"What do you mean he's not here?" I screamed.

The lady in the gift shop must have heard me, because she was looking nervously my way. I smiled and waved until she waved timidly back.

Hillary, however, was not impressed. "You speak English," she said without looking up. "Which word didn't you understand?"

"I understand that your job is in jeopardy if you don't cooperate, toots. I'm here on police business."

Hillary slowly turned a page in her magazine. "You don't look like a cop."

"Hernia Police Department, dear. If you don't believe me, let me use your phone."

"You're supposed to have a badge. Do you have a badge?"

"It's in the car, dear." All right, so it was a lie, but a young man's life was at stake.

"Then I'm afraid I can't help you."

She turned her attention back to her magazine and was immediately captivated by an ad for perfume. While Rome burned down around her, Hillary Clinton ripped back a paper flap and rolled her wrist around on the page. The scent that reached my nostrils smelled like the dead squirrel I found in the rain gutter last spring.

It may surprise you to learn that patience has never been my forte. It certainly surprised me when I reached over the counter and grabbed her skinny wrist. Not the one that smelled like a dead squirrel.

"Where is Thomas Arnold?" I demanded through clenched teeth. My adrenaline was pumping.

At last, I had Hillary's undivided attention. I don't believe in reincarnation, but if I did, I would want to come back as someone who was big and strong and had a viselike grip. Either that, or a natural blonde for whom wearing a bra was a necessity, not a privilege.

"Hey, you're hurting me," Hillary whined, but she didn't scream, or try and jerk away, so I knew I was well on my way to obtaining her cooperation.

I squeezed harder for good measure.

"Okay!" she gasped. "You win. The guy you're asking about just left with his parents."

I let go of her wrist. "He what?"

Her newfound respect for me began to fade before my eyes. "You're not going to make me repeat everything, are you?"

I thought for a moment. "Were his parents Amish?"

"Oh, *please!* Give me a break," she said

and returned to her magazine as if nothing had happened.

Buffalo Mountain runs north and south, and Highway 96 between Bedford and Hernia runs right alongside it. There are no parallel roads to connect the two communities. Had there been, I would have succumbed to temptation, taken the one least traveled, and pushed my pedal to the metal. Don't get me wrong, speeding is a sin, and the Devil is on a first-name basis with those folks who do so just for fun, or can't be bothered to get up in time to drive to their appointments at the legal speed. But neither of those situations applied to me that afternoon, and I was on a sacred mission to save a life, so I pressed the pedal anyway. If I got a ticket, I would drop it in the offering plate at church.

I assure you that I neither swore nor gesticulated as I barreled along at almost twice the speed limit, although I had occasion to do so more than once. Tourists might think of Highway 96 as bucolic, but it can be an obstacle course when there is a life on the line. I deftly dodged Delbert Detweiler's demented dog, which darted out into the highway, but wasn't quite as successful with Rachel Rickenbach's Rhode Island Reds. I made a mental note to give Rachel the recipe for Freni's famous chicken salad. Fortunately the cars I needed to pass were more cooperative, and I didn't encounter any buggies.

About five miles out from Hernia the highway curves in close to Buffalo Mountain and begins to follow the lay of Slave Creek, with many quick twists and turns. The fields give way to woods here and some of the old trees hang over the road forming a virtual tunnel. This is the most dangerous stretch of Route 96, and Susannah and her friends refer to it as Accident Alley. I was slowing down a mite to take the first turn when I saw a familiar car ahead. It was the Dixonmobile.

My first reaction was to let off the brake and step on the gas. I would ram the fiends from behind if necessary. But that would undoubtedly injure poor Samuel, and besides the diabolical duo hadn't a clue I was on to them. No, much better to hang back and follow them. When they made a left turn on Zweibacher Road to get to the Kauffman farm, I'd zoom on past them and then, for better or for worse, get Melvin. And Zelda, too, whether she was done helping her mama or not.

A few people have accused me of being inflexible in my thinking, and I'm beginning to think they are right. Even though the Dixonmobile didn't turn left to the Kauffman farm, I nearly did. I mean, my eyes saw the criminal car sail right on past Zweibacher Road, but my brain apparently didn't — not until I was halfway into the turn. The corrective maneuver I attempted defied the law of physics and made me a staunch believer in miracles. Although my BMW bucked like a bronco, and I lost a quarter inch of rubber from my tires, I was able to continue my pursuit almost uninterrupted. A faithful Christian, I didn't forget to thank the Good Lord for inventing antilock brakes.

Because of my near mishap, I was ready when the Dixonmobile made an abrupt right turn on the gravel lane that winds up Stucky Ridge. That's not to say, I wasn't surprised. I had just assumed the diabolic duo would be headed for the Kauffman farm. Why I had assumed that, I don't know. Let's just say that my aging gray cells don't do their best thinking careering on a country road at ninety miles an hour.

I slowed down considerably since there are no roads that intersect that gravel lane. There was no need to worry about me losing them, and I certainly didn't want them to discover that I was on their tail. Believe me, my decision to reduce my speed had nothing to do with the damage gravel was capable of inflicting on my vehicle.

At any rate, with the slower speed my senses returned. Yes, of course, Stucky Ridge, and Settler's Cemetery in particular, made perfect sense to commit the dastardly deed. The historic cemetery was hardly used anymore, and at that hour of the day one wasn't likely to find spooning couples on the picnic side, either. The copse of woods between the two areas was the perfect place to dump a body. If their car was spotted and they were later questioned, the Dixons could claim they had driven up for the view.

My slow speed assumptions were correct, and as I emerged from the last curve I spotted the Dixonmobile parked at the far end of the left fork of the gravel lane, alongside Settler's Cemetery. I stopped and turned off the engine while I considered my options. The safest thing for me was to turn around and drive into Hernia for help. But if young Samuel was alive — and I had no reason to believe he wasn't — a brash frontal attack on my part might be what was required to keep him that way. After all, the Dixons had no reason to suspect that I knew

340

what they were up to. I could simply drive up the road and park beside them. My pretext could be a visit to my parents' graves. Somehow I would find a way to wrest Samuel from them and get him to safety.

I am not a screamer by nature — just ask Aaron Jr. — but I let out a holler that was heard two counties away when Dorothy Dixon tapped on my window with the barrel of her gun. Then like the fool I never suspected I was, I stupidly rolled down the window at her request.

"You're quite a clever woman, Mrs. Miller," she said. "You know, you might even be bright enough to be a writer. Too bad you won't get the chance to find out."

I was still gasping, aftershocks from my mega-scream. "It's — Miss — Yoder — now. How did — I mean — your car —"

"Oh, that. You thought we didn't see you? Well, then perhaps you're not as bright as I thought. Maybe you should aim for being an editor."

"But I stayed way behind you!"

"You're driving a bright red BMW, for crying out loud. Astronauts on the space shuttle could have tracked your progress."

"You left a pretty messy trail yourself," I said, and knocked my standing down from book editor to literary agent.

"Yeah, well, who knew that Flower had it in her? Blackmail! And just because Angus likes to take a few creative photos now and then. They bring in good money, you know. A lot more than the ones he sells to so-called legitimate publications. Or my children's books, for that matter. And Angus is good."

"How could he do that? He's a father, for pete's sake!"

She seemed positively shocked. "Angus never photographed *our* children. He's a wonderful father. And I certainly never do anything to harm them."

"Thank heavens for that at least. So, what was Flower to you, their nanny?"

"Very good, Mrs. Miller."

"Yoder," I snapped.

She smiled. "We sponsored Flower — her real name is Mei Wua — on a student visa. She worked for us as an au pair girl while she went to college. Then like you, she got to poking around. But" — she laughed pleasantly — "that's all ancient history."

"No it's not," I said, and reduced my IQ to that of a book reviewer. "Flower's new roommate showed up, and she's not the giving-up type. Not to mention there's a coal room full of pornography back at the inn. Oh, yes, and let's not forget the license plate we found with your husband's fingerprints on it."

She blanched. "You searched our room?"

I nodded which, of course, isn't the same as lying. Frankly, I was impressed with their cleverness. Throwing the telltale tag away back home in Philadelphia was a stroke of genius. Well, she was a writer after all.

"But you know," I said, thinking aloud, which is a very foolish habit, "it didn't make a lick of sense for you guys to leave Flower's body at the intersection of North Main and Elm. Why didn't you just leave her in the Festiva?"

"The Amish boys," she hissed. "Flower left us a message on the windshield of our car telling us to meet her downtown at midnight. She thought it would be safer there."

"Little did she know," I said sadly. Hernia doesn't roll up its sidewalks at dark, it keeps them permanently rolled up.

"Angus had just — well, you know what."

"Strangled her," I hissed. "He strangled her with pantyhose. Were they yours?"

"They were my best pair!" she wailed. "Guaranteed not to run, but they did."

"You poor dear. Go on."

"Well, anyway, those stupid boys came along. There wasn't time to put her back in the car. I had to jump in that damn car and drive it away myself. I don't drive a stick shift, and it about gave me whiplash."

"Remind me to cry, dear."

"It wasn't easy catching up with the boys after that, but we lucked out Tuesday night and followed them up here. They have one of those Smiley Faces on the back of the buggy. I didn't think they were allowed."

"Teenagers are given more latitude," I said, and then regretted having opened my big mouth. She didn't deserve an explanation.

"They were smoking cigarettes and drinking beer! Can you imagine that?" Her free hand tugged at her tube top, which apparently was too tight.

Her self-righteous attitude infuriated me. One boy was dead, the other had nearly died, both thanks to her, and she begrudged them a moment of teenage rebellion?

"You two-faced —"

"Get out of the car!" I could hear the safety click off.

I opened the door. I would like to say that I flung it open so fast that Dorothy didn't have a chance to get out of the way. But I had nothing to do with knocking her down. The truth is, I owed it all to Dr. Brack.

When the gun discharged, the bullet hit a metal support in the brace I was wearing, ricocheted, and then grazed Dorothy's left temple. She fell like a ton of Freni's pound cakes. Except for a sore rib and a throbbing headache due to the noise, I was virtually unscathed.

The diabolical duo were not professional criminals, and the gun I picked up from the ground was the only one they had. When he heard the misfired shot, Angus came running and was within range before he realized it. What Angus didn't know is that I could no more have pulled that trigger than shared a bed with Aaron Jr. one more night. Some things are just not right — killing another human being and illicit sex rank right up there at the top.

Dorothy was stunned, but didn't even have the courtesy to pass out. Restraining both Dixons would have been too much even for me, so I did the only thing I could. I hopped back in my car, and with the door still open drove it straight at Angus. He threw himself to the ground, as I knew he would, but it wasn't a comfortable landing, and the last time I saw him — at the arraignment — he was still limping.

Samuel Kauffman was alive and lying in the backseat of the Dixonmobile. Dorothy had done a pretty good job of tying him up with hospital adhesive tape during their getaway ride. In fact, had she not been in the backseat, trussing him like a turkey, I doubt if they would even have noticed me following them. Needless to say, Samuel was frightened, but otherwise unharmed. In fact, his overall condition had improved so much that after a quick once-over by the doctor, he was reunited to the loving bosom of his family.

As for the terrible twosome, the state police picked them up on the turnpike less than an hour later. All three children had been left behind at the PennDutch. It was perhaps the nicest thing the Dixons had done for their children in ages.

CHAPTER TWENTY-EIGHT

It was a small family gathering, just Freni, Susannah, and I. Of course given the fact that Susannah was my sister, and Freni our double second cousin, and each of us was our own cousin, as well as a cousin to each other's cousins, it was a crowded table after all.

"So," Freni said, helping herself to another banana boat, my favorite comfort food, "you really are closing the inn for a week."

"I have to," I said, trying hard not to crack a smile, "I have no cook. You quit, remember?"

"*Ach,*" Freni said, "I was mad. I'm over it now."

I patted her arm fondly, nearly causing the banana to fall in her lap. "I need a break anyway. I finally got through to London, and she said she understood. The truth is, she was thinking about canceling anyway. Wills has his first polo match Thursday, and Harry gets his braces off the next day. She sounded happy to stay home."

"*Ach,*" Freni said, "those English and their children."

"Mags, how come you didn't tell me *she* was coming?" Susannah whined.

"So, they are going to put the children in foster care?" Freni asked as she tore open a packet of saltine crackers.

"She would never do that!" Susannah gasped.

I couldn't help but chuckle. "Not *her*," I said. "Freni was talking about the Dixons. They're in temporary foster care, but I think there's an aunt somewhere that might come into the picture."

"Yah," Freni said with satisfaction. "Blood is thicker."

"Than what?" Susannah asked.

I turned to Freni. Sometimes the Christian thing is just to ignore my sister. "You'll be happy to know that Shirley Pearson's company is going to make a bid on the Miller farm. There might not be a Wal-Mart there after all."

"No Wal-Mart?" Susannah wailed. "But they sell the cutest little lace panties!"

"Yah, the farm will be good news," Freni said. She blushed. "Did you speak to the doctor?"

I patted her arm, and a slice of chocolate-covered banana flew across the room. Freni didn't notice, and I pretended not to, either.

"Of course, dear. Dr. Brack will be mailing a custom-made brace to you within a week."

Susannah howled with laughter. Shnookums howled, too, until I gently prodded my sister in the bosom with a fork.

"Shhh," I whispered.

"It isn't that, Mags," Susannah said, only slightly subdued. "It's the two of you and those stupid braces. You make it sound like there's something to them after all."

"One of those braces saved my life," I said hotly. "In fact, Terry Slock was so impressed with it that he's abandoned his idea of beginning a new religious cult and is going to do TV ads for Dr. Brack."

"Ugh," Susannah groaned, "what a waste."

"Religion might have done him some good," I said. "He dabbled in pornographic films, you know."

Freni looked lost.

Susannah clapped her hands to her cheeks. "You're kidding!"

"I'm afraid not."

"Like what?"

I glanced at Freni. She was discreetly glancing away. There was no reason not to tell Susannah, since we were all girls, just having a bit of girl talk.

"*Her Cup Runneth Over.*"

"Oh, that."

"You saw it?"

"No, but Melvin did. At a bachelor party. He said it was boring."

I supposed that was good news. "Well, anyway, Terry said that in his brief excursion through that end of the business, he came across some of Angus Dixon's filthy work. He tried to tell me the day of the flash flood, but he said I wouldn't listen."

"So, what else is new?" Freni and Susannah chorused.

I glared pleasantly at them in turn. "I sort of miss the young man. I hope he has a brilliant new career selling braces."

"TV ads with his shirt off," Susannah drooled. "The man is a hunk."

"He's an aging baby-boomer, for pete's sake. Besides, you already have a boyfriend. You shouldn't be lusting after anyone else."

Freni read the pain in my voice. "*Ach,*" she said sympathetically, "it hurts about your Aaron, doesn't it?"

"Only a stabbing pain in the gut whenever I think about it. I felt relieved this morning when I finally put Pops on the plane. Maybe now I can start putting that all behind me and concentrate on the future."

"To new beginnings," Susannah said and

raised her water glass.

I obliged her by clinking my glass against hers. "To new beginnings."

"Yah," Freni said and took a bite of banana.

"To my marriage to Melvin," Susannah said, and in the process knocked my socks off.

Shnookums howled mournfully.

CHAPTER TWENTY-NINE

BANANA BOATS

INGREDIENTS

bananas
peanut butter
chocolate syrup
family and friends

DIRECTIONS

Peel bananas and cut in half lengthwise. Spread one of the halves with a thick layer of peanut butter. Press the two halves together and drench with chocolate syrup. Eat in presence of family or friends.